The Director Dilemma

PEMBERLEY PRODUCTIONS
BOOK ONE

E.G. VEROT

*To those who have spent countless hours daydreaming about the
extraordinary stories that Jane Austen shared with the world.
I am one of you, and this is one of my daydreams.
I hope you can see yourself in this story.*

*To Colin Firth, thank you for being the ideal leading man.
I hope you know just how much love you have inspired.
For me, you will always be Mr. Darcy and now Mr. Henry
Brooks too.*

Please note this book contains adult themes and situations. There are some sensitive themes in The Director Dilemma that readers may find triggering.

This book contains mentions of past cheating (not between main characters).

You will also find tension, spice, and a happy ending.

Thanks for reading!

-E.G. Verot

One

WHAT IS MY TYPE? Fictional men.

If a man has a pulse, consider me no longer interested. I've learned the hard way that you can't trust a man with a heartbeat…or black curly hair sticking out of a baseball cap in the cutest way. Those are the type of guys who will become your friend in middle school when their family moves into the neighborhood, start dating you in high school, and continue the relationship through college. That is until your senior year in college when you are vacationing with *his* family, and his father takes pity on you and divulges that you are not his son's only girlfriend. Tearing apart the world as you once knew it.

From that point on, I have exclusively reserved my love and admiration for the fictional men I read about in novels or see on the big screen.

Let's be real—even TV screens are so large these days they can be considered big screens too.

Well, I suppose that heartbreak isn't the only reason I have been single since college, I chose a field that kept me so busy I wasn't interested in adding anything else to my plate. Having spent the last fifteen years of my life teaching in classrooms of varying grades with curriculum constantly changing and never being able to catch up with the endless professional development required, I had zero energy left to put into a romantic life.

That is beyond developing an intense love for the leading male characters I read about in novels.

How I envied the teachers who were able to maintain a work-life balance, but for me, it never came. That is why, this past June, I put in my notice that I would not be returning in the fall without a moment of regret.

Searching for a new job only took a couple weeks. I found a remote professor position at an international university. Now thankful I decided to pursue that master's degree in educational psychology.

When the official offer came, I was provided with a list of countries in which I could work virtually. England was the first on the list, and I didn't bother looking any further.

Living in London is a dream I never thought possible, and honestly, it still doesn't seem real. At the age of thirty-seven, living a completely different life than I was six months ago. I have been finding myself. It's been a month since I decided to move from my small hometown near Syracuse, New York, and I'm still a little unsure of myself. In a new country, city life has been an adjustment, but it is exactly what I needed.

I feel refreshed and more optimistic than ever, but the loneliness is starting to weigh me down. Sure, my friends and I are still in constant contact, chatting via multiple applications at once and Facetiming a few times a week, but nothing compares to a night with everyone on the couch under blankets, a glass of wine in our hands, and our favorite romance movies playing. I could call my mom again—surprisingly, she's not gotten sick of my multiple calls a day…yet.

As I look out onto the busy streets of London, the view is ever-changing but also becoming reliable. Cars zip through the narrow streets while people crowd the sidewalks, moving in and out of different paths on their way to their next destination. A sight I'm so thankful to have, I could sit here and people-watch for hours, and sometimes I have.

Just then, my phone rings with a call from my best friend, Ellie, who works for a minor league baseball team back in the States.

"Hey, El! Don't you have a game tonight?"

"Yes, I just wanted to say hi, and I missed you." Her breath exaggerates her words, indicating she must be running around the ball field. Ellie and I met in grade school and clicked instantly. Aside from Mom, I'm the closest with Ellie. Neither of us has a sister, which has allowed us to develop a close bond over the years. Making her feel more like family than a friend.

"Aw, I miss you too." I love these random calls from her. I miss her company just as much as I miss my mom's. We've talked about her coming to visit once I am settled and after the playoffs, of course.

"Oh, and I saw the parasite at the grocery store today. He asked about you. I told him you were dead." Her voice thunders with pride. The parasite, as my friends—not—so lovingly refer to my one and only ex-boyfriend, the one who forced me exclusively into the arms of fictional men, John.

"Thank you, a gesture I always appreciate. Hopefully, this time, he believes you." Yet, after the first one hundred times she told him, he still isn't convinced.

"I've got your back, girl. Okay, gotta go, *bye!*" She always emphasizes the bye.

"*Bye,*" I respond before hanging up.

In an attempt to clear out each and every bad vibe clouding my aura, the move also provided much-needed distance from those who I no longer needed in my life. John was accurately nicknamed the parasite because he is the one guy who continues to stick around long past his welcome. Early in my teaching career, I wasn't concerned about running into him because I barely left the house. Conveniently for John, the following summer, two mutual friends of ours began dating. He had continued to reach out to me, but once they had started dating, he had even more reason to try to be there whenever I went out with my friends. Another issue with my small hometown, there are only so many bars and restaurants.

As the years went by, the anger faded. I may have forgiven him because I didn't have the energy to be upset any longer, but I never forgot and had no intention of getting back together. He did, however, work his way back into my regular social schedule. John became more of a matter of convenience, especially on those handfuls of lonely nights over the years. As much as I tried to tell him it was just a one-time thing, he always held out hope for us. I wish I had better judgment those nights, but it's been years, and I have no intention of looking back.

Now, I find myself with a new career and the possibility of having time for a new relationship, that is, if I can get over my fear of getting hurt again and my deep commitment to my fictional boyfriends, *who have yet to break my heart.* I want a completely fresh start. I need a new setting for my story, a new location where I don't have the evidence of my only attempt and failure at a relationship.

On this cloudy evening, I find myself spending another weeknight in my London apartment. It's not big by any means, but big enough for me. Luckily, a furnished place was available when I was moving, which cut down on costs. The kitchen is set just inside the door, sharing the open space with my living area. With the modest size of the bedroom, I was surprised to find how spacious the bathroom was when I moved in. Sure, it's not large enough for multiple people to shower at once, but I don't feel cramped in it, either.

I've added my own personal touch with a few plants by the window in my living room and a TV to watch my favorite movies via streaming services. There is an empty corner that would be perfect for a bookshelf where I dream about seeing my collection of novels proudly displayed with bookish knickknacks all around them. Unfortunately, that will have to wait. It was too costly to bring all of those heavy books with me, but I did bring a few of the essentials I can't live without and my e-reader, of course.

Looking over at the clock, I realize my mom will be expecting a call in about ten minutes. She will ask if I've made any friends, as she does each time we talk, but tonight I have an answer for her. I don't have any new friends for her yet, but I do have a plan. My phone buzzes, and it's a text from her.

MOM

Hi Honey, I can't video chat tonight, I'm still in the waiting room at the groomer.

LUCY

Hey, Mom! That's okay. How's it going?

MOM

Good, just waiting for the dogs. Is it raining there?

A common question I get due to London's famous reputation when it comes to rain.

LUCY

Not at the moment, but it was earlier.

I look out the window to be sure my answer is as accurate as possible.

MOM

Have you left your apartment today?

LUCY

Yes! I went back to the coffee shop around the corner from my apartment again.

MOM

Oh good! Did you make any friends there?

LUCY

Well, I think the barista is starting to recognize me, does that count?

MOM

Lucy...

LUCY

Sorry, mom. I did have an idea when I was there earlier. I think I'm going to go when the weather is nice and sit outside with a book while I enjoy coffee in the evenings or maybe during my lunch.

MOM

Well, it's a start to get you out of the house I suppose. When are you putting this plan into action?

LUCY

Tomorrow if the weather allows.

MOM

Does the coffee shop have indoor seating?

LUCY

Yes, but I think I would prefer to sit outside.

MOM

Well, good luck! And try to look friendly!

She can say what she wants, but I think Liz, the barista at the coffee shop, should count as making friends. We address each other by our first names. I did have to give her my name for my orders, and I have been there almost every day for the last couple weeks. And her name is on her name tag, she didn't technically share that information.

Still counts.

Two

LUCY

THANKFULLY THE NEXT day delivers clear skies to accompany my optimistic walk down the street to the Regency Roast Coffee Shop. This is my go-to coffee place, not only because of its proximity to my apartment but also because of its name.

My love for Jane Austen was a heavy contributor when selecting my new home for the international move. I spent years of my life dreaming of the English countryside she would write about in her books. Sure, I've watched the movies based on her books, but I knew I needed to experience these locations for myself. Now, I just have to get myself out to the countryside to see those views with my own eyes *and pretend I am a heroine in one of her stories while I'm there.*

With my e-reader tucked safely in my bag, I spot an empty table in front of the shop that I plan to occupy after I get my order. These outdoor tables fill up quickly, but tonight, it appears I may be in luck.

The large wooden framed door takes some effort to

pull open, but it's worth it for the delicious coffee aroma that waits behind it. The cozy café is decorated with neutral colors and art to complement the dark wooden benches lining the walls with small tables and chairs on their opposite sides. The middle of the shop is occupied with four-person square tables with the exception of one large table that sits about eight. Tonight's crowd clearly prefers the indoor seating.

Checking the counter, it appears Liz must have the day off. I order a cold brew coffee with light cream from a young man whose name tag I purposely ignore. He puts a little too much cream in, but I'll survive. Not everyone can have Liz's skills. Luckily the small table outside is still open, I quickly settle in with my coffee and my e-reader. This is what I consider a perfect night out on the town.

My mom's advice rings in my head—"Look friendly!"

How can I look friendly?

I recall a conversation that I had with Ellie.

"You have to work on your resting bitch face. It frightens people away."

"I don't mean to. I can't very well sit here constantly smiling either, Ellie. I would look creepy!"

"No, don't smile. Just pretend you're in a photo shoot, getting your picture taken. How would you school your face for that?"

I can always rely on Ellie for good advice.

Baby steps, I'm out of the apartment, that's enough for today. I open the e-reader to the last super spicy novella from one of my favorite romance authors.

The roar of laughter from the group of twenty-something friends coming out of the coffee shop catches my attention. Making eye contact with one of them, I share a small smile and go back to my book as they take seats at the table next to me.

Throughout the next half hour, their lively conversation continues. Enjoying my book, I don't pay much attention to the topics of their discussion. That is until one of the men in the group leans back in his chair toward my table. I look up and he introduces himself.

"Hi! I'm Oliver Brooks."

Look at that! Am I making a friend? My mom will be so thrilled. As I sit there getting excited over the potential of making a new friend, I remember he's waiting for a response.

"Hello, Oliver. I'm Lucy Taylor."

Be friendly, be friendly. Don't blow this. They must realize I'm in my thirties. If these super cool twenty-somethings want to be your friend, do not miss this opportunity!

"Nice to meet you, Lucy." He turns toward his friends to introduce them as well. "This is my brother, Finn." Finn waves—the similarities in their features are obvious —both handsome British men. Although there are differences, Oliver has dark brown hair that has a bit of a wave at the top. Finn's hair has more red tones mixed in with the brown. Their striking smiles shine back at me.

For anyone who wants to be surrounded by British men with their good looks and flirty accents, I highly recommend moving to England.

"This is my stunning girlfriend, Hannah." The beautiful young woman next to him lifts her hand to wave and calls, "Hello, Lucy!" Her natural beauty glistens despite the cloudy evening while long dark braids cascade over her shoulders.

Oliver continues pointing to the remaining woman with breathtakingly red hair, "And this is Mia, Finn's girlfriend."

Mia gives a brief nod before saying, "Hi there!" It's difficult to tell any of their heights, but Mia is more petite than the rest. She reminds me of one of those young, hip influencers who knows exactly how to do thier makeup and wears all the latest trends.

Two couples. So not necessarily a friend group, but rather a double date with two brothers and their partners.

Oliver turns his attention back to me. "I'm sorry to interrupt, but my friends and I need your assistance. You see, when we come here and sit for hours, we sometimes like to make a game out of different things. We noticed you are reading and we each guessed as to what it could be. The losers have to buy coffee for the person who guesses the closest to your book's genre."

"Oh!" There is no way any of them guessed a spicy book about a one-night stand between strangers at a bar. I can't tell them that, at least not yet, maybe if we become friends, but not when we first meet. I have to think of something that makes me sound approachable and friendly. "Sure, I'd love to help."

Why can't I think of a single book that doesn't have sex or dragons or both at the moment?

"What are the guesses?" I ask, hopeful their guesses will help me think of something.

Finn stretches as he chimes in. "I can't tell you that, Lucy. We don't want you to sway your answer to meet one of ours. It's a rule we all agreed on, can't change it now."

"How about instead of us talking between the tables,

you bring your chair over here and join us, Lucy?" Hannah suggests.

Is this happening? *Be cool*, I tell myself. "Sure, thanks." I rise and close my Kindle and place it in my bag so I can carry my coffee and chair over to their table.

"So, what's the book?" Finn asks as he leans over the table. He is clearly the competitive one in the group.

I open my mouth, willing a title to come out, but before it becomes awkward silence, Mia speaks up. "We need proof, we want to see the book."

Oh no, that's a death sentence. *Well, I'll have to find another coffee place after this.* Opening my e-reader, I swipe up to my library and look through my current reads. That's when I spot it. The only book currently in my library that could save me in this situation. I completely forgot I downloaded this the other night, but I'm so thankful I did. It was already at thirty-two percent, it's not the book I would have selected to define myself to a new group of people, but it is the best I can come up with at the moment.

I open the book and turn the screen toward them. The title at the top read *The Great Gatsby* by F. Scott Fitzgerald. All four explode into laughter as Hannah raises her hands clearly in victory.

Not wanting to intrude too much on their time, I only stay another half hour before excusing myself to turn in for the night. But not before Hannah insists we exchange numbers so we can meet up again.

Mom will be so proud.

Back at my apartment, I receive a text indicating I have been added to a new group chat with numbers I don't recognize, but then I read the messages.

HANNAH

Hi Lucy! This is Hannah. We will all let you know who we are so you can save our numbers. It was great meeting you!

MIA

This is Mia. Should we plan for the same day/time next week?

FINN

Finn here, Hannah, remember to send your coffee order for next week. My treat since I was way off with my guess. Oh, and the other number is Oliver.

I smile as I read the texts. I was worried at first our age difference would become apparent the longer the night went on, but the opposite occurred. Learning early in the evening that they are all in their late twenties helped. I managed to forget I was ten years their senior by the end of the night.

Despite the move being exciting and loving my new job, having a group of friends here makes me feel like I'm finally settling into my new life.

Three

HENRY

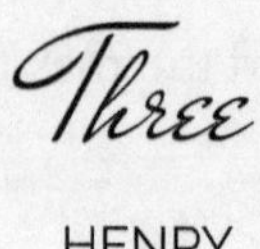

THE SUN SWEEPS through the break in my shades as I lay in bed contemplating starting my day before the alarm goes off or hitting the snooze button. After short deliberations, it becomes apparent that I won't be able to fall back asleep. May as well start the day.

The house is quiet with the exception of the sporadic gust of strong wind racing along the rear side of the house. Living alone at my age is not what I had planned for myself, but I can't complain after finding this beautiful home in a small town an hour outside of London. It's not quite living in the country, but with so few people living here, it sometimes feels that way.

Ever the multitasker, I reach into the shower and start the hot water while I brush my teeth. As the steam begins to fill the room, I lean back on the sink, letting it rid my body of its morning chill.

As the world becomes more connected, I enjoy the peace showers provide. A time to truly reflect with nothing but my own thoughts as the scorching water relaxes my muscles. My feet test the temperature before I walk under the multiple jets cascading warm water over me.

In these moments, I am most grateful to my former self, who decided to get the largest shower option when renovating the house. I can still remember the contractor's look when I picked this one.

"That one? It's big enough for five people." He chuckles.

"Oh, is it? That might come in handy…" I respond with a wink, thinking about my extremely busy social calendar.

"Well, cheers to you, sir," he says with a grin that is a mix of jealousy and admiration.

When I purchased and remodeled this place, I was a somewhat newly single and a famous movie director living in London. I was never wanting for a body to warm my bed after my divorce, but that was years ago when I was trying to distract myself from dealing with the consequences of my failed marriage.

At one time, I was sure I would be with my wife until my dying day, but things never work out how you expect them to. We married in our early twenties, caught up in young love, and instantly had the boys. After years spent growing apart and being frustrated with each other, we finally decided to separate. I loved her—still do, as the mother of my children—but we didn't know how to love each other as anything other than young people in love without a care in the world. It was the impulsivity that drew us in and before we knew it, it was too late. We grew to want different things out of life and that is clear now more than ever.

This setback, as some may call it, has brought

simplicity to my life that I was craving when I was married.

Since then, I have had no desire to make myself that vulnerable again and closed the door to romantic relationships. Sure, I am an expert at portraying love on the big screen, but the more I think back, I'm not sure it even exists on its own outside of young love. It's easy to *love* someone when you're living in the moment and making every decision on a whim without any responsibilities.

Now, years later, I have pulled back on my social life, only going out while I'm in London. My time spent in my home is just for me and my sons when they visit. That's not to say I still don't enjoy the passing company of an attractive woman. I exclusively date with no expectation of love, and that is as far as I'd like to take my companionship. Which still provides the thrill of the first date but none of the disappointment when you get to really know each other.

It didn't take long to get back in the game, but it was a learning curve when it came to pulling. As a gentleman, I am always sure to share my intentions with the women I plan to bed. I am not looking for anything serious, but they sometimes have trouble letting go after our nights together. That's understandable, I'm sure to show them an amazing time.

The issue became glaringly clear after bringing women back to my London apartment when they tended to stick around too long. Each one was a lovely lady, but they didn't always respect my intentions. After that, I decided to give up my apartment in London and make the estate outside the city my permanent residence.

Now, when asking a woman out, I am able to share that I'm visiting with family and don't have a place to take her afterward. It is a genius plan. Hence why I always stay with my sons, Oliver and Finn, when I am in the city. It ensures that when I do have a date, if we decide to take things further then we go back to her place, allowing me to make a quick break in the morning.

Unfortunately, that means I never had the chance to test just how many women would fit in this shower at one time. I shake my head as I leave the shower, "What a pity."

After dressing for the day, I settle into the kitchen with my morning tea and enjoy the view of my garden through the window above the sink. When my bachelor days first began, I was in town every weekend, but as time passes, I find myself making the trip into the city far less often. Oliver and Finn insist I visit at least once a month, but they don't understand how much I enjoy the quiet here.

They aren't the only ones who are on my case about heading back to the city. My agent, Mark, has been calling with job offers for the last few months. I don't know why he keeps calling—he knows I'm not interested. There's a stack of movie scripts by my door for recycling; regardless of my disinterest, Mark insists on sending them, hoping one will catch my eye. I've directed more movies than I can count. The scripts vary between genres—some dramas, a comedy, but most are romance movies. Romance is my specialty, at least it was before I quietly retired. They keep insisting, "I get back out there" in the film industry. I just don't have an interest in sharing love stories anymore, especially not these modern subpar stories. No need to ruin my perfect reputation as a director.

Finishing up my morning tea, I grab the pile and head out the backdoor for my morning walk, tossing the scripts into the recycling right outside the door.

To ensure these morning walks are the most relaxing part of my day, I leave my phone at home so I can clear my mind and enjoy the scenery. A cool breeze glides across my cheek as a reminder that October will soon be coming to an end and winter is not far behind. My fingers chill while I tighten my scarf, quickly stuffing them back into my coat pockets as soon as it's fixed. After letting a shiver roll through me, I continue on my usual route. Living in a small town affords privacy. Today, I do not cross paths with any of my neighbors, but when I do, we share a simple nod and continue on our way. Passing by the small bakery with rich smells of fresh bread tells me I am just about at the end of my walk.

Once returning home, I grab my phone and sink into my favorite chair beside the fireplace. Moving a little closer to the heat in hopes of ridding myself of this chill, I swipe my frozen thumb across the screen.

There is a missed call and text from my youngest son, Finn.

FINN

Morning!

He knows I hate texting. I close the app and call him. "Good morning, Son."

"Hey, Pop! I was just calling to check if you wanted a ride in on Friday?" I squeeze my fingers on the bridge of my nose. I forgot I told them I would visit this week. I suppose we did make plans.

"No, that's all right, I will drive in on my own. Same time?"

"Yeah, that's fine. We have some things planned for the week, but don't worry, nothing too elaborate."

I don't disguise the sigh. "All right, I'll see you on Friday. Take care!"

<hr>

"We are heading out to the coffee shop after dinner, Dad," Oliver says as we set the table in the townhouse they share. I'm always pleasantly surprised they keep such a large place so clean. With three bedrooms, two full baths, and a large kitchen with its own dining room and living space, it still manages to look like a hotel each time I'm here. They were so messy as young boys, especially during their teenage years. I suppose they could have grown out of that while at university, but I have a feeling they only keep it this clean because they both have girlfriends who visit often. I clearly raised smart men—no woman would enter this place if it looked as messy as their childhood bedrooms.

"Can't we order those in?" I ask. I don't particularly want to sit at a coffee shop this evening.

Finn rolls his eyes. "We are meeting the girls there, you were asking for them before, and now you get to spend time with them." I do enjoy their girlfriends, Hannah and

Mia. I suppose it will be nice to be at the coffee shop late at night.

Oliver perks his head up as he remembers something. "Oh, and you get to meet Lucy! She will be there too."

Before I can ask who Lucy is, Finn chimes up, "I'm winning tonight. I know I have a solid guess, and I'm going to win."

"Win what? And who is Lucy?" My fingers drum on the top of the counter as my concern grows at an exponential rate. My sons have pulled sneaky setups with me before. They don't oppose my "hook-ups," as they call them, in town, but they do bring up "worrying about me living all alone in that big house" and how they'd feel better if I had someone as if I'm a senior citizen. Falling in love and getting married at a young age meant I became a father young as well. Having just turned fifty, I don't consider myself a fall risk and am confident I can handle myself well enough alone.

Finn turns to me, his eyes sparkling, and he grins. "Oh! We forgot to tell you about Lucy. She's this nice lady we met at the coffee shop. She's American and moved here by herself about a month ago. She used to be a schoolteacher in the States. We asked what brought her to town—she always dreamed of living in England and once she finished her teaching career, she took the plunge and moved here. I think she is teaching university classes now." He barely stops to catch his breath as he goes on about this woman. If she just finished her teaching career, that would mean she picked London as a place to live out her retirement.

"She reads at the coffee shop where we double date,

and we would try to guess what she was reading when we were bored, so one night, I dared Oliver to ask her what she was reading. He did and we've kind of brought her into the group after that."

Well, it doesn't seem to be a hook-up at all. It sounds like my boys have befriended a lonely, older woman. Pride washes over me; my sons have done a nice thing, and she must have a good sense of humor to put up with them on more than one occasion. The more I think about it, the more I want to befriend this elderly woman too. Might be nice to have an older female companion.

"So what is it that you will win tonight?" I am still puzzled about that part.

Oliver leans over, "Well, we've continued trying to guess what Lucy is reading at the moment. Her favorite hobby is reading. I think her only regret about moving here is that she couldn't bring her library with her. She mostly uses her e-reader."

"So you just pick book titles out of the infinite amount of books she can be reading. How can you ever guess correctly?"

"We mainly guess genres," Finn answered. "Hannah won that first night."

"What was she reading when Hannah won?" I asked.

"*The Great Gatsby*" Finn shakes his head and mutters, "Typical American."

Could be worse—she could have been reading a romance novel. *The Great Gatsby* is certainly not a romantic book. If anything, it's a cautionary tale against it. "Interesting, well I'm looking forward to our evening then."

As we turn the corner, the Regency Roast Coffee Shop appears to our right. The establishment's choice of name always makes me chuckle. I spot Hannah and Mia at a table right inside the window. Greetings are exchanged as we enter, and I sit and begin looking around for the older woman.

"Does Lucy take a taxi to get here?" I ask the table.

Mia answers, "She usually walks. Her apartment isn't too far. Just a couple of blocks in that direction." She points in the opposite direction than we came.

"Oh wow, she walks here…by herself," I say. I guess she isn't as fragile as I was thinking. Good for her, a woman of her advanced age.

I hear the chimes of the coffee shop door open and look up. In walks a beautiful, tall woman with long brown hair. She's bundled up in a black peacoat that hugs her curves with a long scarf that runs the length of her body, meeting the top of her boots at her knees. A matching hat sits on the back of her head. Perhaps she is also planning to sit in the shop while enjoying her order. I'm sure the boys wouldn't mind if I slipped away to chat her up. She meets my eyes and I'm locked in her trance. Tonight might turn out better than expected.

Before I can decide how best to make my move, I hear Hannah shout, "Lucy! We are over here." The woman turns to Hannah and approaches the table.

This is Lucy…

Well, fuck.

Four

LUCY

IT'S TOO chilly to sit outside, but I embraced every moment of the brisk walk here. How I enjoy this time of year. In anticipation of cold weather and coming out tonight, I treated myself to a houndstooth pattern hat and matching scarf at a local boutique I discovered downtown.

Still a few steps away, I spot our group behind the Regency Roast Coffee Shop decal at the large table to the right of the door. Before anyone observes me walking up, I notice the addition to our usual group. He's at the head of the table, sitting next to Oliver. He's gorgeous. Well, my definition of gorgeous. Sure, Oliver and Finn are good-looking men, but they are young. This man is older than them, older than me if I had to guess. His hair and his beard match predominantly brown with gray strands spread throughout. It's ruffled like he had been wearing a hat before coming here today. I bet he looks even sexier in a hat. A broad chest hovers over his folded arms on the table in front of him.

Pulling the heavy door open, I keep my eyes on the

handsome stranger as I enter. The bell above my head chimes, catching his attention. His brown eyes meet mine and I can no longer remember my name. A connection is made instantly, my body feels the push from the universe. I want to walk right over there and curl up in his lap and then never leave it.

"Lucy! We are over here," Hannah yells, and my eye contact with the gorgeous man ends. How long was I staring at this man? It feels like it could have been hours, but as I look at my friends there is no sign of awkwardness in their expressions. Okay, act cool, *try* to act cool, and look friendly.

"Hello!" *Careful walking—now is not the time to trip over your own feet.* I look around at each of my friends, avoiding eye contact with the sexy stranger for now. Someone needs to speak up and introduce us. I look at Oliver next. He's sitting next to this man. He's dropping the ball here. Wait, why am I waiting for an introduction? This isn't a Jane Austen novel. It's the 21st century, and I can introduce myself! Yet, I'm having trouble thinking of the perfect flirty line to say when…

"Lucy, let me introduce you to our father, Henry Brooks," Finn finally speaks up. Their father? He continues, "Dad, this is Lucy Taylor. We told you about her earlier." *Wait. Wait. What?* This man is their father. I need to shut down the endless DILF jokes running through my head.

Finally, I return my gaze to my friend's extremely attractive father. Oh, man. "It's nice to meet you." I play it cool and don't wait for his response, "Does anyone need anything? I'm going to go order." With a round of "no's" and "no thank you's," I notice Henry has his head down in Oliver's direction. Mr. Sexy doesn't need anything. I hang my coat on the back of my chair at the far end of the table and head up to the counter.

"What were you thinking orchestrating this?" Henry asks Oliver, not as quietly as he was obviously intending.

"What are you talking about?" Oliver answers, sounding genuine.

"Is this another one of your setups? You know that type of woman I prefer to date? She's nothing like them," his father replies.

Woah…well, fuck you very much, you handsome shallow jerk. I should have known he was too hot to be a decent human being. Also, did he think this is a setup? If it is, Oliver and Finn are playing a long game just to introduce their dad to someone. They wouldn't do that. At least not without telling me.

"Hi Lucy, what can I get you?" Oh, it's my turn. I must have zoned out. I rush toward the woman with blue pixie-cut hair and a kind smile.

"Hello, Liz, can I please have a hot cocoa for here and my usual ice coffee to go?" As the weather has gotten colder, I've started ordering something warm to drink and an iced coffee for the following day to enjoy from the warmth of my apartment.

While I'm waiting for my drinks, I need a plan of how to act after overhearing that man declare his disinterest for me. Ugh, the universe can be so cruel. Why does he get to be my dream guy in the looks department and with an awful personality? I wonder why he is even here. He must be visiting, but I'll get more details from Hannah and Mia later. Hopefully, he isn't staying long. I have no interest in spending much time with a man who feels I'm so *not his type* that he needs to declare it out loud.

"Here ya go, Lucy." Liz hands me a mug and saucer with my hot chocolate topped with marshmallows and the to-go cup with my coffee.

I thank Liz and head back to our table. There's no way I'm going to acknowledge what I heard. These are my friends and I'm going to enjoy my evening. I'll ignore that cranky, old, *attractive* man for the rest of the night.

During the next two hours, most of my conversations are with the girls. Oliver and Finn pop in and out of our discussions, but they are mostly focused on their dad. It isn't until they guess what I'm reading that Henry decides to acknowledge me again. Finn explains the game to his father and prompts him to make a guess and I grab my e-reader from my bag. Henry declines, "I don't feel it would be right for me to assume Miss Taylor's reading preferences."

"Seriously, Dad. Just pick a book genre. Join the fun," Oliver encourages.

"A dictionary," Henry says with a smirk on his face. It would be considered a very handsome smirk in a more agreeable context.

Everyone else makes their guesses, then I turn my e-reader to show them the cover of *Beowulf*. Having first read the epic fantasy novel in high school, I find myself going back to it year after year, like an old friend. Mia wins, and at the next gathering, she will not need to pay for her tea, not that she ever does—Finn always picks up the tab for her. Their mother must be romantic because it's becoming more clear by the moment that they didn't get it from Henry.

"*Beowulf*. I'm impressed, Lucy. If you don't mind me asking, what was the book you read before *Beowulf*?" Henry asks, showing me more attention than he has since I first entered the coffee shop.

"*Persuasion*. It's a Jane Austen book." Not many people recognize the title as it is one of her lesser-known novels.

Henry's eyes begin to roll and are soon followed by his entire head. Someone's dramatic. "Well, I take back what I said."

The disgust on my face must be clear, Oliver interjects, "Dad, don't start." He turns to me. "Don't take it personally, Lucy. My father here prides himself on his self-proclaimed fridge heart."

While Henry continues to scowl at his son, I take this advantage to poke the bear. "That's a shame. So you're not a romantic?" Henry meets my eyes.

"Love, as you so call it from your books, and I assume the movies and TV series that you watch regularly are manufactured to appeal to those who believe in such fairytales."

"Spoken like someone who has had their heart broken," I reply. His head jerks back in my direction, and his eyes lose their confidence for a brief moment. "I believe in the way Jane Austen's characters make me feel just as much as I enjoy spending time with Beowulf and Grendel. It doesn't mean I think they are real, but the enjoyment they bring to my life is very much real."

For the remainder of the evening, I avoid Henry's gaze until it comes time to say goodnight. Buttoning my coat, I thank everyone for another wonderful night, then look down at the table to grab my to-go iced coffee. When I look up, those deep brown eyes are staring back at me.

Careful, Lucy, don't get lost in those eyes.

Okay, I've got this. With a small smile that keeps my teeth concealed, I tilt my head as if I am addressing an elderly person, letting my snarky tone come through. "It was a pleasure to meet you, Mr. Brooks." Before he can answer, I turn on my heels and walk out the door.

Since leaving the coffee shop, I feel like I've made multiple attempts at shaking Henry Brooks and his beautiful physical features from my memory, but each one was a failure. In an effort to distract myself, I've already changed into my pj's, completed my before-bed routine, and now am trying to decide what to read. I tried to return to *Beowulf*, but now knowing it is a book Henry approves of, I've temporarily lost interest.

As I mindlessly scroll through my e-book collection, my phone's text alert goes off.

GIRLS GROUP CHAT

HANNAH

Sorry about that Lucy.

MIA

We should have warned you.

Be cool, don't show these girls that you were too affected.

LUCY

Warned me about what?

MIA

Finn's father. I saw that look you gave him when you walked in and all the looks you sent him throughout the night.

Damn it.

HANNAH

Don't worry, it's not you. That's the effect he has on most women. It's the reason he's so rich.

MIA

His comment about love being manufactured… *eye roll emoji*

LUCY

Am I missing something?

HANNAH

laughing emoji

MIA

Let's just say he's made a career of making millions of women fall in love lol

LUCY

That's surprising with his personality. I remember you guys saying he was in the film industry… I can only assume he starred in silent pictures.

HANNAH

You've got Internet access. Take a look!

LUCY

It's not porn, right?

MIA

You won't know until you look. ;-)

LUCY

Fine, goodnight ladies!

I put my phone down and grab my laptop. What if it is porn? Well, I guess I'll see it in the search before I click on it and open it.

Deep breath and I type "Henry Brooks career" in the search bar.

The results start loading and they are more upsetting than porn sites. I can't do this alone. The clock shows a little after 12:00 a.m., but back home, it's only 7:00 p.m. I send a text to Ellie, my best friend.

LUCY

Hey, if you're free, I need to talk to you ASAP

My phone rings mere seconds later. "What's wrong?!" she yells into the phone, always the dramatic one.

"Besides the fact that I met the hottest man ever and realized he is the worst person on the planet." Okay, maybe I am being a little dramatic too. It's her fault—she brings it out in me.

"You're going to have to give me more details or at least a name. Also, before we move on, that's not an emergency. Word your texts better!"

"Henry Brooks. Look him up."

A pause and a few catcalls come from the other line. "He's fine. Did he try to murder you? Why is this man the worst to ever walk the world?"

I start from the beginning and share that Henry is Finn and Oliver's father and then I go into details about his overdramatic declaration that I am not the type of woman he would date.

"What an ass."

"Yes, I've decided to hate him for all time, but there's more. Much worse…look at the films he has directed!"

After a brief pause, she shrieks. "How could he!" Now, she understands my pain.

Filling the laptop screen in front of me is a long list of films directed by Mr. Brooks. Among them are some of my favorite romance movies throughout the years. Especially the Jane Austen adaptations. "How does a man like that understand romance so well?"

"Have you looked at what he does in his free time? It looks like this guy has an endless stream of models at his disposal," she mentions. Figures, I don't need to look it up myself to have guessed that…but I take a look anyway.

"I know he was married for years to Finn and Oliver's mother, but all they ever said about it was that it was a messy divorce. I suppose she no longer lived up to his model standards and left."

"Who knows." She sighs. "So, should we kill him?"

I laugh, another best friend trait, willing to commit murder the moment a guy insults you. "Not yet. His crimes, while extremely offensive, do not warrant such action."

"I'm only a call and a ten-hour flight away," she reminds me.

"I will keep that in mind. Thanks, Ellie. I'm going to try to sleep."

"Goodnight, Lucy."

I've already given up on real-life romance, he can't be the one to burst my love of fictional romance too!

How can a hopeless romantic survive with this knowledge?

How could someone capture some of the most passionate performances in film history and have such a poor perception of love?

Five

HENRY

IT WAS *a pleasure to meet you, Mr. Brooks.* Her words repeat in my head during my silent walk back to the boys' townhouse. *Mr. Brooks.* I don't pay attention to how far we've walked, just following behind Oliver and Finn with my head down, noticing the light from the street lamps above us.

Miss Taylor spent most of the night refusing to meet my gaze and acting like I wasn't even there at times. I suppose I was a little harsh when we discussed her books. I let my head lower and shake briefly, remembering my lack of manners, but I couldn't help but be disappointed to hear she was *one of those individuals.* Someone who is expecting a knight in shining armor, which leads me to believe is the reason she is single. At least, I think she's single. Finn mentioned she moved to the UK alone, but she could have found someone here. My body tenses at the thought, but immediately, I push those thoughts to the side and remind myself that I don't care if she's single or not.

Normally, I have no opinion about the interests of the

women I date as they always turn the topic of our conversations to me and my career. Frankly, it usually helps to talk about my career when I'm trying to close the deal. Women are so quick to assume I am just as romantic as the men in my movies. That I will die for them, change my life for them, or swear my love to no one but them. Which are claims I never make—it's not my style to lie to women just to go home with them. I'm perfectly honest up front, but some are more determined to get a chance to experience great love with me. Reality hits them like ice water the next morning when I depart, just as I said I would.

When it was time for Lucy to leave the coffee shop, our eyes finally locked, and I forgot my frustration with the boys for bringing her. Yet, she was quick to remind me of my annoyance as her lips twitched in a grin before they opened to reveal her snarky American tone. *It was a pleasure to meet you, Mr. Brooks*. She held our mutual gaze for just a moment longer before breaking it and walking out the door. I sat frozen as the bell over the door rang, and Oliver elbowed me, "You okay, pops?"

There was confusion on his face as I turned to him. "Yeah, just fine." I spent the rest of our time at the coffee shop planning how I would scold them when we returned to their place.

After hanging our coats in the entryway, we file into the kitchen. I lean against the counter and cross my arms. Finn is the first to notice "Oh boy, looks like we are in trouble, Olly!"

Oliver leaves his head buried in the refrigerator, "Yeah, what did we do now?"

"You spoke of her as if she was a senior citizen! I don't know what type of scheme you two are playing at—"

Oliver cuts me off, "What are you talking about? We never said anything like that."

Finn chimes in, "If that's the picture you painted based on our description, that's on you."

"How many times do I have to tell you I don't need or want to be set up." The volume of my voice grows louder than I anticipated.

This is a sore subject for many reasons. For one, I have no problem acquiring female company regularly and on my terms.

Another reason, the boys don't understand, and I'm glad they don't. As little as I think of love and relationships, they couldn't be more opposite. What they don't understand is that we are different. A happy ending is not in the cards for everyone. They are both head over heels for their girlfriends, and I couldn't be more elated for them. I'm thankful they found someone to love and care for, as they will do in return. I don't want my boys to end up alone and grouchy old men like me.

Finn shrugs his shoulders, "I hate to break it to you, Dad, but this wasn't a setup. Lucy has been hanging out with us for weeks now. You came in to visit, and we invited you to join our regular activities."

I can usually tell when they are lying, which I am starting to think that they aren't since Finn appears to be telling the truth. When he was younger he had some pretty obvious tells when he would lie. He would rock weight between his legs, yet he's standing perfectly still. I look over to check his brother's expression.

Oliver sighs, "He's being honest, Dad. Sure, we would love you to find someone, but we've given up on trying to set you up quite a long time ago."

Finn moves to stand tall, "Not to mention, we like having Lucy around. She's trying to start a new life for herself. We aren't interested in ruining that new life before it even really gets started."

"Ruining?" I question.

Oliver replies, "She said something about a bad breakup before she left the States. We know what kind of relationships you have and that's not what she needs right now."

I hadn't considered this on the walk home, but hearing it is upsetting. How I act with women is my choice. Being married to their mother for twenty-two years was enough time to teach me what I didn't want. In the eight years since I've found casual dating works best for me. I know what relationships are supposed to be like, but I just don't want that. If I decided I wanted to pursue Lucy, I could be a good partner.

Hypothetically, of course.

Before my mind can wander too far in the fantasy of what dating Lucy could be like, Finn takes advantage of the silence, "Don't worry, Olly. Pops was quick to offend Lucy and wouldn't stand a chance with her now anyway." He turns to me, "But you need to work on your manners if you are going to spend more time with us during your stay. We have plans with Lucy all week, and I won't have you being rude to our friend."

When did the roles reverse, and why am I being spoken to like a child? I can act perfectly well when I am not the victim of an ambush like I was tonight. I suppose now that I know she isn't interested in dating, I could relax a little around her. "What happened with that relationship from the States?"

Oliver responds, "We don't have many details, but it's not our story to tell. Just know that she's pretty torn up about it."

Finn smiles, "If you want to know more, you're going to have to ask her yourself, which means you'll need to be nice to her and probably become her friend."

After last night, I find myself content to be in the company of one of my closest mates. Max Shaw still looks every bit of the leading man at fifty as he did at twenty. Sitting back in his chair in the small café with confidence radiating from him in his clean, pressed suit that complements his toned physique—sans tie—leaving the buttons open at the top. His shaved head and oversized glasses round out his signature look.

Early in his acting career, he was overlooked, but when he continued to shine as the leading man in all of my movies, he quickly found himself in high demand. We were inseparable in our younger days after meeting at University. I've been thankful every day that I was rooming with this shy American kid. A dynamic duo who were at the top of our careers and shared many personal achievements throughout our friendship.

We both married and started our families very young. His marriage ended far sooner than mine. He and his wife

Veronica met during his brief time on Broadway. She was a dancer in the show and they married within six months of meeting. During their three years of marriage, their two beautiful daughters, Anna and Emily, were born. Max and Veronica put a pause on their careers to start their family. Being away from dancing and the stage took a toll on Veronica, and just six months after Emily was born, she left Max and the girls to return to the stage.

I tried to be there for him as best I could, but he was never the same again. Since then, we haven't spoken about Veronica, and Max has never shared any intention of dating again. He raised the girls with help from family, and as he got older, he took on more and more roles. When we would do movies together, the girls would always come stay with us. They are practically sisters to Oliver and Finn.

As for his current acting career, like mine, he has slowed down, looking toward retirement. He spends most of his time with his daughters, who are now grown and starting their own careers.

"So what brings you to the UK this time, Max?"

"Aside from your warm company?" he says with a slight smile.

"I was reminded just last night of just how unappealing my company can be, so I know it's not that."

"I've always told you, you need to work on your first impression…and your second and third impressions aren't usually great either." He smirks at me. "You come off gruff." Max loves to bestow his wisdom as the older of the two of us by six months. *Well, I'm taller.*

"What's going on?" I ask.

"Didn't Viewmont call you yet?" Viewmont is a production company we've worked with for years, but I haven't heard from them since we wrapped our last film years ago. I shake my head at Max, and he continues, "They flew me in to discuss the movie. I asked if you were involved, and they said they are still in talks with everyone. I assumed they only called me because you were already signed on."

"What movie? I haven't heard anything from Mark." Sure, during our last call, I told him to leave me the fuck alone. Yet, if Max was involved, he should know I'd want to be informed.

"Oh…Henry…" This wasn't good. *Why is he hesitating?* "They are making a new adaptation of *Pride and Prejudice.*"

My shoulders slump and my chin falls to my chest. It's the most famous Jane Austen story and arguably the most popular love story ever told. These adaptations are wildly coveted among actors and directors. I've spent my entire career begging Viewmont Productions to let me have an adaptation of *Pride and Prejudice.*

"Call Mark now, I don't mind." Max is a friend like no other. If he hadn't been contacted about this movie, would it have been made without me? I pick my phone up and try to ignore the knot in my stomach.

The rings stop, and I hear a booming voice on the other end. "Mr. Henry Brooks! What a pleasant surprise."

"Viewmont is doing a new adaptation of *Pride and Prejudice.* Have they called you?"

Mark stutters to answer, good. My anger has translated over the line. "Henry, this is the first I've heard of it. Are you sure?"

"Yes, I'm sitting here with Max, who just met with them about casting."

"I'll call right now."

I hang up. I don't want another moment wasted on getting that movie in my name. After a deep breath, I take a large drink of my water and try to compose myself. The waiter brings our lunches, and I'm suddenly no longer hungry. I know better than to expect an immediate call back from Mark and try to calm myself.

"Aren't you a little old to be Mr. Darcy, Max?" I turn my attention to my friend, who has a mouth full of his bacon, lettuce, and tomato sandwich, which he almost chokes on while laughing at my joke.

"Well, based on your dating history, younger women appear to be interested in older men now. I might just be able to pull off the handsome owner of the famous Pemberley estate."

Could this be one of those adaptations where they are changing everything? That is a trend I've noticed lately.

After chewing his bite and taking a drink of his water, Max continues, "Unfortunately, they did not ask if I would play Mr. Darcy or Mr. Bingley. I think I would have been great as Mr. Bingley back in the day. He was always my favorite character each time I read the book. Anyway, I was asked to play Mr. Bennett."

"Congratulations, my friend. You will be great in that role!"

Max gives me an exasperated look, "We'll see."

"What does that mean? I assumed you were already signed on," I asked.

"I let them know I won't do it unless you are directing.

I haven't signed anything yet." Loyalty is a strong component of our friendship. I can't let him down. He deserves this role. I am determined to get this job. Surely, the years of our professional partnership and the considerable amount of money I've made them is enough for Viewmont to have me as the director.

Pride and Prejudice will not be the one that got away.

As I turn the key in the lock to the boys' townhouse, the smell of popcorn fills my lungs. They know it's my favorite snack—they must be up to *something*. Letting the delicious scent guide me, I find a crowd around the kitchen island. My sons are here with Hannah, Mia, and Lucy.

My entrance has gone unnoticed, so I take this moment to lean on the door frame and watch the newest addition to our group. Her long brown hair falls in waves down her back as she leans over to grab a carrot off a tray in the center of the island. Permitting myself only the quickest of glances down her backside, I am startled from my admiration by Finn yelling, "Let's play Uno." As they laugh, Lucy is the first to notice me. She straightens her stance immediately and says, "Hello," with a smile that isn't quite friendly, more like she is planning something.

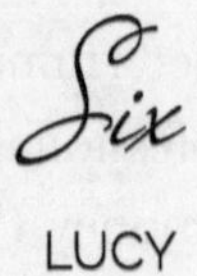

LUCY

DURING MY SHORT time spent in London, it feels as though every experience is new, but at the moment, I find myself in a very familiar environment. Growing up with a large family who spent most of their time together at game nights, we all became a little competitive…well, very competitive, actually. While I have been able to keep that side of me at bay since my new group started our game nights, tonight, with Henry's presence, I worry that covering it up will prove to be quite the problem.

Henry is the first to take his seat at the large round table that allows for poker games on one side and a flat surface for board games on the other.

We've only exchanged pleasantries until this point in the evening, but as I pass him to find a seat at the opposite side of the table, he pulls out the chair next to his and says, "Here." He meets my eyes with a challenge in his gaze, intensely watching and waiting to see if I will take his direction. Never one to back down, I sit quickly and thank him.

Perhaps he has a plan to win the game by distracting me with his good looks, and he does look exceptionally well in those dark jeans and black Henley.

Nope, I will not *be distracted. I must remember his personality.*

Mia picks the first game since she is the current winner, and she goes with Finn's suggestion of Uno. I may have downplayed my skills in a few games the last time we played.

As the cards are being dealt, Henry takes the opportunity to lean in, engulfing me in his intoxicating cologne. Every inch of my body tingles as I inhale the woodsy scent. It has been far too long since I've been this close to a man. This is unhealthy. He's like a weapon.

"Have you ever played before?" he asks with slight condensation.

It was on his suggestion that I sit beside him, which in Uno terms also means he is directly in the line of fire to receive my draw two and draw fours. "Yes, I've been playing with everyone here since joining their game nights, and it's quite enjoyable." Not a lie, but I withhold my years of experience, watching for tells in those I am playing against. He will learn that even if I can't guarantee a win for myself, I can be sure to save all my draw four and draw two cards for him.

The smug look on his face tells me he is now certain that I will not be a real threat in this game, and he moves his attention to the cards he was dealt. Of the first five games played, I don't win every game but make sure he always loses with a handful of cards.

Coincidentally, Henry suggests a game change soon after, and we move on to trivia, yet this is a team game. Of course, the couples pair up and leave Henry and I to be partners. While Oliver and Finn are setting up the board, Henry and I make our way to the kitchen to top off our drinks.

"May I?" He holds his hand out for my glass. I oblige his kind offer. "You've played Uno before…" He guesses as he pours my white wine with his sleeves pushed back to his elbows.

Distracted by the view, it takes me a moment to answer, "Yes…for years."

"And our next game, should I assume you have all of the trivia answers memorized as well?" His forearms are on display filling his short glass with whiskey.

"Sadly, I do not."

"Should I try to arrange a partner trade? Or are you hoping to switch so you can be sure I lose yet again?" He looks at me with a weary look.

"Please, don't hold back. Continue sharing how deceitful you think I am," I scoff.

He looks so good tonight.

No, I need to be diligent and not think better of him solely based on his physical appearance.

He follows me back to the table and pulls my chair out for me. These manners are something a girl could get used to but I must remember, he's just being polite. He leans forward to say, "Oh, I don't trust you at all—I thought that was obvious." He returns to his seat next to mine. Thankfully, I'm able to contain the shiver his close proximity encourages.

"Do we need to separate the two of you?" Oliver asks with a stern look at his father.

Henry answers, "Not at all. Stay partnered with your love. I'm sure Lucy and I can endure each other's company for the remainder of the evening." I can't help but let my eyes roll as I take a larger-than-normal drink of my wine. At this rate, I may need a refill before we have a chance to answer a single question.

It is our team's turn to ask a question to Finn and Mia, Henry takes the card and begins to read. I lean my head slightly in his direction to check for the correct answer. Without looking up, Henry puts his arm around the back of my chair and brings his hand and the trivia card between us. I feel a smile creeping on my lips at his kind gesture but halt the action before anyone else can notice. Even after Mia answers correctly and Henry discards the card, he doesn't move his arm from behind me.

It must be the wine causing my serious lapse in judgment, but I am finding myself enjoying his closeness far too much. As each turn passes, I become less focused on the trivia and more so on Henry's close proximity. If I turn too much, it could appear as if we are snuggling like a couple. I can't have that. I don't need to look like one of the many women who fall all over him, but as the game continues, the distance between us grows naturally smaller. I should know better, but I do nothing to stop it.

During our final opportunity to answer a question, my shoulder is against his side. My wine glass sits on the table, only half finished, and I realize I can't even blame that for my actions.

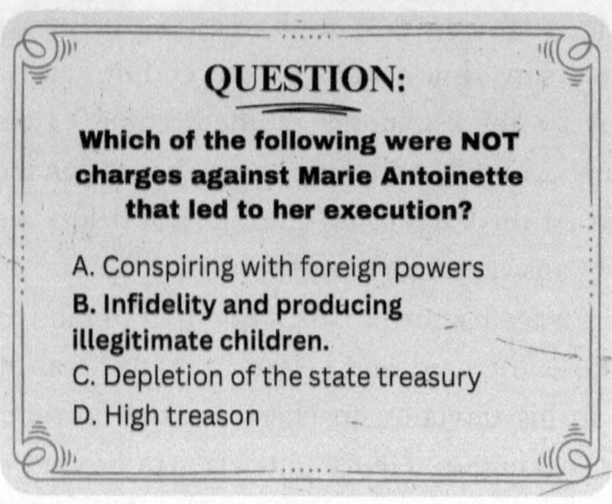

"Our answer is C." Henry's voice is firm with complete confidence.

"It is not!" I exclaim louder than is needed, but I'm not going to lose this game on a question I am absolutely certain I know the correct answer. We both sit up straight to argue face-to-face.

"Excuse me?" he asks as he places his glass on the table.

"You're wrong." It's that simple, and the rest of our party begins to make taunting sounds at my confidence.

"I am not wrong. I believe as Europeans we know a little more about our history than what they teach in the States. Isn't your country the one who glorifies the act of dumping tea in large bodies of water?"

Why must this man be absolutely awful?

He's so much more attractive when his mouth is closed. Not that I would have a shot with him if he were a good person. I am very much *not* his type.

"Fine, go ahead. Use your answer, and then the loss is on you." I turn to the room, "You are all here to witness."

"Our official answer is C," Henry says directly to Mia, who still holds the card in her hand.

As he does this, I pull out my phone and send a quick message to the group chat.

LUCY

The correct answer is B.

Mia starts to shake her head as Finn, Oliver, and Hannah pull their phones out to check the message they just received. "The correct answer is…B." She gives my partner a sympathetic look, "Sorry, Henry."

"You're joking, Mia." He laughs in an annoyingly sexy way.

"Nope."

She hands him the small trivia card, and I begin to stand. I'm not sure where I get the courage, but as I begin to leave the table, I stop behind Henry's chair. I rest my hands on the back of his chair while he faces away from me, still looking at the card. Leaning close to his ear, I whisper, "Looks like you owe me a coffee, at the very least. Sorry, *you* lost the game." Before he can reply, I move into the kitchen while I call for a cab and then assist with the cleanup.

"Ellie, I'm telling you, the man hates me." My kind friend always assumes everyone is flirting and in love with us.

"I don't know. You said he sat with his arm around you

the other night." I guess that's a best friend's job, to try and make the best of things that are bothering us.

"He had his arm around my chair…not me," I clarify. "Also, we've run into each other twice since that night. The following day, when I ran to the coffee shop, he was sitting at a table by himself. I know he saw me. We looked right at each other, but then, when I began to say something, he put his head down. Message received." It is clear then that his politeness will be limited to when his family is around…and that doesn't bother me at all.

"Maybe he's just shy because his feelings for you are getting so strong!"

"Ha! Yeah, that totally explains the interaction we had yesterday when we saw each other at the library. I think he was so startled he only spoke to end the conversation before it began. He was leaving the library and continued on his way after a 'have a good day' and let the door close in front of me."

"I'm sticking with him being nervous." Ellie stays firm. Something is getting lost between our international phone call. If she were here, witnessing Henry's indiscretions, she would understand what I'm trying to tell her.

"Yes, the super famous playboy of London is very nervous around me, an online college professor whose only local friends are his sons and their partners," I say with a huff as I stretch out on my bed.

"Well, he doesn't live there, right, so you don't have to endure him much longer. Just try to avoid him."

"Do you think that will really help?"

"No, I think it will make you mysterious and make him fall even more in love with you."

"Thanks, Ellie…on that note, I think I'll get some rest. Enjoy the rest of your day!"

"Sweet Henry dreams!" She hangs up before I get a chance to argue with her. Ellie is a constant supporter of love and all things romance. I suppose I am too, but certainly not with Henry.

I haven't watched any of Henry's adaptations of Jane Austen's work since meeting him. I'm too worried it will somehow alter the films or perhaps alter the way they make me feel. Still not having the nerve to do it, I grab a book instead.

What more can a girl want than to fall asleep with Captain Wentworth…

Seven

LUCY

I **TRIED** everything to get out of this dinner tonight, but Mia and Hannah insisted. Holding out hope of not attending until the last minute, I hadn't made time to shop for a cocktail dress. After many outfit try-ons in front of my mirror, an off-the-shoulder top with a flower that hides my bare left shoulder and flared black dress pants with heels are deemed the winners.

We arrive in separate cars and I notice Henry immediately, standing by the entrance with Oliver and Finn. He looks mouthwateringly handsome this evening. Sure, I've found plenty of photos of him on the Internet wearing suits to movie premieres and award shows while Googling him late at night when I know I shouldn't be, but nothing compares to experiencing this with my own eyes. Concentrating all of my efforts at hiding my awe, I trip over my own feet. Luckily, the source of my distraction is close enough that he wraps an arm around my waist and pulls me upright, stopping me from falling to the ground. Heat engulfs my body at his touch. I can feel it moving up to cover my cheeks as I thank him and rush into the restaurant. Henry remains silent as he walks in behind me.

The restaurant's earth tones and dim lighting barely distract me from the million thoughts running through my mind. Once we arrive at the rectangular table, I pause for the couples to choose their seats first. Shock and suspicion overtake me when Henry touches my back to lead me to the closest chair and holds it out for me. I take my seat, slowly letting my gaze sweep over his suit again. "Thank you," I say when our eyes finally meet.

"Of course," he answers with a nod.

Will he sit next to me again? Before I have a chance to stop myself from hoping that he will, Henry takes the seat on my left at the head of the table. My heart flutters.

I'm going to have a very stern talk with my stupid heart later.

It is particularly quiet on our end of the table, with sparse small talk. After Henry finishes eating, he sits back in his chair, looking anywhere but at me. I hate how much that upsets me. I catch myself multiple times trying to think of topics for us to discuss, but I stop myself. Wasn't my desire to avoid him the reason I didn't want to come in the first place? He's giving me a reason to not talk to him, so I should be overjoyed. The food is exquisite and I am enjoying the ambience this restaurant offers for a nice dinner out with my friends.

"Isn't this place amazing!" I try to encourage conversation with Henry but fail miserably when he nods without looking at me as a reply. Aside from the odd interactions with him, I'm quite enjoying my night. I even tried a dish I've never had before, artichoke risotto, which was exceptional.

We wrap dinner up quickly, exiting the restaurant to find a large SUV outside waiting for us. "Mia didn't want to worry about us taking two cars, so she insisted on this," Finn explains.

"It will be fun." Mia is the first to jump into the very back seat. Hannah follows her while Finn gets into the front passenger seat.

"Lucy." Henry grabs my attention as he stands next to the vehicle's backdoor, holding out his hand to me. I take it, and that heat from earlier returns but this time is joined by butterflies fluttering in my stomach. I slide into the middle row of seats and move over to sit against the opposite door that faces the busy, traffic-filled street. Henry follows behind me to sit in the middle seat with Oliver at his other side.

Henry fidgets trying to get comfortable in a seat no one in the history of car passengers has ever found to be comfortable. "Are you going to be all right?" I ask, trying not to laugh at his squirming.

He turns in my direction and lays his arm across the back of my seat. "I'm fine."

I overhear Finn sharing the best route to our next destination with our driver. Behind us, Mia is going on about the new bar we are heading to next. She's already been a few times with work friends, but she swears they "aren't as much fun" as we are.

The close proximity to Henry reintroduces me to his cologne, the woodsy smell I almost convinced myself I had imagined the other night. If Ellie could be here now, she would find some crafter to make me a candle that smells like him or just send a bottle of the cologne to me with instructions to spray it all over my bed.

The rest of the ride goes by quickly, and soon after, we are pulling up to the bar. After exiting, the group makes their way inside, and eventually, Henry and I find ourselves in the middle of a large U-shaped leather booth while the two young couples file in on either side of us. Mia squeals and does a little dance in place when the waitress delivers a tray of small glasses filled with clear liquid. While the others are devouring their shots, Henry orders, "I'll have a scotch and open a tab." He hands her his card and turns to me.

"A merlot, please." Well, if he is paying, he can buy me a fancy glass of wine.

Once the waitress has moved out of the way, Finn, Mia, Oliver, and Hannah immediately make their way to the dance floor. I had assumed once the others left and more space became available within our booth that Henry would have moved down, but he remains just as close as he was when everyone was squished in. One slight move on either part, and we will be touching, either at the shoulders or legs. As much as my body craves it, my mind understands that, logically, it is unnatural to sit this close with so much space. Thinking better of it, I decide to slide down and put distance between us.

With Henry's closeness throughout the car ride and entering the bar, multiple brushes occurred, each setting my skin on fire and lingering long after he moved. I am beginning to hate him not just for his sour personality but also for how attracted I am to him. Which is partially his fault. He could work at not looking so good all the time. Who am I kidding? He probably looks this sexy the moment he wakes up in the morning. Okay, I need to shut down thoughts of him in bed immediately and turn my attention to INXS roaring from the speakers located in every corner of the dance floor.

Trying to distract myself, I shuffle down just a few more inches and reach for some gum in my purse, hoping to be discreet. Of course, the gum packets have a way of hiding under everything else in there, and I catch Henry watching me out of the corner of my eye. I move the e-reader to the side, and he starts to say something, but it's too difficult to hear over the song lyrics from "I Need You Tonight" by INXS blasting out of every speaker. I lean in a little and ask, "What's that?" with my hand by my ear.

Henry closes the distance I just put between us by placing his arm around the back of the booth this time. *What is with this guy and his arm move?* It's déjà vu. He leans to my ear, his warm breath sending shivers down my spine. "Do you not spend enough time reading? Is it necessary for you to have that here?"

Struggling to think clearly, I take the opportunity to speak directly into this ear. Two can play that game. While leaning in, I also place my hand on his leg. "Habit when I go out with couples." Hopefully, this answer was vague enough to keep the conversation going. *I shouldn't want that.*

Henry moves his arm from resting on the back of the booth to around my shoulders to allow him to get even closer to me. I sit up straight and look forward as he asks, "Did you not know I was coming?"

I answer, returning to my position of leaning into his

ear and my hand finding its previous position on his leg. "I assumed you would, yet you aren't shy about your lady killer reputation. Honestly, I'm amazed you haven't swept one of those girls at the bar off their feet by now. They look like your type." I nod my head in the direction of three young twenty-somethings sitting at the main bar who haven't taken their eyes off him all night.

He doesn't follow my gaze but continues to focus on me, sliding his hand down my lower back, applying just the slightest amount of pressure to pull me toward him, and then his mouth is back at my ear with a soft nudge of his nose against my ear. "You think me so rude to leave you here alone?"

My body takes over, and I shiver at his words and proximity. I could declare it's from a chill, but I'd rather not admit the action to him at all. He leans back with a smirk on his face. Sure, he earned that smirk, but it's time to shut this down.

When I lean in to respond this time, I keep my hands in my lap. "Well, you now know I do have the company of endless characters in my purse. You are free to make one of those girls' dreams come true tonight." I lean away and watch his face. The volume of the music starts to quiet just as the rest of our party makes their way back to our booth.

Henry moves his arms back to his side as the girls start asking for recommendations to send to the DJ via the club's app while Finn orders another round for the table.

About a half hour passes, and conversations flow between everyone. It appears no one noticed our close conversation while they were dancing.

"What do you think of this place?" Hannah asks, leaning close so I can hear her.

"It's great," I answer while noticing two of the girls from the bar walk by our booth, looking directly at Henry. When he notices them, they smile and wave.

I move to grab my drink from the table and study him from the corner of my eye as he politely acknowledges them with a nod but doesn't linger with his attention. Of course, why would he—it's like fishing in a barrel for him.

"Mia really is in her element." I nod my head toward Mia for Hannah to follow. She's at the end of the booth, dancing with her drink still in one hand raised above her head and her dress swaying with her hips. That girl is her own party. So confident and brave—I find myself a little jealous of her ability to just stand up and dance by herself.

Finn is seated at the end of the booth, staying at arm's length of Mia, yet not even he can keep up with her energy. Oliver and Henry are chatting to themselves and I notice Henry looking beyond Oliver's shoulder in the direction of those girls at the bar. Ignoring the burning sensation in my chest, I bring myself back to reality. Henry is conceited and arrogant, and I am not his type. Remembering his words from earlier when he said he wouldn't go talk to them because I was here. Perhaps I am keeping him from what will surely end as an exciting evening. Or worse, he will go over and pick one of them up in front of me. For some reason, I decide I do not want a front-row seat to Henry's seduction of one or both of those blondes.

Hannah and Mia announce they are running to the ladies' room. I jump up to join them, taking this as my chance to leave without any fuss. On the walk to the ladies' room, we approach the exit doors. "Hannah, Mia, I'm getting a bit of a headache. I think I'm going to call it a night."

"Oh no, you can't leave yet. They didn't even play your song!" Mia pleads. "You haven't danced yet."

"Next time, I promise you will have my first dance." I feel bad leaving when she is so upset, but I think half of it may be the numerous shots she's had this evening. I know she's in good hands with the boys.

"Mia, if she has a headache, she should go home and rest." Hannah's voice is consoling. "When her song comes on, we will dance and send her a video and she can watch it tomorrow when she is feeling better."

I whisper into her ear a very specific goodbye message for her to share with Henry. "Thank you, both. Send the guys my best!" And with that, I move through the exit to grab a cab back to my apartment.

As I leave the bar, I notice a group of photographers standing outside. They raise their cameras as I open the door but quickly lower them when they realize I am not anyone important. This place Mia picked must be really popular with celebrities. I didn't notice anyone famous, but then again, it was poorly lit inside…and if I'm being honest with myself, Henry occupied all of my attention.

Eight

HENRY

AS THE LADIES in our group take their leave, I notice the line at the bar is finally thinning out. Grabbing Lucy's empty glass, I make my way to get us each a refill as we are the only two not exclusively drinking random shots.

While I'm grateful Finn and Oliver and their partners are enjoying themselves, I'm just not that age anymore. I far prefer a quiet evening with cocktails and good company. Specifically, the company that places her hand on my leg while she whispers with a seductive tone into my ear.

My muscles feel rigid, perhaps stiff from sitting for so long, yet walking doesn't help much. I'm anxious to return to the booth…and her. Taking a deep breath, I try to work out the feelings that accompany her proximity while making my way to the front of the bar. Couples move around me, heading in the opposite direction toward the dance floor. *Would Lucy like to dance?* The bartender pulls me out of my thoughts. I place the empty glasses on the bar and order another scotch for myself and a merlot for her.

As I'm waiting, a couple of young blondes approach to introduce themselves. The braver of the two holds her hand out to me, I shake it but don't pay attention as I look over her shoulder to check if Lucy is back at the booth yet. The other, more subtle one leans her side against the bar while twirling a strand of hair around her finger. Turning away from them, I check for the bartender's return, and thankfully, he approaches with our drinks.

"Put it on my tab, Henry Brooks," I instruct the bartender. I point out the booth just to be sure. It's still only occupied by Finn and Oliver. The bartender nods and turns to the other patrons.

The blondes are looking at me expectantly—I suppose I could give them a little something. They are certainly my type, and any other night I would have added their drinks to my tab too and remained at the bar with them, but not tonight. "Have a great night, ladies," I say, quickly walking away before they have a chance to respond.

Finn and Oliver are sitting at the other end of the half-circle booth. I remain standing so upon Lucy's return, she can move into the booth before me. I place the drinks on our table and notice Mia and Hannah returning. I look for her, but Lucy is not with them. "Where's Lucy?" I ask as soon as they are close enough to hear me.

"Ugh," groans Mia. What does that mean? Is she sick, uncomfortable, upset—did she leave with another man?

Thankfully, Hannah responds quickly. "She wasn't feeling well. I think the loud music gave her a headache. She caught a taxi and headed home for the night."

"She left?" I sigh. Why did that question come out sounding so disappointed?

"Yeah, she wanted me to tell you that she hopes you and the lucky lady you pick have a fun night!" she says with kindness as she slides into the booth next to Oliver. Yet, did Lucy mean them with the sweet tone Hannah relayed it, or was it meant as a jest?

I follow behind them, now sitting at the corner end of the booth while the two couples snuggle in deeper. In an attempt to push down my unexpected emotions, I drink Lucy's wine in a couple of gulps. Music continues to play as I wallow in being the only single person among the couples.

Something that never bothered me before.

One of the blondes, not surprisingly the forward one from the bar, approaches our booth. I wonder if she deserted her friend. She gently touches my shoulder as she walks past. If this is what Lucy thinks of me, who am I to correct her.

After saying my goodbyes to my party, I follow the blonde to the bar, downing my scotch in one shot as we walk. This is exactly how I like to end my evenings when I go out in London, but something is missing. I don't feel the thrill of excitement I usually get when meeting a woman at a bar. This is absurd. Why am I still thinking about my sons' friend who left? This is who I am. As Lucy said, I should have a fun night.

The sun is too bright, and my head begins to pulse as an extremely annoying alarm goes off beside me. Before I can open my eyes, I feel a body crawl over me, followed by a loud bang as a hand slams down on the clock beside me. The momentary silence is welcome as I try to regain my wits. Yet, it is short-lived.

"I'm late for work!" she shrieks. "I have to get ready."

Finally opening my eyes, my vision is blurry at first, but the view becomes clearer when the bare body of the blonde from the bar last night launches into a room I recall is the bathroom. This is the perfect out for me. It's always such a pain when they want me to stay or have breakfast. As shuffling noises come from the other side of the door, I quickly dress myself.

Usually, I feel pretty well after a night like this, but not today. The pit in my stomach grows more painful the longer I stand here, facing the reality of my poor actions from last night. Knocking on the bathroom door, I call to her, "I'm heading home now. Thank you for a fun night."

She pokes her head out with only a towel wrapped around her. Modesty is welcome—it sets boundaries. "I put my number in your phone last night. Let's get coffee sometime."

"Great," I lie. "Have a good day."

"You too," she replies, and I take my leave.

When I get outside and look around at the familiar street, I remember her place isn't too far from the boys' place, and I decide to walk back to clear my mind a little. It just so happens that this route does include Lucy's apartment. It's early, and she had a headache. Surely, there's no chance of us crossing paths. I look at the rows of townhomes and wonder which could belong to her.

Our coffee shop is open and filled with customers and I contemplate stopping in but decide against it as it may be obvious to the staff and patrons that I'm dressed in my evening wear from last night at 9:00 a.m. Just then, the one person who would recognize my clothes from last night walks into the street, Lucy.

She notices me immediately and looks me up and down. Any other time, I'm sure I would find this extremely appealing, but in this case, it just feels embarrassing.

"Good morning," I say casually. She can't be surprised. She practically insisted I *have fun* last night.

Her voice is low and snarky, "Sure looks like it was for you." Is that anger I hear, or even better…maybe jealousy?

"Yes, I took your directive and decided to have a very fun evening after you left." I should be asking how her head is feeling, but that's not what I do. No, I make matters worse. "You left early—you can't be cross if your evening was less than desirable."

"My night was wonderful, we simply have different ideas of a good night." I'm sure I could show her a great night…

"It could have been a great night if you stayed" Before I can stop myself, I continue to what? Flirt with her? Antagonize her? "You don't know how it could have ended."

Lucy's jaw drops. "I am certain if I stayed, I would not have been interested in a random man like you coming up to me with an offer of a good time just to do the walk of shame the next morning." That's exactly what I did, but why was she so upset by this? Why was I?

Lucy looks up at me. "You might want to wipe the lipstick off your collar if you don't want anyone else to know that you're just walking home now."

With that, she walks past me toward her apartment. A part of me wants to find the nearest manhole to hide out in for the rest of eternity. The other half wants to run after her, but what would I even say…

Instead of doing either of those things, I continue on my way, feeling worse than I did before.

After a refreshing shower and two cups of coffee, I feel a little better, but still not necessarily happy with myself. Hoping to distract my mind from the morning's events *and how to fix them*, I settle down to check my emails. At the top of my inbox, is one from my manager sent this morning.

```
From: Mark Hill
<mark.hill@hilltalentagency.com>
Subject: P&P
Henry,
I spoke with Viewmont Productions—Can you
stop by my office this week?
-Mark
```

```
To: Mark Hill
<mark.hill@hilltalentagency.com>
Subject: Re: P&P
How soon can you meet?
```

```
From: Mark Hill
<mark.hill@hilltalentagency.com>
Subject: Re: P&P
I'm available now. I'll be in the office
for a couple hours trying to catch up from
my vacation last week.
If you're not free, call Mary, she's in
too. She will get you scheduled.
```

```
To: Mark Hill
<mark.hill@hilltalentagency.com>
Subject: Re: P&P
I'll be there within the hour.
```

The Hill Agency offices have been almost unrecognizable since Mark took over for his father. What previously looked like a professional office building now resembles a shopping mall. The walls have been replaced with glass, and the waiting room is now standing room only, with all of the plants removed and a tablet next to the receptionist, Mary. She has worked in the office since Mark Sr. opened the company. In what has become our tradition, we share an eye roll as I arrive.

"He has you working on a Sunday?" I ask.

"Having two weeks paid vacation was worth coming in on a Sunday," she shares.

We talk about how she spent her holiday while I check in on the tablet, which I feel is pointless because Mark Jr. can see me from his desk in his glass wall office and waves me in.

As I sit in front of the ostentatious glass desk, he begins to stand, an indication this might not be great news. "They are going in a different direction."

The words I was worried I'd hear. "What other direction… It's Jane Austen. How many directions can you take?"

"Any direction away from you. They don't want to associate this great love story with you."

"Excuse me?"

He leans over to grab a folder and then hands it to me. "I had Mary print some of your most famous articles out to show you. The studio feels your rogue reputation will discourage fans from becoming interested in the movie. The public now knows you as a man who has one-night stands with random models and no intention of having romantic relationships. You said yourself, 'It's Jane Austen. It's one of the greatest love stories of all time,' and they want to broadcast all things involved as romantic."

"My private personal life has no connection to my professional abilities and experience," I argue. How dare they ignore the years of professional partnership we have shared, all for some paparazzi photos.

"Your personal life is not private." He points to the folder in my hands. I throw it back onto his desk.

"So that's it. After everything I've worked for, all of my awards, I'm just removed from the conversation because of my *personal* dating history?."

He sits down in the chair next to me and leans forward with his elbows on his knees. Times like these, he reminds me of his father. "Think about the target audience here, Henry. Sure, you'll have teens and young people seeing this movie who will have no idea who you are. But the majority of the viewers are people who are so invested in Mr. Darcy's story that they will be critical of not only the movie itself but the entire production. Those viewers may know your name, and if they don't already, they will once production starts. Advertising has changed. Every step of this movie's production will be broadcast on social media."

This shouldn't be a matter of public opinion based on my personal life. Sure, I've done nothing to hide it, but my work should be the only thing considered when deciding who will direct this. "So it's settled then? They have another director?" I ask.

"No. From what I've been told, they are having trouble finding someone with a clean personal life who does work as well as you."

"You think there is time to change their minds?"

"Possibly…sleep on it. I'm not sure how we can erase how you've been spending the last couple of years, though." I don't imagine I'll be able to get much sleep with this over my head.

Nine

LUCY

THE ENTIRETY of my Sunday is spent trying to distract myself from the infuriating interaction I had with Henry this morning. It's none of my business if he decided to spend the night with one of those women and do a very proud walk of shame the following morning. But did he really have to do it in front of my apartment? I would have rather assumed that's how he spent his evening rather than have proof first thing in the morning.

Now, I'm left wondering which of the women did he leave with, or it could have been multiple women. I know who he is, and he has never denied it. In fact, he has bragged about it. It shouldn't bother me at all who he spent his night with, after all, I did encourage it. There's just some small part of me that enjoyed him speaking into my ear with my hand on his leg last night.

This is why I stick to fictional men!

What was he insinuating by saying I would have had a great night?

Who knows how things could have ended?

Was he suggesting I could have found someone to go home with? Surely, he didn't mean I may have gone home with him.

I could call Ellie for her opinion, but she would run wild with that exchange and even more if I shared our close conversation from last night with her.

Instead, I end up on the phone with my mom and little does she know, the call is greatly appreciated. I think she begins to be suspicious when I am far more interested in the Thanksgiving Day preparations than I have ever been before. I ask and debate each and every option of pie and sweets from our favorite local bakery, contemplate the shopping list for our dinners, and review the flight schedule multiple times.

When I finally end our call, my head feels a little clearer, that is, until I see a text message from Finn and notice a new number has been added to our group chat.

A photo and link to an article fill the text box. The photo is of Henry leaving the bar last night hand-in-hand with one of the blondes from the bar. Well, at least I don't have to wonder which one it was anymore. Under the photo comes another text.

FINN

Is this our new mom?

A couple minutes of silence pass then a message comes in from Oliver. It's a photo of Henry on his walk of shame this morning.

OLIVER

I'm going to guess no. I bet she tossed
him out when she learned she'd have to
deal with the two of us as sons!

That text received multiple laughing emojis from Mia and Hannah. Still no response from the unknown number, but I am starting to suspect it could be Henry. Then, the conversation turns to me.

FINN

Makes me wonder if Lucy truly had a
headache last night. Could it be that she
also snuck off on a secret rendezvous with
a mystery lover?

MIA

big eyes emoji

LUCY

I shouldn't admit this since there isn't any
photographic evidence, but yes. You
figured it out. I spent the entire evening
thinking of one man, and I rushed home to
get in bed with him!

I quickly snap a photo of my well-read copy of *Persuasion* on my pillow and send it to the group. Everyone, including the unknown number, adds a laughing emoji reaction to my photo.

The beginning of the week goes by fairly quickly as my students are submitting their midterm papers. The assignment they have is to watch a movie that features a particular topic we cover in class. Most students decided to focus on trauma and connected it with war movies and some stretched it to horror movies. Other students who are studying education write about the connections within children's movies. Most of my colleagues voice their complaints about grading at the monthly department meetings, but I find it fascinating. I check daily for early submissions and grade them as the students turn them in so I don't get too overwhelmed. Thankfully, I wasn't worried any of them would use one of Henry's movies for their papers. No, jumping into my work has been a welcome break from thoughts of him.

Tuesday evening at the coffee shop is entertaining, as always. Mia goes on about the drama taking place in her office between various coworkers. Hannah shares a new recipe she wants to try for us. Finn and Oliver gush over their ladies as always. To my surprise, Henry selected the chair next to me even though he arrived later than the rest of us. Which I may have kept empty for him.

We don't talk much. I assume there is still some lingering awkwardness between us from his walk of shame. I will never judge the actions of consenting adults, which he and his lady friend surely were. It does, however, hurt when the first man you've felt *something* for since your ex displays similar tendencies. Not that I would accuse Henry of cheating or deceiving women without evidence like the parasite. But it does appear that he enjoys the company of many women.

He is an adult and has every right to do so.

Henry lost the guessing game for my current book, and his sons didn't let him lose discreetly. He confidently guessed that I was reading *Persuasion*, which they immediately mocked him for after. Finn tells him, "You've already lost."

Henry argues, "How can I have lost? She was just reading that less than forty-eight hours ago."

So, I was correct in assuming that the new number belonged to him in our group chat.

Mia jumps, "Yes, and she probably finished it that night."

Then Oliver says, "Rookie mistake."

Hannah and I keep quiet with smiles on our faces.

Ten

LUCY

WEDNESDAY'S WORK day is coming to an end, and I find myself with an unplanned evening with endless potential. Ellie and I had scheduled a chat tonight, but she needed to reschedule. Something came up with her baseball team's trading deal…or something. I don't follow baseball, but I know she can get busy in the office, even during the off-season.

There is something special about knowing someone since you were a kid and watching them grow and mature into a professional. The pride for them is unexplainable. Ellie is very passionate about keeping the fans engaged in the off-season. Last year, she said, "It's easy during the season to connect with the fans, but in the off-season, that's where it takes creativity to keep those fans engaged."

I've finished my lectures for the day, and now I'm sending out reminders that Friday is the deadline to submit midterms to those students who haven't already sent me their papers. I can't blame those who are waiting until the last possible minute. Who hasn't submitted papers at 11:59 p.m. on the due date?

My phone buzzes next to my laptop. It's the unknown number from the group chat, Henry. I forgot to go back and save his number.

HENRY

Hi. Having a good day?

This is extremely odd, but I'm too intrigued to ignore it.

LUCY

Yes, thank you. And you?

Dots pop up under his name. My mouth falls open to see him typing his response immediately.

HENRY

It's waiting for you if you can sneak away from your desk.

Under his text is a photo of a cold brew coffee next to what I can only assume is his hot coffee in a mug on a dark wooden table that looks very familiar. A particularly sweet gesture from a man who is the opposite of sweet. I sit back in my chair and take a few moments to decide how to proceed.

LUCY

Is this a trap? Are you trying to lure me out just to lecture me on the negative points of Mr. Tilney?

Although, how could he argue Mr. Tilney? Not only is

the leading man of Jane Austen's *Northanger Abbey* perfect, but Henry himself directed Max in the role and knows there is nothing bad to say about such an admirable character.

HENRY

I have your number now, Lucy. I don't need to trap you into coffee to discuss the ridiculousness of the fictional men you are so infatuated with.

This is simply a friendly gesture.

LUCY

Hmm... it is a tempting offer...

My curiosity gets the best of me, but I don't let him know immediately. I grab my coat and head out the door. As I approach the coffee shop, I pull my phone out and send him a text.

LUCY

Alright, but just in case, I'm going to let my boyfriend, Fitzwilliam Darcy know where I am... Just in case your intentions are not of a gentlemanly manner. ;-)

I spot him before he notices me. He is seated at a bench table where the chair on the opposite side had been claimed by another table. I suppose he expects me to sit next to him, so odd how he always does that.

He looks down at this phone, presumably to read the text, and I notice his lips twitching slightly to one side while he reads. What a sight, but I can't linger like a creep watching him. While he is distracted typing a response, I pull on the heavy door, and the bell above me ruins my discreet entrance. I can feel my phone buzz from his response but I decide not to check it.

Just as I suspected, he moves down on the bench, allowing me to slide in next to him. I hate to admit it, but I quite enjoy sitting next to him.

I thank him for the coffee with an inquisitive look.

"I must share—I do have a specific reason for asking you here this afternoon." He looks down at his coffee as he talks. His knee is jumping beneath the table next to mine.

"Is everything all right?" Could something be wrong? He is acting out of sorts.

"Oh, sorry. Nothing urgent. Everyone is fine, in good health...it's more of something I need your...advice with..." Puzzled, I silently wait for him to continue. "As you know, I've made a career of directing movies, romance movies, to be specific."

"Yes, that was an...interesting discovery for me, but go on." I notice his face fall.

"I've recently been informed that the production company, my production company, the only one I've worked with for years, has decided to make a new adaptation of *Pride and Prejudice*."

I can't control myself. I cheer loudly. "That's so great!"

"Yes, I assumed you would be pleased to hear that. I was too. It's the one adaptation I've been trying to make since my career began."

"You'll be directing it?" I feel my skin blush, realizing instantly that my tone was not very kind.

"No, it doesn't look like I will be," he says with a sigh and sadness.

"I'm sorry."

"No, you're not." It's not anger in his voice but defeat. "Can I ask why?" He leans closer to me and almost whispers, "This was the very reason the studio turned me down. They do not believe the viewers and fans of Jane Austen's work, individuals like yourself, would want to see it if you knew I was the director." Ouch, that was harsh of them.

"Can you explain your disappointment at the thought of me directing that?" As he asks, he leans closer and talks quietly to avoid being overheard.

"Henry, I adore your movies."

"Then what is the hesitation?" His posture goes rigid as he sits up to put distance between us. Almost as if he knows what my answer will be.

"After meeting you—"

"Yes, I know I was unpleasant when we met, but I've not met the majority of the viewers of my movies." His lips push into a thin line and I notice his jaw clench.

With a slight laugh, I continue, "True, you weren't very friendly upon our first meeting, but that wasn't it. I did some Internet research on you. You've been very public about your ideas of love, which is your right to feel as you do. Yet, you seem to have a different view on romance than what the fans of romance movies, especially Jane Austen fans, would want."

His shoulders slump, and he turns his body to face forward once again. "That's what the production studio said. They are planning a social media campaign, and they worry it will bring the things you're referencing to light." With a huff, he continues, "Why can't people look at romance movies the way they experience other things, like a roller coaster? It's all manufactured to make you feel a particular emotion."

"Well, that's a very objective way of looking at it. I suppose you are quite good at it, but *Pride and Prejudice* means so much to people. I think we want to know it's in the hands of someone else who cares for it as much as we do."

"I do care. That's why I want to direct it," he says as his hand bunches into a fist on the table.

"Aside from a career perspective, do you truly care about sharing this love story with the world? I think they may be looking for someone who has a more outward romantic side," I ask, trying not to sound too jaded.

"Well, how do you suggest I change people's perception of me to appear more romantic?" he asks with an exasperated tone.

"Well, first, do you even remember how to be romantic? I assume you've been in love at some point in your life." I've hit a nerve. His face shuts down, and he turns to look over his shoulder.

After a deep breath, causing his broad shoulder to rise and fall, he turns back to me. "It's not about real love. It's about manufactured love. I have learned very few people can notice a difference. At least not when watching movies or even following someone's personal life."

"And you think you could fool people with your manufactured love approach?" I ask with disbelief.

He smirks to himself while placing his coffee on the

table to turn his body toward me. He places his arm behind me and leans slightly forward. His dark brown eyes move from my eyes to my lips. I lick them without reason as his gaze moves back to my eyes again. Without breaking eye contact, his fingers graze mine as he places my drink on the table next to his, then gently takes my hand, and his thumb begins soft strokes over the back of it.

The connection sets my body on fire, and I struggle to remember where we are or what a truly dislikable person Henry is when he speaks. Which reminds me of his mouth just as he opens it slightly to say my name in a hushed, seductive tone, "Lucy."

My heart begins to race as my brain tries desperately to maintain composure. He raises a hand to my cheek while the other continues to hold mine. With a soft caress, he moves my face to the side and breaks our eye contact only to gain better access to my ear. He leans in closer, and as I look around to the other customers no one pays us any attention, but why would they? We appear to be a normal couple cuddling in the corner.

Then, he begins to speak, only to me, at a whisper's volume but with a deep and certain tone, *"In vain have I struggled."* My heart stops. To hear the words I have replayed over and over in their mind, being spoken directly to me, this must be a dream. *"It will not do. My feelings will not be repressed."* I lean closer to him as his lips brush the top of my ear before he pulls back. Strong fingers under my chin, guiding my face back to his, but this time closer than we've ever been before. Our lips are a moment away from each other. Those burning eyes, now darker, speak directly to my soul. *"You must allow me to tell you how ardently I admire and love you."*

I'm breathing again, at a more rapid pace than I would prefer to do in public. His hand drops from my chin as the other releases mine as he grabs his coffee, and smirks before taking a drink.

"Feel confident in my abilities now, Lucy?"

Well, I certainly can't claim to be unaffected. He must notice the flush on my face, but I need to play it cool, if only a little.

"I'm appreciative that you stopped before telling me all the reasons why I am not good enough for you." A nervous laugh escapes me. I'm stalling, trying to regain my senses.

His expression is all business as he asks again, "You didn't answer my question. Have you changed your mind on my ability to manufacture the romance needed for this film?"

"Yes, I suppose you would be the right person to direct it." I do not want to elaborate and tell him how unbelievably sexy that was. Also, I don't want this adaptation to be poorly made. The anguish readers feel when their favorite book is mangled in its transition to the big screen is something I don't want for *Pride and Prejudice.*

Yes, that's the only reason, not how he left me breathless.

"Then, tell me. I can't possibly demonstrate my talents to every Jane Austen fan, and quite frankly, I do not want to. How can I win their approval?"

Why do I feel my lips curling up into a small smile when I hear he doesn't want to whisper in other's ears? I know why, because that was an experience I will never forget and it's only for me.

"What if you were to lean into the social media aspect the production company is looking for?"

"I don't have social media," he says with absolute resolution. There is the stubborn man I know.

"Yes, I know," I say with a pointed look. "But you can get one and create a new image for yourself. Right now the only thing the public knows about your life after your last movie is the photos of your nights out on the town. Perhaps show them more. Or manufacture a different image."

"How would that make me romantic?" This man clearly doesn't understand the potential of social media.

"You don't have to necessarily be romantic. Just give yourself some depth. You can just post a couple photos so people can know another side of you. They don't need to be long or have any captions, for that matter, just something other than the paparazzi shots. Simple things, like your morning coffee, making dinner with your sons, or a book you are currently reading. Maybe even a photo of *Pride and Prejudice* on your nightstand could slip in there. But not at first that would be too obvious. It could easily be done without even posting your face. Give the public a glimpse into a more wholesome and possibly romantic side of Henry Brooks, even if it is manufactured."

"Hmm.. Let's get a professional opinion." He grabs his phone, taps it quickly, and holds it to his ear. "Hi Mary, it's Henry Brooks. Is Mark available? Yes, it's urgent… Thank you." He looks around the coffee shop to check that no one is watching but turns to me and relays the social media plan into the phone in a hushed tone.

When he puts the phone down, he smiles up at me. "Mark, my agent, thinks it might work."

He pulls out a notepad and pen from the bag I didn't realize was sitting behind him. With his pen in hand, he asks, "Will you start over with the list of pictures I'll need to post?"

"Well, first, you'll need to get an account."

"Oh, should we do that first?" he asks.

"Not exactly, let's get the list together, then Oliver and Finn could probably assist with the account setup later. I'm not sure how to go about verifying your accounts, but I'd bet Mia would."

"All right." Before I can start listing photo ideas, he leans closer and says, "Thank you. I wasn't feeling optimistic this morning, but I knew if anyone could help, it would be you."

I feel the blush coming back, reclaiming its territory over my neck and face, but my brain steps in before my misguided infatuation can take over again. "Yes, lucky you have a Jane Austen fan in your proximity."

"No, I'm lucky to have a Lucy Taylor in my life." Matching his words, his gaze is more serious than I was expecting.

As he said before, he believes love is manufactured for the media and not real. Yes, I will need to repeat that to myself every time I think about him whispering Mr. Darcy's words in my ear.

"Yes, of course, let's get started on your list then," I

say in an attempt to move the conversation along before my hopeless romantic heart gets control of me again.

Later that night, I receive many texts from Finn and Oliver, cursing my name for placing the task of bringing Henry into the social media age on them. It's not long before I receive the request from the "Henry Brooks - Official" account, pleasantly surprised to see that it is already verified. Very impressive. I take note of the very handsome black and white headshot they used for his account photo. I'm sure that alone will gain him many followers.

Eleven

IT'S BEEN two weeks since joining the innovative world of social media, and I'm already experiencing the impact. Lucy was a genius to suggest this and her photo ideas are incredibly simple and yet getting tons of attention. The account shows I have over a million followers, but that can't be correct. Aren't there more interesting things to do on the Internet than watch for a random photo I post each day?

Mark and I have been in contact, but there has been no movement in either direction from Viewmont Productions yet. I can handle no news—as long as they haven't signed someone else, I still have a chance in this race. Although I am no less angry, they are making me put on such a show, simply for a chance at the movie that I have earned the right to be their first choice after working for them most of my career.

In addition to virtual popularity, Lucy and I have been in daily contact, even though I suppose she has already sent enough photo ideas for weeks' worth of content. I like to get her approval on them before I post. Sometimes, she comes up with catchy captions, others she insists need no caption. "It's better to leave it a mystery," she says.

We are getting closer. Aside from the social media posts, we have started sharing the events of our days with each other, and joking has increased as well. I look forward to seeing her name on my phone.

GROUP CHAT

HENRY

10 reasons why Captain Wentworth is the worst Jane Austen leading man. Click Here to Read.

Before anyone else can reply, Lucy does.

LUCY

10 ways to protect yourself and your health during a ONS. Click Here to Read the Article.

HANNAH

Sorry, Henry. Nice try, but Lucy just taught us all not to mess with her! *laughing crying emoji*

OLIVER

laughing emoji

MIA

face with tears emoji

HENRY

What is an "ONS"?

FINN

rolling on the floor emoji

One Night Stand, Pop.

HENRY

Shots fired, Lucy.

LUCY

You came after my personal life, so I came for yours!

HENRY

Reading alone isn't a relationship

LUCY

Neither is what you're doing.

Lucy messages me individually after our "battle in the group chat," but surprisingly, it's not to further antagonize me.

LUCY

Hi! I had an idea for new content on your accounts. Do you have any set photos from movies you previously directed? Reminding people of your passion and the amazing work you've done in the past might get them wanting more.

HENRY

Yes, of course. I believe there are a few here in London. I'll look for them. Great idea!

LUCY

Thanks

HENRY

Will you be joining us Saturday night? For dinner and drinks?

LUCY

Yes, I'll be there. Hannah and Mia are taking me shopping on Friday to get more "dinner clothes," as Mia says. See you then!

HENRY

Enjoy the shopping.

Saturday night arrives, and our limo pulls to a stop outside of Lucy's apartment. *Now I know which one is hers.* Hannah offers to run up and grab her, but I ask her to text Lucy and let her know I'll be coming up to get her. "She's in apartment number two," Mia yells with her head out the window.

At the top of the outer stairs, there is a buzzer with a button next to the number two. I press it, wait, and then her sweet voice comes through the little speaker. "Hi! I just need a minute, and I'll be right down." Her voice wavers as it comes through the speaker. She sounds almost nervous.

"It's Henry, I can come up and get you."

Lucy's voice returns, "Oh, sure. I'm up the stairs to the right."

The door clicks as it unlocks, and suddenly, I feel a tightening in my stomach as I ascend the short staircase. Once at her door, I give a quick knock and she opens almost immediately. I'm struck motionless. Again, she selected an item that bares her shoulder. This time, it's not a top but a stunning black dress that hugs her curves as it flows down her body. As I regain my composure to face her, I notice she too, is admiring my attire.

"Please come in, I just need to grab my coat and bag." As she turns to grab the missing items from her outfit, I notice the high slit in the skirt of her dress, revealing mile-long legs, perfect to provide access to her luscious thighs. I catch my breath, trying to regain my composure before she sees me so…distracted. If this dress was something purchased with Mia and Hannah, I may need to encourage them to take more shopping trips together.

As Lucy reenters the room, she moves with little coordination, attempting to hold her purse while pulling her coat on. I jump to her rescue, grabbing the coat and assisting her into it.

She thanks me, but something about her is shy tonight as she continues to fidget with her coat even once it's in place. Perhaps it's the formality of the evening. I offer her my arm. Relief and excitement flood through my body as she slips her arm through mine.

She holds onto me tightly as she carefully descends the steps outside her building. That's when she notices what is waiting for us. "A limo?"

"Well, with everyone dressing so formally, I decided it would be better to have more room to sit without being on top of each other," I explain.

"How thoughtful," she responds.

I open the door for her to slide in. "You can go straight in. We have the back seat."

I move in next to her and close the door behind me. The overwhelming urge to put my hand around her and pull her close comes over me. *No, that is ridiculous.* Maybe I could just hold her hand? Would she like that?

Enough. This isn't a date.

Stealing a glance, I struggle to look away from her. This may turn out to be a very long night. Here's to hoping I survive it.

At dinner, I can barely focus on my meal while the conversation between Lucy and I flows as if we've known each other for years. We speak not only of the success of my social media presence, but she has many new ideas she shares in attempts to win me the director role I so longingly desire.

It's easy to fool myself into thinking she is doing this for me and my professional pursuits, but I know that she is really doing it for Jane Austen and her characters. Regardless of her motives, I find myself thankful for any reason to have her here speaking with me.

During a pause in conversation, I take my chance to get to know Lucy better. "I don't think I ever asked, what motivated your international move?"

She smiles at me with flushed cheeks. "It wasn't one specific thing, and when everything in my life felt like it was pushing me toward change, I figured why not just make the move." Her face relaxes. "It's always been a dream of mine to live in the UK." Given her love of Jane Austen's work, it's her obvious destination of choice.

"Do you miss your friends and family? That's an awfully brave move to be so far away from everyone you care about." Hopefully, my question isn't too obvious, but I'm trying to get more information on the relationship she spoke of with Finn and Oliver.

"I call my mom just about every day, and I'll be visiting her for the holidays. As for my friends, we are still in regular contact, and hopefully, they will be coming in to visit soon." She turns to look over at the rest of the party. "I'm very fortunate to have made such great friends so soon after moving here." She beams in their direction.

Lucy answered my questions without any indication that she was in a relationship prior to leaving. Could it be that she is still so broken up over this heartbreak she can't bear to speak of it? My jaw clenches as my mind fills with fantasies of destroying the man who could hurt her so much. Although, without such heartbreak, I would have never found myself sitting next to her tonight, admiring that beautiful dress and the breathtaking smile on her face when she looks in my direction.

It is a long-standing joke that I do not believe in love, and she claims to only be interested in fictional men. We are the two outcasts in our group with four individuals who have found a true love connection. I stand firm on my take on romance, but a small part of me is relieved that she has not voiced her intention to date since we've met.

I daresay I am enjoying our new friendship, but I know better than to want it to be anything more.

Well, after seeing her in this dress, maybe a little more.

Twelve

HENRY

I TRY to rid myself of the memory from the last time we went out and the events that followed, tonight is a new night. I am not sure how it will end, but it will certainly not end as it did then. I shake my head to bring myself back to the present. This bar is different from the one we last visited. When we enter it is far more crowded and takes more time to make our way to the booth Mia has reserved for us in the back. I make sure Lucy is in front of me with Oliver in front of her. There are too many people—*men*—in here. I want to keep an eye on her.

She turns her head over her shoulder and catches my eye. "Looks like tonight you'll have plenty to choose from." She tilts her head in the direction of the large group of young women on the dance floor. Nothing about those women tempts me in the slightest and not just because of what paparazzi photographs may come of it, but I am enjoying my time with my family and don't want another night of Lucy and I going our separate ways. I will be the one to get everyone home at the end of the night, and that includes Lucy.

Shaking my head, never looking away from her, I lean in. "Keep walking," I say with a firm tone while placing my hand on her lower back, giving the slightest bit of pressure. She laughs and follows my directions. "Good girl," I whisper. She shivers under my touch.

The booth we are given is in an L shape with two square tables in front of us, allowing for people to get up as they need. This is much better for our large party and much less restrictive.

Lucy and I take the two seats at the bottom of the L shape, with me on the end and Hannah on her other side. After our drinks are delivered, Mia raises her glass in cheers to another amazing evening and then passes something to Lucy. I noticed quickly it's a pain reliever. "Take it now," Mia yells, "No headaches tonight. We are partying until the sun comes up."

Lucy laughs and places the package in her tiny handbag.

"No e-reader tonight? Won't your fictional boyfriends miss you?"

She smiles up at me. My breath catches, and before I can look too deeply into why that is, she answers, "The bag isn't big enough for it. So sadly, I will not have their company to fall back on."

"No need, I plan to provide you with constant and exceptional entertainment this evening." I have no plans of leaving her side, but I'm not sure if she believes me.

"Take a photo of the table with the drinks," she says with her glass in her hand.

"I thought we were trying to put distance between the pub scene and myself."

"The bars were never the concern—it was the company you were keeping. This is a nice night out with your family. It shows your fun side and that you are spending time with your sons and their partners. You can caption it 'An entertaining evening with my family' and then link their accounts." Even in this poorly lit bar, her eyes sparkle as she shares her idea. I don't hesitate to take the photo while she sips on her red wine.

The waiter comes to take our order for the next round of drinks and yells loud enough for us to hear, "And for the couple at the end, same as before?"

Together, we reply loudly, denying being a couple. The waiter doesn't care. "Okay, not a couple, same drinks as before?" he says, with intense exasperation. We both nod quickly with everyone's eyes on us as we avoid eye contact with each other.

Hannah attempts to engage us both in a conversation before Oliver quickly cuts her off and whisks her away to the dance floor.

"Care to dance?" I ask Lucy, trying to sound confident in my request.

"With whom?" Mischief crosses her face, and then she looks away from me as if searching for a dance partner in the crowd. *Cute.*

I stand and offer her my hand. Her face falls a little. Did I offend her?

She grabs it and tugs on it for me to sit back down, but her efforts are in vain, and I use my strength to pull her up in front of me. She wasn't prepared and neither was I, for how close we are. "Let's dance," I say while my mouth is a breath away from hers. I don't give her the chance to answer as we make our way to the dance floor. I remember her mentioning having dance lessons when she was younger—maybe I could impress her a little.

The dance floor has varied between sets of club music and variations of contemporary streamlined music. I believe the switch between the two is to allow for each group to break for drinks and whatnot. I appreciate that. The twenty-something celebrities Mia has been fawning over since we arrived have finally moved off the dance floor and into their seats at the bar and various booths like ours.

As the music begins, I pull Lucy into my arms, and she moves with a delicate ease. *Oh yes, she knows how to dance.* Sure, we've touched before, but holding her in my arms is causing my body to heat with a fire I haven't felt in a very long time.

While it was an admiral plan to impress her, it's glaringly obvious she is the impressive one. It is as if her body is connected to my thoughts. She turns with precision, sways her hips in time with mine, and holds her posture solid, yet is flexible with each move I make.

The hours fly by like minutes, but after checking my watch, I realize it's well after midnight. Lucy catches my action and asks, "What time is it?"

I've been deprived of her touch since we parted after our last dance, but now she's provided me with another opportunity. I hold my wrist up, but just out of her reach. She gently grabs my wrist and pulls it in for a closer look, just as I wanted her to.

"It's late, I think I'll be heading home soon," she says, making a grand gesture of letting me know before disappearing again.

"One moment," I tell her with my pointer finger up in hopes she won't disappear the moment I turn around. She nods.

"Finn, Oliver." I wave them toward me. It may just be my advanced age, but I believe the music has continually increased in volume since we arrived. They both lean over to hear me. "Ready to head out?" They know I had intentions of us all leaving together. Looking back at their girls, who are leaning toward each other in the booth, showing signs of depleting energy. They nod back at me. "I'll call for the car. Should only take them a couple of minutes."

Returning to Lucy's side, I take advantage of the loud music, drape my arm around her shoulder, and pull her close to speak directly into her ear. Just as I had hoped she rests her hand on my leg as she turns her body in toward mine. Electricity runs through me at her touch. "I just messaged the driver and said we are ready to leave. He will let me know when he is here."

Reluctantly, I begin to pull away from her. As I do, her lips brush my cheek as she leans in to speak with me. Those soft lips caress my cheek with the most delicate of touches, but I know their touch will leave a lasting impression, strong enough to ingrain in my memory forever. "You don't have to leave because I am. I can get a cab."

Absurd.

Never will I allow her to leave a shared evening alone again. Escorting her safely to her apartment will be a far better experience than I can have with anyone in this bar tonight. "We are leaving together," I say firmly while looking directly into her eyes as a promise not to act as foolishly as I did before.

It seems to have the opposite effect on her. It looks as if she snaps out of a trance and pulls her hand from my leg quickly. Did I say something wrong? Could she have plans to meet someone after? Perhaps our time spent dancing has caused me to be more comfortable than she is with our new friendship.

I look around to the rest of our party, but they don't appear to have noticed. At that moment, my phone buzzes. It's the driver letting me know he's outside. We make our way to the exit, and Lucy begins to struggle with her coat again. I jump at the chance to assist her.

Finn and Mia are first at the door, followed by Hannah and Oliver, and then us at the end. As soon as Finn opens the door, flashing lights begin to flood the entrance lobby. He closes it and looks back at me. Finn and Oliver are familiar with this situation, as are their partners. No one enjoys it, but we all know what to do.

"Fix your hair, check your makeup. Looks like we are all about to get our photos taken tonight." Finn always tries to break these tense situations with a joke.

Then I turn to Lucy, whose face has lost some of its coloring. My stomach sinks at the effect this is having on her. Placing my hands on her shoulders, I lower my face to meet her eyes. "You don't have to acknowledge them at all. Just stay very close to me, keep your eyes forward or down, and we will get to the car as soon as possible."

"Why are they here?" She's still trying to process this, and the longer we stand in here the more suspicious the photographers will become.

"I believe it is due to the many celebrities inside tonight."

"I didn't notice anyone famous, well, aside from you," she says, and my heart flips a little. That place was filled with celebrities, including many handsome young men whose attention she caught without even noticing. Could that perhaps be because I held her attention all night?

No, don't go down that road.

"We are all going to leave now. Once we get in the limo, everything will be fine," I pause, "I'm sorry about this." I doubt it will be the last time I apologize to her for this. "Stay close to me, all right?"

She nods and moves to my side. I give Finn a nod, and he opens the door again. My left arm goes protectively around Lucy's waist as we exit the bar. She leans her body against mine as we begin our swift walk to the curb where the limo awaits. Photographers begin yelling my name, I ignore it, but it clearly has an effect on Lucy. With her right hand, she grabs onto my suit jacket as if to pull me closer to her. I lean down to whisper in her ear, "You're doing brilliantly, just a few more steps." I feel her slight nod as she looks forward.

She shuffles into the limo behind Hannah. I practically leap in behind her. Once the door is closed and we are en route, Oliver breaks the silence. "Welcome to the family, Lucy."

Hannah leans over and pats her knee. "You did well. The first time that happened to me, I froze in place, and Oliver and Finn had to practically carry me to the car."

Lucy's smile returns to her face and I find myself now indebted to Hannah.

The short ride is spent with Mia listing the celebrities who were in attendance and what they were wearing. Everyone is shocked that Lucy didn't notice a single one.

I help Lucy out of the limo and walk her up to her apartment. She stops just outside her door, keys in hand, and turns to me. Before she can say anything, I say, "Lucy, I apologize about the photographers, I should have realized they would be out there."

She grows distant once again like she was earlier when she pulled her hand from my leg. "No need to apologize, Henry. Thank you, I had a wonderful night." Her tone sounds rigid and almost practiced.

"Yes, of course. Goodnight then."

She quickly unlocks the door and hurries in. Before closing it, she turns back and says, "Goodnight." I wait to hear the lock and make my way back to the limo.

Thirteen

LUCY

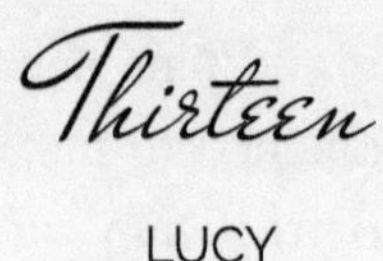

THE SOUND of my text message alert pulls me from my peaceful slumber. Without looking I roll onto my opposite side and pull the covers over my head. If it is that important, a real emergency, they would have called and not text. It can't be anything urgent.

After hours of tossing and turning, sometime after looking at the clock at 4:00 a.m., I must have finally fallen asleep. I don't know what time it is now, but I do know I need more sleep. Flipping over without checking my phone, I attempt to get more rest.

But then, the text alert sounds twice more.

With a loud *ugh*, I roll over to check it.

I laugh as I remember Ellie changing John's contact name in my phone to her nickname for him.

THE PARASITE

I was just wondering if you're coming
home for the holidays.

Maybe we could catch up, spend some
time together…I miss you.

Hell no. I'm not answering. I can't believe I woke up for that. I roll over and pull the covers back over my head. If only John knew his competition here.

No, not competition, because there is no situation where John would have a chance, and I would have to be seriously interested in Henry, which I'm definitely not. *He's not fictional and will certainly break my heart.*

And more so, he is certainly not interested in me.

To top it all off, neither of us is interested in any kind of relationship. Well, I suppose Henry is interested in similar types of relationships John has.

No, that's not fair. I shouldn't compare the two. Henry is upfront with his partners that he is not looking for anything serious. According to everyone in our friend groups, John promises hearts and flowers to the girls he dates in secret. Whenever I ask if he's dating someone, he denies it and never brings dates out when we hang out with our mutual friends.

I need to get my mind off of the two of them. It was difficult enough to stop thinking about Henry last night after admitting to myself that I'm starting to enjoy his company. He whispered in my ear again, *only because the music was too loud to hear him otherwise.* The volume of our conversation was not enhanced when I put my hand on his leg, *but that didn't stop me.* He didn't seem affected by it anyway. And I should not be affected by it either. *But I am…*a little.

Enough, I'll count sheep until I fall back to sleep to keep myself from thinking of him.

A few hours later, I hear my text alert go off again. Looking over at the clock, I notice I've slept until the early afternoon. Picking up the phone, I find the text that woke me this time.

HENRY

Coffee?

I smile. I much prefer waking up to a text from Henry than…well, anyone else. He apologized so many times last night after we left the bar. I'm sure he's offering coffee to make up for it, but it didn't bother me as much as he thinks. I certainly didn't enjoy it and didn't want to deal with the paparazzi again, but it was not his fault. I'm not angry or upset, what he was noticing was my reaction to the confusing feelings I can no longer ignore. There were moments when the evening did feel as if we were on a date. A very good date, probably the best I've ever had. Which makes it even more sad that it wasn't a date at all.

I need some distance to process the events of last night and decide to decline his invitation.

LUCY

Hey, I'm sorry, but I can't today. I'm staying in to grade papers.

I hate lying to anyone. It gives me a pit in my stomach but I can't very well tell him the real reason I want to stay home.

Dressed in lounge pants and an oversized sweatshirt, I make my way to the kitchen and grab a glass of water before heading to my final destination for the day, my couch. An uneventful Sunday is just what I need. Maybe I'll order takeout later so I don't have to run to the grocery store.

When I queue up my favorite streaming service, the first movie in my Watch Again category is *Persuasion*, which Henry directed. I have seen the movie so many times before and this might be the longest I have gone between views.

I push the play button and tell myself this has nothing to do with Henry.

Sure.

Just as I'm watching Mary tell Anne that Captain Wentworth said Anne looked so old since he last saw her, he barely recognized her, the doorbell buzzer rings. It must be a takeout delivery for one of the neighbors—they always ring the wrong apartment.

Not wanting to leave the warmth of my soft blanket, I keep it wrapped around my body as I wobble to the intercom.

"Hello?" I say, waiting for the delivery person to reply.

"Lucy, it's Henry. I have coffee." I freeze in place, still clutching the blanket around me. He continues, "I would like to come up and speak with you."

"Okay," I say as I push the button to unlock the main door then I bolt to my bedroom to change as quickly as possible. Thankfully, I never got around to putting away my clean laundry and am able to frantically pull on a pair of jeans and decide to leave the sweatshirt on. In front of my mirror, I quickly pull the bun out of my hair and race against time to brush it out. I have just enough time to put makeup under my eyes to conceal my dark circles from the night before and a little mascara before he knocks on my door.

Two quick spritzes of perfume and a last check in the mirror, "Good enough."

I open the door and immediately realize my appearance is not good enough. Henry looks like a model. All black from head to toe with a fitted winter jacket over his athletic pants and a solid black ball cap. It's as if each time I see him now, he looks like he just walked off a magazine photoshoot. In his right hand, he has a carrier with three drinks, and on the left, some newspapers and magazines are folded under his arm.

"Hi, welcome," I say as I move out of the doorway for him to enter my apartment. He looks around with a soft smile on his lips until his eyes land on my TV.

I forgot to turn off the movie. Great, as if I wasn't flustered enough by his unexpected visit, now I can add embarrassment to the list.

Henry's smile grows slowly as he turns to me. I can feel the heat rising from my neck into my cheeks. I walk over to find the remote that was hidden well under my blanket when I threw it in haste earlier and immediately turned it off.

Desperate to change the subject. I ask, "Is everything

all right?" It is extremely odd that he is showing up at my apartment.

"You don't know yet?" he asks, still holding everything in his hands.

"Don't know what?" I move toward him and extend my arm. "Would you like to put the drinks down? Or perhaps help carrying your reading materials?"

"Yes, of course. My apologies." He lets me grab the drink holder out of his hands but holds the folded papers close to his chest.

"Are we expecting someone else?" I ask, pointing to the three drinks.

"Oh, no. I didn't know what you would want so I asked Beth to make your typical order. She handed me a hot chocolate and a cold brew coffee and said to trust her."

Before I can stop myself, an awkward joke leaves my mouth. "In Beth, we trust!"

He smiles. Butterflies start to dance in my stomach, but thankfully, my brain quickly shuts them down. He must be bringing bad news to bring me drinks to my apartment. I put my iced coffee in the fridge for later and then carry our drinks into the living room.

"Would you like to sit, and then you can give me the bad news." I move to my couch, expecting him to sit on the larger one next to it, but he sits next to me instead.

Before he can say anything, both of our phones buzz with text messages. We pull them out to check, and we have a new message in the group chat.

FINN

Lucy, are YOU our new mom???

Multiple photos of Henry and me from last night pop up under Finn's text. One with the title "Who is Henry Brooks's newest leading lady?" above the photos.

Since our encounter with the photographers last night, it never crossed my mind that the pictures would be printed anywhere. I've been too consumed with thoughts of Henry and our evening. When I look up at Henry, his brows are creased with concern.

"I'm sorry." It's the only thing I can think of to say. We have been working so hard to paint an image of a family man who spends his weekends with his kids or at home reading. Now, I've ruined it for him, and people or, more importantly, the production company will think he is back to his playboy ways.

"You're sorry?" He looks from the papers back up to me. "Why are you sorry? I put you in this position. I know how much you value your private life."

I hadn't thought of that. I look at the picture again. There are a few photos where my full face is visible and others where I'm looking at Henry with more emotion than I want to admit at this moment. In every single picture, Henry has his arm around me, some I'm holding onto his jacket looking forward. But the most incriminating are the ones when we are speaking to one another or making eye contact, "gazing into each other's eyes," as the caption states.

Henry continues while I am lost in the photos. "I am very sorry. I hope you can forgive me."

No need for him to apologize. I needed this slap of reality more than I realized. "It's fine. I'm just sorry if this jeopardizes your chance with the movie."

"Quite the opposite actually…" he says quietly, as if to himself more than me.

I allow my hands to loosen from their grip on the papers, dropping them on the table in front of me. I take a few sips of my hot chocolate before turning to Henry. "How so?"

"Well, I was with my family. It wasn't the typical night in town for me. Every publication includes photos of Oliver, Finn, and the girls."

Relief settles in me. I'm glad I didn't cause too much damage. "Well, that's a relief." Looking back at the papers, I ask, "Do you think these will be published in the States? How famous are you?"

"Apparently not that famous—you didn't know me before we met. Just my work." He leans back on the sofa, coffee in hand, while the other arm takes its place on the back of the loveseat.

"Good point." I risk another glance at the photos but don't let my eyes linger.

"My agent called this morning—he was the one who alerted me to all this." He waves his hand in the direction of the papers and magazines. "He feels we could expedite the studio's decision if I, we, were to…lean into it."

"I don't follow."

Henry adjusts his position as he places his coffee back on the table. Then begins running his hands down his thighs. I'm briefly distracted by the action but am pulled out of it when he blurts out, "What if we didn't deny this."

"Denying would imply that people are even asking." Could this be a bigger ordeal than I realize? "Are people asking?"

"Well, Mark, my agent…"

"Yes, I remember. Keep going." I shouldn't be so short with him. He rubs the back of his neck, and the view of his muscular arm makes my stomach twist.

"Yes, the publicist Mark recently employed for me since our social media plan began said that this is getting a lot of traction from my recent rise in popularity." He stands and begins to pace behind the chair that separates my living room from the kitchen. "Mark asked if you were…if we were…together."

"And what did you tell him?" His answer doesn't mean anything. He must have told him the truth. Surely the cocky Henry Brooks didn't date women like me. Why would Mark even question it? He must not know his client very well.

"Mark suggested a solid, committed relationship, broadcasted on social media, of course, could be the final push we need to get Viewmont Productions to give me the role." *More like the final nail in my coffin.*

"Did you tell him we are together?" He avoided the answer once—I will not let him do it again.

He stops and leans over the back of the chair. I begin to assume the worst as he is putting a large piece of furniture between us before answering. "I told him that it's still new."

"What's still new?"

"Our relationship."

Standing but not making the move to be any closer to him, I say, "Our relationship? Funny, I wasn't aware we were in a relationship." I can barely contain the emotions at odds within me. The less intelligent half gets delighted at the idea of us being in a relationship, *lying about being in a relationship,* but the far more rational side is furious over the fact that he feels he can say such things about me for his own selfish needs. Without my knowledge!

Henry stands up straight, readying himself for this argument. "It's not a bad idea. You have to admit that."

"Sure, I suppose if you were to get into a relationship and post endless romantic dates, it would gain the attention of your target audience, but you don't want a relationship."

"Correct. It would be unfair and unkind of me to find someone to date just to use them for my own personal gain. Which is why this might be the perfect solution. You would be the perfect solution. You are aware of how I feel about love, and you are the creator of this persona that has been so successful and most of all, you aren't looking for a relationship either."

He's right. I don't want a relationship, but do I necessarily want to pretend to be in one with him, either? *It could have some perks* but also can turn into a disaster. "What are you suggesting?"

"We let people think we are in a relationship." He watches my face closely, slowly moving from behind the chair toward me. "You can plan romantic posts for the social media accounts, dates we can be sure paparazzi will photograph, and…" he pauses with a smile on his face, "you get to tell people you are dating one of London's most eligible bachelors."

Arrogant asshole.

"What more could a girl want…" I take a few steps away from him and move to the window.

Do I really want to be known as Henry Brooks's girlfriend until he fake dumps me, and then I have to go back to my normal life?

Could this affect my job?

How would I explain this to my mom, or worse, my friends? But more than that, I can't help but think back to how I felt this morning. When my day started out so crummy, I did the same thing I've done for years, put on comfortable clothes and watched my favorite Jane Austen adaptation. Within minutes, I began to feel better, and Henry had a hand in that.

"It was a joke, Lucy. Well, the last part. I know this is a selfish request. What can I do for you? How can I get you to agree?"

"I want time to think through all of this before I answer."

"Of course. Thank you for even entertaining the idea. I know I'm not the most tolerable person to be around, but you'll only have to pretend to date me for small amounts of time. The rest of the time, you can go back to barely enduring my presence." He smiles at me as he moves to the door. "Thank you again."

"Sure." That is all I can say as he closes the door behind him.

Fourteen

LUCY

THE AWNING in front of the restaurant does little to protect me from the rain. Everyone warned me about the ever-persistent precipitation when I decided to move to London, but I don't mind it at all. I've even found umbrellas that match my coats and accessories.

Standing on either side of two puddles that look dangerously close to meeting in the middle and drowning my shoes, I still can't find myself upset at Mia for suggesting a weekly girls' night—just for the three of us. *"Mondays are such a drag. I think we need to change that, and what better way to do so than to look forward to a night out with the girls?"* Like always, Mia is correct. I've spent most of this dreary day looking forward to their company.

As I pull out my phone to text Mia, Hannah approaches, clutching her umbrella tight and rushing over to me and the awning. She's going to be discouraged when she discovers it offers barely any coverage. We stand close together and line up our umbrellas above us to double the barrier from the rain.

"How was work at the publishing house today? Any new books I should keep an eye out for?" Hannah's job sounds like a dream come true. However I don't think I would make a good publisher, I love almost every book I read and struggle to be critical with them.

"Very well, thank you." It's so refreshing to me when I come across people who truly enjoy their professions. It's far less common than we are made to believe as children. "Yes, in fact, I think you would be very interested to hear about a new trend popping up in our contemporary romance genre."

"Oh, do tell—"

"Ladies!" Mia yells from her taxi window as the car pulls to a slow stop in front of the café to not splash us with the puddles. She jumps out of the car, and the three of us quickly make our way into the café.

Once we take our seats and order, Mia announces our next destination for the evening. "I have decided what we will do after, we're going shopping!"

"Isn't this weather a little difficult for shopping?" Hannah asks.

"Yes, I do believe this calls for a rain check on our shopping plans."

"Before you cancel our plans, let's see what it's like when we leave," Mia pleads.

Hannah and I both agree. Our dinners are delicious. It's a small café with a long menu of sandwiches and coffees that ended up being too much for us to decide. We order four different sandwiches—a turkey club, sausage sandwich, chicken salad, and classic cheese, and then cut them up so we are able to try each of them.

"Hannah, you were just about to tell me about the new books you are reading at work," I remind her.

"Yes, we are finding an increase in modern-day retellings of Jane Austen's books," Hannah explains. "I'll be sure to recommend those authors, I believe a couple already have books that are published."

"Speaking of romance…" She turns in my direction. "How are you doing with the response to the photo of you and Henry from the weekend?"

"What response?"

Has Henry spoken with her or perhaps Finn about his manager's prediction?

"It was all over the Internet and each of my feeds, but maybe that is because I search the Brooks name regularly for anything on Finn and Oliver."

That's a relief, we didn't go into details of what our staged relationship would involve, but I'm not sure I want to bring my friends into our charade, but I don't want to lie to them either.

"I'm managing. Haven't thought much about it since yesterday." I've tried to preoccupy my thoughts with *anything* else.

"Oh, yes, sorry about Finn's joke. I don't think he meant any harm," Mia explains quickly.

"Not at all, it was funny!" I try to reassure her.

"You didn't answer, so we figured it was still a touchy subject," Mia asks.

I look over at Hannah, but she doesn't indicate anything off about yesterday either. They must not know Henry came to see me. This could be my answer to him keeping it a secret from everyone. "Yeah, it was a little surprising. I simply forgot to answer him. I'll have to think of something witty to respond."

After finishing our dinner, Hannah brings our attention to the front window of the café with a frown, the rain has picked up. "I think it might be best for us to call it a night, Mia."

Mia slouches in her seat with her chin down as she lets out a sorrowful sigh.

"Next time we will be sure to visit twice as many shops," I promise her with hope of a better time.

Mia and Hannah share a cab and I am lucky enough to find one for myself. Normally I'd take every chance I can to walk the streets of London, but I'd prefer not to catch a cold before traveling home for the holidays.

The storm grows stronger, and the temperature continues to drop through Tuesday. It's decided in the group text to cancel for this week due to the weather. I'd much prefer snow to icy rain. Even though I haven't left the house the entire day, I still have a chill I can't shake. Without plans for this evening, I spend the day making soup to enjoy it while curling up on the couch with a new book, one Hannah recommended to me.

Just as I find myself tucked in and starting to warm up, my text alert sounds.

HENRY

Should I still guess what you are reading?

LUCY

Sure, if you'd like, but I'm certain it is not a book you will be familiar with.

HENRY

Well, let me tell you what I hope you are reading…

LUCY

So you've been giving this some thought?

HENRY

Dear Lucy, you have consumed my thoughts since we parted on Sunday.

LUCY

Wow, you are pulling out all the tricks today.

Please tell me, what is it you hope I am reading?

HENRY

Romance…

LUCY

Why would you hope for that?

HENRY

To prepare for your role as the love of my life.

LUCY

Interesting. Here, I assumed you were the love of your life.

HENRY

Unfortunately, I am not looking for a comedian, Miss Taylor.

LUCY

Does that mean I'm no longer being considered for the role?

HENRY

Sadly no, you are the only qualified candidate. I must have you.

LUCY

You must have me? In what capacity?

If I were to accept the role, what would be expected of me?

HENRY:

;-)

The gentlemanly thing would be to let you set your expectations first.

LUCY

I believe you already have something in mind. Let's start there.

HENRY

I was thinking of staged (by you) photos of us to post to my social media accounts.

Possibly, a few outings (or dates, I believe they are called).

LUCY

Yes, I have heard of the term, dates, as well, I believe it refers to couples going places together.

HENRY

This is why I am hopeful you are reading romance. I believe we will both need to brush up on the subject.

To make this romantic caper appear
authentic.

LUCY

Yes, this will take elaborate planning and
great efforts on our part.

HENRY

Just think how proud you will be if we can
pull off a ruse as grand as this.

LUCY

Grand, you say?

As grand as the great staircase of Rosings
Park?

HENRY

Yes, I believe it will be just as grand as
Rosings Park itself.

LUCY

It will not be easy to convince others that I
enjoy your company…especially those
who know you personally.

HENRY

I understand the extensive torture this will
be for you. My apologies. In return for your
troubles, I promise to deliver the most
exquisite film adaptation of Pride and
Prejudice you've ever seen.

LUCY

Well, that's a very presumptuous promise,
Mr. Brooks!

HENRY

I'm a confident man. I thought you knew
this by now.

LUCY

I believe it's spelled A-R-R-O-G-A-N-T.

HENRY

Once again, with the comedy.

LUCY

I do believe relationships involve humor and laughter. This is a skill I can utilize IF I decide to agree to be in a fake relationship with you.

HENRY

I'm not sure, but I'll spend the rest of my evening researching typical relationship behaviors in the hope that you agree.

Goodnight, Lucy.

LUCY

Goodnight, Henry. Best of luck with your research

Fifteen

LUCY

"YOU'LL NEVER GUESS who just texted me," Ellie screams into the phone. Well, if it's going to be one of these calls, it's time to switch to speaker phone. I drop it onto my bed and continue to braid my wet hair. Ellie called just as I was getting out of the shower. Knowing I won't be on camera with students this afternoon, I washed my hair after my morning classes ended. I'd rather let it air dry, and loose braids always make for great waves in my hair.

"Who texted you?" I ask, running through the possible suspects in my head.

"The *parasite*," she screams John's nickname, and I'm thankful I decided to put the phone down.

"That's awfully brave of him. What did he want?" I never did reply to his texts the other day. Maybe he has moved on and hopes to make a pass at Ellie. Even though she is the last girl on this Earth who would fall for him. He's dumb enough to think he could pull any girl, even the ones who hate him.

"A lot, actually, all about you. And he sent me this! Hold on, I'll text it." Now finished with my braids, I pick up the phone as one of the paparazzi photos of Henry and I come through. Oh course, it's one that shows my face is in full view while Henry is whispering in my ear. "What is going on? Are you two an item, and you never told me?"

I should have told her sooner, but she has been busy with work, and I've tried my best to not think too much of it. Well, time to face the music.

"*Lucy Taylor!*" Last names are only used in our friendship when one of us is in trouble with the other. "Are you dating this man and keeping it from me."

"I would never keep that from you. You work in PR. You know that the paparazzi can make photos look like much more than they really are."

"I need more of an explanation than that!"

"Of course, we were all out to eat that night and then went to the club after. When we were about to exit, paparazzi were waiting outside. Apparently, there were a ton of celebrities inside, but I honestly didn't notice any. Maybe because it was so poorly lit there."

"Lucy! Back to you and *Mr. Love Isn't Real, but I make movies about it.*"

"Yes, well, as you can imagine, I didn't know how to react to the paparazzi. He was just being kind and trying to get me to the car without allowing time for me to freak out. What looked like a sweet whisper in my ear was him saying something like, 'Don't look at them, we are almost at the car.'"

"Oh," Ellie says, clearly the truth is a letdown for her.

"Yes, it looks far more romantic than it was, I promise you."

"So nothing is going on between you two?" she asks.

"I mean, I guess we dislike each other less than we previously did, but that's about all I have to report." If I go through with the fake relationship, I'm going to need to lie to her and tell her we are together. I get a sinking feeling in my stomach at the thought, but it won't last long, and I can tell her the truth as soon as it's over. I assume that once he gets the director position, we will be able to end the ruse. "Wait, what was it that John texted you?"

"Oh, him. He faked concern for your safety, saying you hadn't replied to his texts, and then he saw you photographed with a man. He worries you are being held against your will." I picture her eyes rolling as she speaks. "I answered him so it wouldn't become your problem."

"What did you say?"

"I told him you were perfectly safe, that you and I are in constant contact. And as for that man in the picture, it's none of his business." Pride fills her voice. "And then I called you immediately because what you are doing with that man is *my* business."

I laugh and agree. "Yes, I know. I should have told you sooner, but aside from getting our photo taken, there wasn't much else to tell."

"Yeah, yeah…I expect a full run down when you come home next week. And hopefully, you'll have something more juicy to share about your grumpy director."

"He's not mine." It's common practice between us to start referring to men in our proximity as "ours," but this matter is so sensitive that I know I need to clarify…if only to remind myself.

"If you say so, but if I hear from John again, I'm going to tell him you got married and to get a life."

"All right, you do that," I encourage her.

"I have to go—at least we cleared that up. I shouldn't have to say this, but I expect to be made aware of everything going forward."

"Understood. Enjoy your day."

We end with our traditional "Okay bye" to each other, and I notice I received some texts while I was on the phone with Ellie.

THE PARASITE

> Hey, is everything alright? I'm getting worried I haven't heard back from you.

> I know you are probably busy with work, but I want to be sure you know how much I miss you.

I close the text window and try to put him out of my mind, but I just can't. Of course, he saw a photo with me and is now getting insecure that I might have finally found someone else. I've encouraged him to settle down with someone else for years, and he always adamantly refused because he believes "we are destined to end up together."

I pull up the paparazzi photos and try to imagine them from John's view. I can understand how he and most people would assume there is something more between Henry and me. What would John say if we publicly announced a relationship, a *fake relationship*? If I agree, it can't just be for that reason. John's not worth all that energy. *But it would be a nice benefit.*

It's time to give Henry an answer, he has been plenty patient with me and hasn't tried to rush me at all. I wanted a different life, that is why I moved here, but there haven't been any big challenges here aside from adjusting to the new location. I enjoy my job greatly, but it doesn't challenge me the way I'm accustomed to in the classroom.

I want Henry to get this movie—his career accomplishments have proved he is the best man for the job, and recently, he has proved he still has what it takes. As grumpy as he can be, he was a complete gentleman when we were bombarded with the paparazzi.

If I'm being honest, the moment he mentioned another *Pride and Prejudice* adaptation, my heart sped up. Of course, I want this movie made but I want it done correctly. Far too many times, jerk characters have been labeled as Mr. Darcy and uptight girls as Miss Elizabeth Bennett, but they are so much more than that. And there is nothing more exhilarating than hearing the actors recite your favorite lines from the book. When the scripts are completely changed, it still has the potential to be a good movie, but it's not the same as when the book comes to life.

I can do this. What's the worst that can happen? *A lot.*

No, I'm doing this for Jane Austen. She's not here to have a say, so I will try to act in her best interest.

For Jane! *And Henry.*

Sixteen

HENRY

I LEFT London a few days ago in an attempt to calm my nerves about whether or not Lucy will agree to the fake relationship. The hour-long drive provided relaxing scenic views that always reinforced my decision to move to this quiet town.

The anticipation of Lucy's answer is getting the best of me, not that I would ever share that with her. I can't pressure her into an answer. If she agrees, it will disrupt her life. It's a tough decision she needs to make, and I can't interfere with her choice. The benefit this could bring for me greatly outweighs her benefit of getting an enjoyable movie out of her favorite book.

Perhaps I can even provide her with a better dating experience than she had in the past with her ex from the States. While nothing has been confirmed, I've completely written him off as a fool. Without her ever mentioning him, I have filled in the blanks with a villainous story of my own. How could he let her slip through his hands, let alone end it poorly?

With Lucy, I would woo her without concern that she is wanting for anything. We could simply enjoy each other's company without any expectations of a romantic relationship while continuing to build on our friendship.

I check my phone again to see if she's reached out, even though it's been sitting next to me for the last ten minutes and hasn't made any notification noises since I last checked. I worry if I stayed in London, I would have made excuses to visit her. This is why it was imperative to come back to my home.

I need something to occupy my mind, I'll find a book to read from my library.

While browsing my many shelves, I'm drawn to the one with my copies of Jane Austen's work. The books are old editions, with brown leather covers and wear from the years of attention they've received from their previous owners.

During our many discussions Lucy has encouraged me to think about the significance of these books when they were first published. She often mentions how she wishes she could have experienced it at the time. If only we could discover what their lives were like and how these stories affected them.

Staying away from *Pride and Prejudice*, I move to another favorite of Lucy's, *Northanger Abbey*. A less famous book, but the first Jane Austen adaptation I directed early on in my career. Max played Mr. Tilney, a role that suited him well as he is as kind and affectionate as the leading man himself. I read the book at the time, but not since. I pull it off the shelf and make my way to my favorite chair, which faces the large fireplace.

As my disdain for John Thorpe and his scheming sister returns at an accelerated rate, my phone rings, and Lucy's name appears on the screen. Placing my finger on the page, I close the book to hold it in one hand before sitting up straight in my chair as if she can see me.

"Hello, there," I greet her.

She doesn't bother with a greeting in return. "I'll do it. The fake relationship. I'll do it."

I put the book down on the table—*I'll find my page later.* "May I ask what brought upon what seems to be a sudden decision?"

"I don't think that's necessary. I do, however, have one condition, a request, really."

"Name your price, Miss Taylor." I would give her anything she asked for.

"If you get the job, I want to visit the sets, all of the sets. And I want you to talk to me about it. The process, how each day is going…I want to feel a part of it. As much as would be allowed for someone who isn't actually working on the movie."

"Of course." Of all the things she could ask for that I would have agreed to without hesitation, she simply asks to be involved and included in the production. She didn't have to ask for this—I would have included her anyway to keep her included in all areas of my life.

"Okay, thank you." A brief nervous laugh follows. Did she expect me to exclude her from it? She continues, "So, where should we begin? I am leaving for the holiday on Monday. I'll be in the States for the week, coming back on Saturday."

"Oh, yes. I remember. I'm no longer in London myself. I came home earlier in the week. I suppose I will stay for the duration you are out of town, then we can plan to regroup in London once you return."

"Henry, do you want to…do you think…"

"What is it?" I ask, nervous she already regrets her decision. If she changes her mind, I will respect her decision, but in this moment, fear floods my body and it has nothing to do with the movie.

"Do you want to talk about this false relationship we are committing to?" She pauses but continues quickly before I can respond. "Will this secret stay between the two of us, or do you plan to let your family know?"

"I haven't thought of that. I suppose it would be best to keep it between just the two of us." A slight thrill runs through my body at the thought of the two of us sharing a secret.

"Do you truly think Oliver, Finn, Hannah, and Mia will believe us? Even with us being more civil to each other lately, I don't know if they would fall for it." She makes a good point. "Not to mention, if we claimed to be a couple, they would expect displays of affection between us."

"Yes, I suppose you make a good point." Displays of affection would have been nice, but I concede without argument. "We can explain the situation and ask them to keep that information to themselves."

"There is one other person I would like to tell, my best friend, Ellie. She won't tell anyone, but it would ruin our friendship if I keep this from her." The worry is gone from her voice. This is more demand than request. It's very appealing.

"Understood," I reassure her.

"Thank you. Do you have any other concerns or boundaries you want to discuss?"

"Given our lack of interest in real relationships, I think we can skip the typical 'let's not fall in love speech,' don't you think?" I insist. Which is why she is the perfect woman to share this venture with.

"Yes, of course. Honestly, if you do get the job. I have grand plans to reacquaint myself with someone I've had feelings toward for years..." *What?* "Mr. Darcy." Of course, she is looking forward to expanding her feelings for a fictional man. Maybe acting as a fictional boyfriend, I will give Fitzwilliam some competition.

"You can't see me, but my eyes are rolling," I tell her with a laugh. "And try to remember that whatever it is Mr. Darcy is doing that makes you feel something for him, it's me behind him pulling the strings."

"Oh, don't do that! Don't ruin it," she whines into the phone. "Anyway! Since we won't be in the same location for some time, we can still begin posting tonight if you'd like."

"Explain."

"Do you have a fireplace?" she asks.

"Three." I'm looking at one right now.

"Gross. Bragging isn't necessary."

"My bragging is now your bragging, *darling*. You can go back to the States and brag about the new man in your life who has a home in the UK with three fireplaces. Two downstairs and one in my bedroom."

"Well, with this being your first post about our *relationship*, dear, we should try to keep it clean. Pick one of the downstairs fireplaces, preferably a lounge. Grab wine glasses, fill them with wine, and place them on a coffee table in front of the fireplace. Then lower the lights and take the photo."

"Sounds like you may have hidden talents as a director," I say with pride. I wouldn't have thought of this, but now that she said it, it makes complete sense. "And what am I to do with two glasses of wine after I finish the photo?"

"Drink them. Alone." Both are more orders, not requests from Lucy. "Please don't mistake this next statement for any personal investment on my end for your personal life, but if you are to be in a committed relationship, you can not be found by the paparazzi 'cheating' on your girlfriend."

"No need to get jealous, *my love*. I am all yours for the foreseeable future." Since running into Lucy on my shameful morning walk home, I haven't been interested in meeting anyone new.

"Great," she says with sarcasm. "You can post the photo this evening if you'd like, and I will send you more ideas as I think of them. I think you should continue with the family photos and the old ones for movie sets as well."

"All right, I'll send the fireplace photo to you before I post to be sure I captured your vision."

"Well, I think that sums up our plan. Have a good night," Lucy states as if she is ending a business meeting.

"One last thing, Lucy. Thank you. I greatly appreciate your assistance in this matter, and if it works, I'll never be able to thank you enough. With that said, if at any point this becomes too much and you want to stop, just say the word."

"Thank you, Henry."

"Goodnight, *love,*" I emphasize the endearment and it clearly works because she hangs up without another word.

Seventeen

HENRY

IT'S early morning when Oliver rings, "Hey Pop, got any plans today?"

"Nothing important."

"I'm getting in the car now and heading your way, thinking we could spend the day together." His words sound rehearsed.

"That's great! Can I ask if anything in particular brought about this spontaneous visit?"

"I'll tell you when I get there. See you soon," he says before hanging up.

What could Oliver need to talk to me in person about? Why didn't we have this talk while I was staying with him? Checking my watch, I decide to run to the local bakery for some pastries for us to keep myself busy while I wait for his arrival.

I'm standing at the top of the driveway when his car pulls in. As soon as he steps out, sensing the anxiety radiating off Oliver makes me even more concerned than I already was. I take a deep breath and open the back door for us. The sound of our chairs dragging against the floor is the only noise in the house as we take our seats at the kitchen table. I can't bear the silence any longer. "Oliver, whatever it is, we will get through it. Just please tell me."

He raises his gaze from his clasped hands on the table to meet my eyes. "Dad," he takes a deep breath, "I'm going to ask Hannah to marry me." Apprehension remains on his face.

"That's wonderful news, Oliver!" Rising from the table, I go to him as he stands, and I embrace him. "I'm so pleased for you!" Pulling out of the hug and holding him by the shoulders at arm's length. I ask, "Why did you look so solemn when you told me? Are you worried she won't say yes?"

"Not at all, Pop." A smile now stretched across his face. "I was worried about how you would react. You've voiced your negative thoughts and feelings on relationships openly for years. I was worried you would think I was making a mistake."

My heart sinks—I didn't realize the effect my words have on my children. "I'm so sorry I gave you that impression, Oliver. I couldn't be happier for you and Hannah. She's an amazing person, and it's clear whenever I am with you that you both care for each other very much."

He pulls me in for another hug and asks, "With your support, I'd like to propose here if you wouldn't mind?"

"Yes, of course," I insist. "When are you planning for?"

"During the holidays, I'd like everyone to be here when I ask her. You and Finn can help with the setup, and that morning, Lucy and Mia can get her out of the house. I'd like to decorate the place with flowers, maybe cater the food, and certainly order from the bakery—she loves sweets." Oliver has thought this through, and the excitement in his voice is clear.

"This place is your home and I'd be happy for you to ask her here. Just let me know how I can help, Olly."

"Thanks, Pop."

The rest of the day, we spend making lists of supplies, what can be shipped prior, and what we will need to pick up closer to the day of the proposal. We also call around bakeries, florists, and caterers.

Over dinner, I share with Oliver the plan Lucy and I have decided to move forward with on social media.

"So you'll post photos that make you look like a couple and take her on dates, but you won't be dating?" he asks, seeming a bit skeptical.

"No, there's no reason to be in a real relationship. My agent believes that if we lean into the idea of me being a romantic man caught up in a very public relationship, it may sway the production company to give me the director position," I explain.

"And Lucy has agreed to all of this?" he asks.

"Yes, she agreed. Most of the content was her idea," I confirm.

"Well, all right. I'll let the others in on this and swear

them to secrecy." He still doesn't look convinced but doesn't bring it up again.

———

I wave to Oliver as he backs out of the driveway and begins his journey back to London. I wish he would have waited until tomorrow, it worries me, him driving after dark.

I have much to plan, but first, I need to be sure one guest in particular can confirm. Finn and Oliver always bring Mia and Hannah up to visit, arriving a couple of days before Christmas and staying through the first few days of the New Year, leaving in the middle to visit their other family members.

HENRY

Do you have plans for the Christmas and New Year holidays?

LUCY

I'll be in the States for Christmas and then most likely back in London before the New Year.

HENRY

Oliver and Finn usually bring Hannah and Mia to stay at my place for the holiday. We would love for you to join us when you get back and stay through the New Year.

While it would be nice to spend Christmas with her, the thought of ringing in the New Year together gives me a thrill. It's been years since I've had someone to kiss at midnight. Not that we would kiss at midnight. That's not included in our fake relationship. But if the mood strikes, I would never deny her.

LUCY

Thank you. Yes, I think I'd enjoy that. Great opportunity to take some photos for your account. Unveiling your new partner for the New Year could gain a lot of attention for your accounts.

She makes a good point—it hadn't crossed my mind to use her visit for our ruse. Regardless, it will be nice to have her here.

With that reminder, I close our text and send a quick email to Mark. Asking if he has heard anything from Viewmont then return to my text with Lucy.

HENRY

When you have your travel dates set, please send them over. I'll arrange for a car to pick you up and bring you directly to my place.

LUCY

Thank you! That's a very kind gesture, but I can rent a car and drive myself.

HENRY

If we want the world to think you are with me, the most romantic man to ever walk the Earth, that man wouldn't make the woman he is courting drive herself.

LUCY

I believe the man you speak of would pick up his love himself from the airport. He would not want to be without her for another moment.

HENRY

If you are already concerned you are going to miss me that much, you just have to ask, and I will gladly come pick you up myself.

LUCY

Sure, you think that.

If that is all for this evening, I have a book to get back to…

HENRY

As do I.

In my reply, I send a photo of *Northanger Abbey* sitting on my table next to me.

LUCY

Is that a stock photo you found on the Internet?

Well, now she is forcing my hand. I need to send a photo of me holding it. I check myself in the camera on my phone. It's not too bad, my glasses are on and my hair isn't too out of place. Some may even say I look sexy, and I would agree. This is the first "selfie" I've taken. It is a very awkward process, especially if you are trying to hold something while doing it. When it's done, I inspect the photo quickly and hit send.

Lucy responds with a photo of her e-reader with

Northanger Abbey open on a surface I recognize as her loveseat with the striped blanket next to it.

HENRY

How can I be sure that it isn't a stock photo from the Internet? Have you even read that book?

LUCY

You know it's not and that I have. I could probably recite most of it from memory.

HENRY

How would I know that?

There is only one way I could know for sure you are reading that book tonight.

LUCY

I'm not sending you a photo of me just so you can ogle at it all night.

HENRY

Is that what you plan to do with the photo I sent of myself?

LUCY

Now I'm considering sending you a selfie with my middle finger on display.

HENRY

Vulgar American.

I love it.

LUCY

eye roll emoji Enjoy your evening with Miss Morland and her adventures at the Abbey.

HENRY

Thank you. I certainly plan to.

Opening the book, I resume where I left off just as Miss Morland is cast out of the Abbey in the middle of the night.

Eighteen

LUCY

THIS IS GOING to be a long day, luckily the London Airport isn't as crowded as I expect it will be when I land back in New York. I decided not to check a bag and only bring a carry-on because I left plenty of clothes at my mother's house before I moved. An announcement comes overhead that my flight will start boarding soon. I pull out my phone to text Mom to let her know—she will be worried and I don't want her arriving too soon to pick me up. As I am looking at my phone, messages start flooding in from the group chat. Hannah shared my flight information with them. As I move to put my phone in airplane mode, I get one more text notification.

HENRY

> Safe travels, Lucy. I look forward to
> hearing from you once you've landed
> safely in the land of traitors.

I smile at his joke—he's always sure not to come across as overly concerned.

LUCY

> I'll let you know when I arrive in the land of the free, away from your oppressive monarchy.

Thanks to a cocktail I had before the flight, I wake up just a couple hours before we land in Syracuse. I typically do well with shorter flights, but flying internationally gives me too much time to think about everything that can go wrong. Good thing I have my e-reader to distract me during the remaining hours in the air.

Before I know it, I'm at my mom's place being smothered with puppy kisses from her two rottweilers. I'd love to have a pet of my own, but with traveling back and forth multiple times throughout the year, I'd have to find someone to look after them. So for now, I'll enjoy snuggling with these two during my visits.

Mom is busy, as always, so I take the opportunity to put my things down in my childhood bedroom. My eyes land on the top shelf of my bookcase, the one that has been dedicated to all things Jane Austen for as long as I can remember. The center space displays my favorite copy of *Pride and Prejudice*. Maybe I should bring that back home with me. It would be nice to start filling my apartment with more of my favorite possessions.

When I return downstairs, Mom is pulling out piles of her reusable shopping bags for us to use tomorrow. We plan to do our Christmas shopping while I'm in this week, and I'll leave everything here so I don't have to worry about traveling with it in December or shipping internationally.

"Thanks for letting me store all my gifts here for a month, Mom," I say as I start loading the bags into the largest one for easy transport. "I'll try to get most of the wrapping completed while I'm here too."

"Of course, sweetheart." Standing and moving to the refrigerator, she pulls a single piece of paper off the notepad and studies it. "Care to join me? I'm running over to the grocery store to get the last few things we are missing for Thursday's dinner."

We stopped doing the traditional Thanksgiving dinner years ago when our family size went down to myself, my mom, and my grandmother. Since then, my mother has hosted more of an after-dinner party for our extended relatives and family friends. We make a smaller "dinner" for the three of us to have around lunchtime and then prepare for our guests. We set up folding tables around the house and in the basement, bringing out every board game and deck of cards we own. My mom and I split the duties of cooking the constant stream of appetizers starting at 7:00 p.m. to give us both a chance to play.

"Sure. I'll grab my coat." As I head upstairs to grab my phone from the charger, I notice a few texts from Ellie with plans for Wednesday night, a couple of messages in the group chat, and one from Henry.

An odd sensation comes over me, and I catch myself missing him, considering what this week would be like if he were here. That's dumb, there's no paparazzi here, and no need for him to be here. But what if he were…

What would he think of my mom and her excessively affectionate, very large dogs?

What would he think of our nontraditional Thanksgiving after-party? Would he enjoy the packed house and my loud friends and family getting far too competitive over a game of Monopoly or a card game, arguing who had their card down first? Maybe he would enjoy the games—he certainly is competitive enough to fit in with this crowd.

What would he think of Ellie? I would like for them to meet, but I would have to make her swear to be on her best behavior. We always tend to misbehave in front of each other's crushes. Not that Henry is my crush, but I think she feels that there is some romantic potential between the two of us. That's just because she hasn't been around us while we are together. Being in our shared company would certainly disillusion any romantic thoughts of us being more than…whatever it is we are.

When I return to London, we will begin posting more photos of the two of us. I have to tell Mom about Henry before things get out of hand, and she finds it suspicious. Our trip to the store will be as good a time as any.

"So, I met someone." I purposely wait until we are stopped at a red light.

"In London? Oh, honey! Tell me all about him!" She turns toward me as she claps her hands together.

"Do you want me to drive, Mom? The light is green." I point up.

"Oh, goodness, no, I'll be fine. We are almost there, but keep talking! What's his name, what does he do for a living, how did you meet?"

Deep breath, you can do this. You just have to lie to your mother about a fake relationship. At least here are some completely true parts. "We met at the coffee shop near my apartment. He's a little older than I am."

"Oh, I can't say I'm surprised. You've always had a thing for older men," she says with a shrug.

"Thanks, Mom." She's not wrong. "I met his sons and their girlfriends at the coffee shop and they introduced me to him when he was in town visiting them. "

"How old are we talking, Lucy?" Her tone is a little more serious.

"He just turned fifty—his sons are in their late twenties." I need to move off this and keep the conversation going so I can get past the lying parts. "His name is Henry. His sons are Oliver and Finn. I'm getting to be close friends with them and their girlfriends, Hannah and Mia."

"Well, tell me more about him. I need more details."

"He's nice." *Lie.* "He lives in a small town about an hour outside of London." *Truth.* "We hit it off the moment we met." *Lie.* "He works in the film industry and directed a lot of my favorite romance movies, actually." *Truth.* "We are just starting to see each other and want to take it slow because we really like each other." *LIE.* "With his occupation, sometimes we could find ourselves in places where paparazzi are and could end up in the papers. Well, we actually already ended up in the papers, but I'll show you those pictures later." *Truth.* "It was no big deal." *Lie.*

"Is he handsome?" she says as if all the other information wasn't as relevant as this.

"Very." *Truth.*

"Well, I look forward to these pictures." She puts the car in park, "Get them out while we walk in."

She pushes the cart while I swipe through the photos I've saved on my phone from the websites they showed up on. Thankfully I didn't have many and swiped quickly past the ones with the "longing looks" between us.

"And he makes you happy, honey?" she asks as I put my phone away and move to take the cart for her.

It was a question I didn't prepare an answer for. "Yes."

As much as I don't want to admit it, truth.

Nineteen

LUCY

IT'S JUST after 9:00 p.m. when Ellie's text buzzes on my phone. The Wednesday night before Thanksgiving is just as big of a holiday in my hometown. With everyone who previously moved out of town back to visit with family, the local bars are jam-packed with people looking to catch up with old friends.

ELLIE

I'm outside! Get your butt out here!

I head down the stairs and grab my winter coat, a bright blue scarf, and a matching hat before stopping to say goodbye to Mom.

"Ellie and her dad are outside. Her brother is working tonight and will give us a ride home after his shift at the bar ends. Don't stay up!" I say as I give her a quick hug before heading out the door.

"If anything happens and you need a ride, call me. I'll come get you. Don't get in a car with a stranger or, worse, a stranger that's been drinking."

"We are thirty-seven, Mom. The time for us to make poor decisions has long passed. We can handle this. I love you."

I hear her yell back, "I love you," as I close the door behind me and run to get into the back seat of Ellie's father's car. "Hello, Mr. Burrell. Thank you for driving tonight."

"Of course, Lucy. You know I look forward to driving you girls. Especially on a night like tonight. How long have we been doing this now?"

"Long enough, Dad, no need to remind us how old we are getting," Ellie cuts her father off.

"I suppose, El." I notice his eyes move to me in the rearview mirror briefly as he asks, "How are things in London, Lucy?"

"Very well, thanks. I've been begging Ellie to bring you and Mrs. Burrell to visit me soon!"

"Well, that would be a nice trip for us to go on. We'd love to visit you." Both of Ellie's parents are enjoying their first few years of retirement. So far they've spent their free time traveling to different ball fields following Ellie's team on away games.

"Yes, Dad, we have to wait until I have a break from my job before spending a couple of weeks in another country. We can't visit all of England in a weekend."

"Good point. We will be ready when you are." He smiles at his daughter. "Well, girls, we are just about here. Shawn is taking you home tonight, right, but if you decide you'd like to leave earlier, just call, I can always come back out and get you both."

"Thanks!" We both say as we get out of the car and

walk into the bar where Ellie's brother, Shawn, is the lead bartender, *Sliders*.

The moment we walk in, we are greeted with a roar of welcome from our friends, people we went to high school and college with, and friends we've met along the way.

That's the nice thing about having a hometown bar, but I'm reminded it can also be a curse when I make eye contact with John, who is currently showing a twenty-something how to hold a pool stick. This is not the first time I've witnessed such a scene, but it doesn't sting like it once did. Quickly, I move my attention back to Ellie and follow her to our usual spot at the corner of the bar.

"Hey, Lucy. Long time no see. How's the king?" Shawn asks as he leans over the bar to greet us.

"He's very well, Shawn. Told me to let you know he's sorry he couldn't make it in to call upon you himself but looks forward to your appearance at his next state dinner."

"You tell him I'll be there!" We both laugh. There is something special about the connection you have with your best friend's siblings, especially when they make you feel like you are a part of the family. "So what will we be having tonight, ladies? Pink wine or your signature cocktails?"

I look at Ellie, we pretend to be having a silent debate, then turn back to Shawn and agree it's a holiday. We will go with cocktails this evening. Before we know it, Shawn places our drinks in front of us. I get my cranberry juice with mandarin orange flavored vodka and two limes—and lots of ice. Ellie gets something that resembles a screwdriver but adds cranberry juice to it. We also each get a large water to drink after every cocktail as a preventative for tomorrow morning.

"Lucy!" I know that yell anywhere—we started this obnoxious name-calling when we met in one of our dance classes during freshman year of college.

"Luna," I answer in response. Standing to meet her, my arms engulf her in a tight hug as soon as she is close enough.

Our bond was formed from that very first ballet class, both pursuing minors in the dance program, but only because they didn't allow us to take the program as a major at that time. Something we fought for each year we attended, and years after our graduation, the university finally expanded the program. Luna now runs the premier private dance school in southern New York State with her two older sisters. She also is the go-to choreographer for most local theater companies in the area. And unlike Ellie, she shares my deep passion for Jane Austen.

"We haven't spoken much since you moved. I need to hear everything about London." We texted a few times but spoke on the phone only once. She has a far busier schedule than I do these days. With everything going on with Henry, I'm guilty of letting this friendship fall to the side.

"I didn't want to text about it, but you must tell me what you are doing with that sexy British movie director!" she shouts loud enough for the entire bar to hear. Which includes John, and as I look at Luna she gives me a wink. Like the rest of my friends, she no longer hides her dislike of him. I don't bother to turn to see if he reacted.

Well, it's obvious those pictures have circulated more

here than I previously assumed. "Yes, Henry." Oohs and Awws come from around us as others start to listen in. "We just started dating."

"I need more details!"

"It's still new—there's not much to tell." Telling them the generic answer I've prepared for this evening. I should have known Luna would never settle for that.

"Well, your British boyfriend's social media account says there's more to tell," Marissa, another friend from college, yells from behind Luna.

"Thanks, Marissa," I say and look to Ellie for help, but she's not paying attention. She's too focused on her phone. I wonder who she is texting. "Well, I hate to break it to you, but those photos are all you're going to get. I like him, and we are keeping it mostly private for now. But thank you for your concern." Trying to end this topic diplomatically.

Luna leans in, "You know I'm only concerned for your happiness, Lucy. But I'm also a romantic who is dying to hear every detail of this courtship. I need details," she pauses, "when you're ready."

As the night goes on, talk of Henry quiets down, and I get to catch up on everyone's lives and how their families are doing. We play some trivia games at the bar before it gets too crowded after midnight.

Ellie gets up to go to greet her cousin, Bex who just walked in. Rebecca, as she prefers to be called in just about every other setting, is only a couple months younger than Ellie. They were often mistaken for sisters when they were younger, but as they grew up, their personalities came out more in their appearances. Bex, as Ellie insists on calling her, is a corporate queen who is working her way up the ladder within a major hotel company. They both wave at me before being bombarded by more locals.

I grab my phone, but before I can check it, I feel a once familiar arm around my back.

"It's good to finally see you here and in one piece," John says.

Before turning around, I flip my phone over onto the counter with the screen down and turn to him. "Yep, I'm perfectly fine."

"It's not like you to ignore me for so long. I was beginning to get worried." The rehearsed concern in his voice makes my skin crawl. Or maybe it wasn't rehearsed —maybe he is starting to get concerned that I'm finally moving on from him.

"I'm better than ever. Thanks for your concern." Trying to cut this conversation short, I purposely don't ask how he's doing.

Thankfully, Ellie quickly comes to my rescue. "Keep moving, Parasite, it's girls night!"

Before I can say much, he pulls his arm away and lifts his hands to show he means no trouble. He turns back to me and winks, "I'll be around—we'll talk later." I ignore it.

Our steady drink rotation of cocktail, water, cocktail, and water continues with a variety of appetizers Shawn makes for us throughout the night. It's a little after 12:30 a.m. when my phone buzzes on the bar top.

HENRY

How are the festivities going?

It may be the drinks, or it may be that I am excited to hear from him and selfishly want to keep him up if it means I get to talk to him a little more. Moving Ellie's drink next to mine, I angle my phone just right and take the photo, then hit send.

"Who are you sending that to?" Her eyes squint with the question.

"Henry. He just texted—he can't sleep and asked how our night is going." She rolls her eyes but maintains a sly smile on her face.

"Well, let's entertain Henry a little more." She takes my phone from me, and my heart stops. What if she texts him?

She opens the camera app and flips it before pulling me close and taking a selfie of us. I reach for the phone, but she pulls away and announces, "Attaching photo and texting 'You're welcome. Ellie'"

Once I wrangle the phone back from her, she winks, "And you're welcome too."

Getting a better look at the photo, we both look great in it. I don't hate the idea of sending it to him. "Thank you," I mutter quietly under my breath.

> Looks like an entertaining evening for you both.

As I am smiling at my phone, deciding what to text next, when that frustratingly familiar voice comes behind me again. "So that's really happening?"

Yes, John. This is what's happening. I'm no longer the lovesick girl who you've kept at arm's length since breaking my heart all those years ago. I'm finally showing interest in another man. That's what's happening.

With more liquid courage than I usually have and after noticing he was waiting until Ellie left her guard position next to me to sneak up behind me, I lose my restraint with him, "Excuse me, but it's none of your business who I'm texting, John! Should I ask you to look at your phone? I wonder how many women you have texted tonight?"

I've never mentioned the other girls to him before, never caring enough to bring it up. I've encouraged him to date again for years, but he's always shrugged it off. I'm not dumb—just because I haven't witnessed him with anyone else, there's plenty of rumors about him with other women.

He just smiles at me. I know better than to give him a grand reaction—he loves it when I do that. He always interprets my "passion," as he calls it, for the connection between us. "You know you are the only one I love." Deny, deny, deny is the method he's going to stick with. That's fine, but I don't need to listen to it.

I get up from my seat and grab my cocktail and Ellie's —we can get water refills later. Luckily, there are two empty seats at the table with Luna and Marissa. I don't want it to appear as if I need protection from my friends —I can stand up to him. I just did. It's his persistence that I don't have the patience for any longer. Shawn will let Ellie know where I went.

Once safe in my new location, I reopen the texts from Henry and look back over the conversation I was enjoying before that annoying interruption.

Starting to feel the effects of the cocktails, I decide to call it a night after I finish my current drink and move strictly to water. I also decide this is a safe time to cut off my texts with Henry. I don't need to keep drinking and then send him drunk texts that I can't take back.

LUCY

Very entertaining. I hope you can get some sleep.

Twenty

LUCY

"YOUR TURN," my mom says as she hugs me from behind while I'm clearing the empty bottles from the kitchen counter and restocking the sweets.

"Already? Did you lose that quickly?" I didn't expect her back so soon from the card game she was playing with my cousins and Ellie.

"Ellie is too good. Are we sure she isn't related to us somehow?" Mom has always believed our bloodline holds a great ability for winning. She assumes others "just don't have *it*." It's too bad that *it* was limited to cards and board games.

"All right, I'm going to see which games are starting next." I walk out into the parlor and straight into John. I had assumed he would come—he and his family have been coming since they moved into the neighborhood when we were kids. I was just hoping to avoid him this evening.

"Just who I was looking for." He moves out of the doorway, sliding his arm around my waist and pulling me to the side to allow his parents to greet my mom in the kitchen. After exchanging pleasantries with them, I move out of John's hold.

I hate to refer to it as a tradition, but since high school, after the Thanksgiving festivities died down, John and I typically end up spending time together. Only once did things go too far—most years, we would just hang out, talking all night. This year, I have no desire to continue with this custom. Hopefully, leaving it in the past for good.

"Grab some food, and enjoy the evening." I move to walk away, but he grabs my hand.

Looking back, he leans in to say, "I didn't come for the food or the games. I just want to spend time with you." I huff in disgust as he continues, "Maybe even convince you to move back home. And you know, I can be very convincing."

At that moment, as if I planned it, my phone rings from the back pocket of my jeans. I grab it to check who is calling, and the photo of Henry holding up his copy of *Northanger Abbey* takes up the entire screen. John has the perfect view, and I'm so delighted I set that as his caller ID photo for more reasons than one.

"Sorry, John. Henry's calling. I'm going to take this." I pull my other hand out of John's and swipe to answer. Knowing John is listening, I put on a show. With a smile, I say in my attempt at a sexy voice, "Hi, Henry. It's so nice to hear from you, I'm missing you terribly!"

John's face falls, and he turns back into the kitchen. I run upstairs to my room so I can explain my odd behaviors to Henry in private.

"Hello, Lucy." Of course, he gives me his sexiest voice. He must think I have him on speakerphone.

Once I close the door behind me, I explain, "Sorry about that. My ex was standing next to me when you called—I wanted to put on a show."

"Yes, of course." Henry clears his throat.

"What are you doing up this late?" I ask.

"I couldn't sleep, and I knew you had your big occasion this evening. I thought it would be good to call, let everyone see that I'm checking in…missing you…to follow through on our story."

"Oh, smart idea." We hadn't planned this, but I'm thankful he did it anyway. "I just came up to my room for some privacy, but I'll be sure to brag about you the moment I get back downstairs."

"Well, there's no shortage of topics in that area." He is confident at first, and then his tone changes. "So your ex comes to your holiday dinners?"

"Well, it's a less formal gathering with friends and family. His parents are here too. I don't think it will be much of an issue." I feel the need to declare there is nothing left between John and me to Henry, but he wouldn't care outside of our arrangement. I doubt he's even considering that anyway.

"All right then," he pauses, "And you're all right?"

"Yes, I'm fine."

"Splendid, enjoy your evening. Send your family my best." Hesitation is in his voice.

"Thanks, I will. Goodnight."

"Goodnight," he says and quickly hangs up. His caller

ID photo fades, and my phone screen returns to the background photo filled with lilacs.

Before I can stand up, there's a knock at my bedroom door. "Lucy! I'm coming in," Ellie yells as she comes through the door.

"How's your hot director boyfriend?" she asks as she lies down on the bed next to where I'm sitting.

"Ellie, he's fine. I just made a big deal of it to try and shake John off."

"Oh, that's right! He's probably looking for a hookup tonight. Well, I think you shook his confidence a little bit. When you came upstairs, he came to talk with me. As if I would help him in any way. That man is delusional."

I don't want to deal with this any longer. "Hey, Ellie… how about a sleepover at your place?"

She sits up and yelps, "Yes!"

"All right, I'll go let my mom know, and then we can slip out before John even notices I'm gone."

"And we'll need to silence your text alerts, at least the ones from John. Don't want to miss any from your British boyfriend!" She yells those last two words down the staircase. I'll have to remember to change my lock code on the phone before I go to sleep tonight. I don't need her texting Henry while I'm sleeping.

Friday morning begins earlier than we would have liked after Ellie and I stayed up far too late last night. It doesn't matter how much older we get—we revert to those teenagers who stay up all night talking when we are together.

Now, armed with our extra-large amounts of caffeine, we are on to the first stop of our shopping trip. Ellie has a drink that is almost the color of milk due to the copious amounts of cream and sugar in it. I ordered my usual—cold brew, black. It works quicker this way and I plan to sip on it between the many shops we plan to visit.

After hours of shopping and too much caffeine in our systems, we reach the last of our stops. "How are you going to get all this back to the UK with you?" Ellie asks as she looks at the numerous shopping bags filling the back of my mom's SUV.

"I don't plan on taking any of it back home with me. It's all staying in my bedroom here until Christmas."

"Did you just say, 'back home' when referring to London?" Her shoulders drop, and sadness covers her face. "Lucy, here is home. I am home."

"Ellie…" After closing the back hatch, I pull her into a hug. "You are home. You always will be."

She pulls away, and we move to get back into the car. Once she is situated in the passenger seat, she says, "I don't blame you if you make London your home with your new boyfriend."

"Ellie, he's not my boyfriend. You know the truth."

"Oh, I think I do know the truth… It's you that's trying to convince yourself otherwise…" She gives me a knowing look.

"Okay." I try to appraise her. "Let's go. It's nap time and then take out for dinner and wrapping these gifts at my mom's place if you're up for it."

"Yes, as long as there is wine… Wrapping grates on my nerves. I need wine if we are doing that."

"Well, then, I guess we have one more stop on the way home," I say while switching our driving route to the closest winery.

After a much-needed nap, Ellie arrives at my mom's and we begin our evening of wrapping presents. My mom has offered to wrap the presents I ordered online for Ellie when they arrive, so I don't need to hide anything from her tonight.

"I can't believe you are leaving already, Lucy. It's as if you just got here," Ellie whines as she selects a roll of wrapping paper with baseballs on it. She must be starting with a gift for her dad.

"I know. I'll miss you, but I'll be back in a month. Then, in the New Year, you must come to visit," I insist.

"That's true—a month isn't that long to wait. And I'll try to get a trip in before the season begins."

My phone is buzzing again, I look down to check it to find more texts from John. He's quite upset that I disappeared last night "before he could say goodbye" and is insistent on seeing me tonight before I leave.

"That guy is persistent, but that's something we already knew." Ellie doesn't pick her head up from her current present. "It feels different this time…"

"What feels different?"

"You and John. You've been mad at him before, even ignored him, but it doesn't seem to be affecting you as much as it once did." I wait for her to bring up Henry, but she doesn't. "Who knows what the future holds for you, but I'm getting the feeling that this might be the time John finally remains in the past."

"Thanks, El. Me too."

Twenty-One

HENRY

THIS DAY IS MOVING at an expeditiously slow pace. It was grueling enough to spend the last week stressing about Lucy in the States and her seemingly over-interested ex-boyfriend, but now I am once again worried about her flying over the Atlantic Ocean. Of course, air travel is a relatively safe form of transportation, but I'll feel better when she lands.

And I can see her.

Checking the clock again, I have roughly a half hour before I need to leave for the airport. She doesn't know I'm picking her up. She insisted Hannah not trouble herself and that she would take a taxi, but I'm too anxious to tell her the good news.

I just hope she is happy to see me. Perhaps she wants time to herself to process whatever it was that took place with the mysterious man from her past who she has such a long history with. I remain in the dark about what occurred between them last year before she decided to move.

What if he realized the enormous mistake he made and wanted to reconnect? If that was the case, I trust Lucy would be honest with me. *Although she could be waiting to tell me to my face.* No, I can't let that negative possibility consume my thoughts.

I need to dress in something that covers most of my prominent features. I'll take Finn's car rather than a driver, that would attract attention. The final thing I grab is the small sign I made to hold and stand next to the other drivers waiting for their passengers. Smiling at it, I'm confident it will catch her attention.

Choosing to leave my snow cap and jacket on while I wait at the bottom of the escalators, dressed in all black, I almost blend in with the other drivers, but I'm not dressed in a suit like they are. Her flight landed about twenty minutes ago, and she sent a message to the group chat to let everyone know she is safely back on UK soil. I chose not to respond and let her think I was preoccupied at the moment.

Lucy's bright scarf and matching hat catch my attention before she turns to face forward. My breath catches at the sight before me. Her long dark brown hair sticks out beneath her hat, curling at the end where it rests on her bent arms carrying her bags. She doesn't look directly at me, but curiosity has gotten the best of her as she scans the names on the signs held up by each of the drivers standing beside me. Then she stops at mine, and her eyes look up to see the man holding the sign that says, "Miss Elizabeth Bennett."

Our eyes meet, and my chest tightens to the point of pain until it feels as if something inside me bursts. During our time apart and only in the dark hours of the night would I allow myself to admit just how greatly I have missed her, but even in those moments, I didn't anticipate this rush of emotions I'd feel at the sight of her. Her smile can be witnessed by everyone in this airport, but it is not for them.

It's mine.

"Mr. Darcy." She approaches, "I just wanted to give you my best wishes for finding your Miss Bennett."

I move to take her bags for her and lean in, "Oh, I've found her."

A faint blush comes over her cheeks, and her lips curl up into a tiny smile. "Thank you, but I can carry them."

I don't bother to acknowledge her comment about her bags as I take them from her. "Let's get out of here. I have Finn's car to take you back to your apartment. Are you hungry?"

"Yes, but I can throw something together later."

"No need, it's taken care of," I tease her.

"It is? How so?"

I'm not giving up on the surprise this soon. "You'll see," I say as we exit the large glass doors of the airport and make our way to the parking lot. Sounds echo through the floors of cars, forcing us to remain silent until we reach the car.

"All right. How was your week?" she asks.

"Nothing of note." While opening the SUV's back

hatch, I keep my attention from her. I don't want to give anything away.

"What's with the grocery bags?" she asks. "Did you get your weekly shopping done before coming to get me?"

I just laugh and walk her to the passenger side to open her door for her.

"Thanks," she says, her eyes focusing on me.

I walk slowly in front of the car, watching her through the windshield, never taking my eyes off her, even as I slip in behind the wheel and smile at her. Something about the two of us, contained in this low-lit small space, makes me hyper-aware of her body. How close she is, how easy it would be to place my hand in hers, to wrap my fingers around her thigh, to slip my arm around her and pull her into a kiss. No one would hear; the garage is filled with parked cars, and the windows would surely contain the sound.

But what if they started to fog?

Careful not to linger too long, afraid I will act on one of the impulses running through my mind, I pull the car into reverse and head in the direction of her apartment.

As we drive through the city, the interior of the car remains dark, which does little to stifle my awareness of her next to me. She hasn't stopped fidgeting in her seat, rubbing her hands up and down her thighs.

"Are you cold?" I ask as I turn the dial to increase the heat.

"No, I'm fine," she answers quickly.

Does she know her unintentional fidgeting is pulling my attention to her legs?

Can she feel this electricity between us?

I place my hand on the middle console, but no closer. I've always found her attractive, even if I denied it when I thought Finn and Oliver were trying to set us up, but after a week without her, I can no longer suppress her lure.

Fortunately, there is an open place to park directly in front of her apartment. I get out with her, but she hasn't caught on yet. "If you don't mind carrying the groceries up, I can grab your luggage."

Her face scrunches up as I lift the strap over my head. "The groceries are coming up? Are they for me?"

"They are for us." As that last word leaves my mouth, it comes out with more breath than I intended.

Us. I'm positive I've used it before in reference to me and her, but this time, it means something different… something more…to me, at least.

She doesn't say anything but moves quickly, opens her lobby door, and then holds it for me. Not one to miss an opportunity, I'm sure to brush her with my body as I move past her, inhaling her familiar perfume. A light and sweet smell of lilies and mandarin and, I believe, a hint of cucumber.

I follow her up the stairs, failing miserably at any attempts to clear my head. As she unlocks the door, I'm swept into a daydream of this moment becoming a regular occurrence for us. Trips to the grocery store together, planning a romantic evening for the two of us. After dinner, we could share a bottle of wine, turn the lights low…

The thunk of the grocery bags hitting her counter pulls me back to the present. Waiting for me to leave her small luggage and bag by the door, she stands still with her arms crossed over her chest, staring at me. The only action she is missing is tapping her foot. "What's going on, Henry?"

"I thought you may be tired after your travel day, and I appreciate all your help with the movie, so I wanted to do something nice and thought I could cook you dinner… this evening."

Maybe she doesn't want this after spending ten hours flying.

She may just want to go to bed or I should have offered at the least to get take-away.

Cooking in her kitchen and surely making a mess, but I plan to clean up too, might not be what she wants this evening.

I suppose these ingredients will stay for another day. I can offer to come back tomorrow.

Or she can really make this for herself. I don't need to be included. *But I want to be.*

"Oh, that's very kind of you…" She doesn't appear to be put off, but she is not elated either. Her brows furrow. "Why are you being so nice?"

So she does like this offer, she finds it nice. But she knows me better than this. I wish she knew me as the man who would plan a surprise dinner for her, but that's not the case, not yet, at least. "Like I said, I wanted to thank you."

"Did you hear from the studio?" Of course, she figured it out. She's far too intelligent to keep anything from her, but also, I'm bursting to tell her. It was difficult enough not to call her the moment Mark called and again when I first saw her at the airport.

I move from the kitchen and stand before her. Keeping my emotions reserved and reluctantly keeping my hands to myself, I share. "They called last week."

She grabs onto my arms and my body responds to her touch as if it was the air I need to breathe. "Do you have something you need to tell me?" How I'd like to grab her wrists, to place them behind my neck, bringing her closer to me. The endless emotions I've had day and night since she left flash through my mind, and I want to tell her each and every one of them, but this is not the time for that. No, she asked about the movie…

"You've put so much work into turning my reputation around…"

"Tell me! You got it?"

"I did." I don't know who moves first, but within an instant, her arms are wrapped around my neck and my arms around her waist.

This is bliss.

"Henry, Congratulations! This is wonderful news." She pulls out of our embrace and I attempt to hide my disappointment at the loss of her touch but continue to bask in her closeness.

"Yes, I begin on Monday. I found out a few days ago, but wanted to tell you and thank you in person. I asked Viewmont not to release a statement until next week. I wanted to be the one to tell you." She pauses, seeming surprised by what I said, and then takes a small step back.

"That explains the dinner. I was beginning to worry— the Henry I know wouldn't do all this," she says with a wave, and I wonder if I may have shown my hand too soon. "Do you mind if I grab a quick shower and change while you prepare dinner? I'd like to get out of my travel clothes."

I gulp like a cartoon character at her mention of showering just a few steps away from me. I could join her, although I doubt her shower is that big. It can't compare to mine. I think she'd like mine. I'm sure she would look spectacular in it.

"Unless you need help with dinner?" Her question pulls me out of my inappropriate daydreaming.

"Not at all. I've got this under control." I turn to the groceries in an attempt to hide my embarrassing reaction. "Take your time."

The door to her bedroom closes behind her as I pull the pasta and other ingredients out of the brown bag. There's another door next to her bedroom that remains closed as I hear the water turn on. It must connect to her bedroom as well. *I'm a grown man.* Many women have showered in my presence. My lustful feelings are obviously one-sided, and I need to cool down. We are friendly… certainly friends at this point. I don't need to ruin this by storming into that bathroom and worshiping every inch of her body.

Shaking away those feelings, I turn my focus on producing an exemplary dinner for the mastermind behind securing the most coveted movie in my career. I put music on my phone and get to work. She mentioned many times about her love for Italian food, so I put in a call to Max, who has become a master chef in recent years. He recommended a fettuccine Alfredo dish that he said was a midlevel dish that I could "handle." Of course, with the water running, I am struggling to remember the order of ingredients for the sauce so I call Max quickly.

Max answers on the second ring. "Henry, how'd the dinner go?"

"That's why I'm calling. I need you to go over the sauce once more." Desperation fills my voice. "Quickly."

"Are you in the middle of cooking? Is she watching you call me? This defeats the purpose of impressing her, you know." As much as I denied it to Max when I asked for this recipe, he saw right through me. *"I know you, Henry. You don't go to these lengths for women. There's something more to it."*

"No, she's in the shower. I'm trying to have it started at the very least by the time she's done."

There's silence from Max's end, then he says, "You're going to have to give more details before I continue."

"Enough, you perverted old man. She just wanted to shower after a day of traveling." Frustration grows inside me. "Rest assured, nothing untoward is taking place in this apartment. I'm just trying to be a good friend and make her dinner. Now, can you be a good friend and help me."

"I have no desire to be that type of *good friend* to you, Henry." He laughs to himself but then continues with the recipe for the sauce. "I'll text it to you now too, just in case you forget again. Enjoy your romantic evening!" And then he hangs up before I can deny it.

Twenty-Two

HENRY

I HEAR the door click open and without thinking, I turn to steal a quick glance at Lucy. She's wearing black jeans and a beige jumper that is a few sizes too big. She looks comfortable, which makes her all the more appealing.

Fixing my face, I let her know, "It's almost ready." She certainly saw me checking her out. "Just adding the finishing touches." I need to stop acting like such a teenager around her.

She steps up beside me and her perfume overwhelms my senses. In truth, this entire apartment smells like her. "How can I help?" she asks.

Struggling to remember how to speak, my response comes out a little gruff. "I've got it."

"Well, then I can set the table." She moves to reach up into the cupboard and begins to pull out plates. "Sorry, I don't have any champagne for our celebration," she says with a frown.

"I brought wine."

"Not champagne?" she asks.

"No, I know you don't care for it." She smiles at my remark and I return it before turning to the sauce preparation.

I need to control myself—this is not a date, it is not a romantic evening. This is simply a thank-you dinner to celebrate the success of her grand scheme. I plate the pasta and carry it over to the small table Lucy has set for us.

I raise my glass to her. "To you and your success."

She replies, "To us, and *Pride and Prejudice*."

"To Jane Austen," I add.

We both smile and sip our wine. Cautiously taking my first bite of the pasta, I'm relieved to find it is delicious, if I do say so myself. I believe I actually did a fine job.

Lucy confirms, "This is fantastic, is it your recipe?"

If this were a date, I would have lied and taken the credit, but it's not, so I proceed with honesty, "No, my mate, Max, shared it with me. Or, as you may know him, Mr. Tilney from my *Northanger Abbey* movie adaptation. And, in fact, you will now know him as Mr. Bennett. After I signed on to the movie, he agreed to the part."

"How exciting!" She beams with a huge smile. "Well, I look forward to meeting him. His portrayal of Mr. Tilney was perfectly done." The way she lights up at the mention of Max in *Northanger Abbey* makes my stomach turn, I don't like the idea of her swooning over my closest friend.

"Yes, I'll be sure to introduce you. Perhaps when we visit the set locations." Max can be captivating, on or off set, but hopefully, she will be too distracted with everything else going on during shooting, she won't have a chance to fall for him.

"Oh, that's right! I would be so grateful to visit the sets. Having spent months in the UK, I had expected to visit more of the English countryside I've spent so much time reading about, but I haven't left the city yet."

"Well, you are planning to stay with me at the end of the month. I don't live in the country, but it's close enough to visit. I'd love to take you sightseeing," I offer while mentally accumulating a list of places to take her.

"Henry…" She puts her fork down and sits back in her chair, then brings her hands to her lap and looks down at them. "What does this mean going forward?"

I pause, thinking of what I should say. Should I tell her that in the last two hours, I've realized I have feelings for her? But what do I want from that? I haven't given myself a moment to think what I would want that to look like. Do I want to jump into another relationship? Does she? She's been open about her disinterest in a relationship since we met. Is she asking because things went better than I realized with her ex, and she is looking to get back with him?

While I'm thinking of every possible option, she must take that for confusion and clarifies, "Now that you have secured the director role, does that mean we will stop with the fake relationship posts?" She turns her face to show no emotions in either direction.

If I say yes and go back to being friends, I will lose most of my reasons for contacting her. I could tell her the truth, Viewmont Productions credited my new social media presence as the reason they decided to go with me, but they didn't make this relationship requirement by any means. *She doesn't know that.*

This might be my way of keeping her close for a few more weeks or months until I can get a better understanding of what is going on between us and if it is mutual or just one-sided.

I lean forward, "Just the opposite, in fact. The studio credited the social media account as the reason they decided to select me for the director, well that and my resume. They would like us to continue to share our love story on social media and Mark recommended more photos of us together, which we already have planned. As long as you are all right with continuing?" I hold my breath, waiting for her answer. If she is planning to rekindle her relationship in the States, this will surely force her to confess it.

"Oh, well." She sits back up and takes a sip of her wine. "Of course, that was the plan all along. I'm all right to continue as we scheduled."

"Well, good. That's settled."

She tries to hide her smile behind her wine glass, but there's no hiding it as her eyes give her away. "So, tell me what happens next. What will you do on Monday?"

"As most of the pre-production has already been in place, I will spend most of December in meetings getting caught up on casting and locations, reviewing the scripts, and making any necessary last-minute changes." Her eyes light up as I speak. "I plan to stay in London with Oliver and Finn because most of the work will be done from the main offices in the city."

"This is so exciting, Henry." She looks delighted. "Don't tell the others, but I think I'm going to be reading *Pride and Prejudice* again soon, maybe even tonight. I'm sure they will guess that with the news that you have the director position."

"Hold that thought," I say as I get up from my chair and move to grab the package I wrapped at the bottom of the grocery bag. Back at the table, I hand it to her. "For you."

She takes the gift and pulls on the large red bow on top. Then, carefully unfolding the paper, her mouth falls open and her eyes go wide. She pulls the three small old books with gold designs on the spine and a solid dark cover away from the wrapping and looks back and forth from the books to me. I purchased this first edition years ago, after I started making movies and real money, it was a promise to myself that I would one day direct that film. Now, that goal has only been achieved thanks to her. They belong with Lucy.

"Henry?"

"You mentioned you often thought about how people felt while reading *Pride and Prejudice* when it was first published. I can't take you back in time, but maybe this book will connect you to the time it was printed," I say to her, still standing next to where she is sitting.

She jumps out of her chair, clutching the book close to her chest as she uses the other arm to wrap around my neck. *It feels like the most natural embrace.* I take the opportunity to wrap my arm around her back, caressing her gently. *This feeling, her in my arms, feels…just as it should.* It must mean something.

Can I consider being in a relationship again? Can I be good for her?

"Thank you," she whispers genuinely into my ear. I

give her one more squeeze, then release her as she pulls out of our embrace. "This is not necessary. It's too much, Henry."

"Nothing will ever be able to convey my appreciation for your assistance in securing the film I've waited my career to direct. Thank you, Lucy."

"I will treasure them," she promises.

Her gaze moves toward the window. "Don't you think this would be a good post?" Before I can answer, she places the books on her chair with gentle movements. Then hands me both of our wine glasses as she takes out her phone and moves to the window. "Come join me." Following her direction, I kneel next to her in front of the windowsill. She leans in close to me and holds her phone in front of us to get the perfect angle that gives us a backdrop of the moon in the night sky above the city lights. We hold our glasses in front of us and smile.

The phone clicks and we both check the photo. *This will certainly gain the coveted spot as my home screen's wallpaper.* She sends it over and instructs me to post it.

"What should the caption be?" I ask.

"I'm not sure. Maybe just a couple emojis—use the pasta and wine and the moon." She smiles. "That pretty much sums up our night…as much as your adoring fans need to know."

After clearing up the dishes, I bid her a reluctant goodbye and make my way back down to Finn's car.

When I arrive at the boys' townhouse, I find Oliver in the kitchen finishing up his dishes and offer to help him dry them.

"Where were you this evening?" Oliver asks.

"I picked Lucy up from the airport and then got her something to eat." Oliver pauses his scrubbing to look over at me. I pretend not to notice.

"Is that your payment for her being the mastermind behind your social media fame?" Oliver asks.

"Of course." I'm not discussing this with Oliver. I don't even know how I would express the feelings I'm having. I have to figure this out on my own first.

"Hmp." He thinks he knows everything. People say he gets that from me, so I suppose I deserve it.

Changing the subject, I tell him, "I did ask about her plans for the holidays. She'll be going to the States for Christmas, then be back before the New Year."

"Do you think she would be interested in spending the New Year with us? At your place?" he asks.

"Oh, yes. She was excited when I asked," I answer.

"I bet," he says as he looks at me with a side-eye. "New Year's Eve will be the perfect night to propose. That settles it. I'll do it then."

"Splendid. I'll call the shops we decided on to finalize the arrangements. You'll still be coming up before the twenty-fifth?" I ask.

"Of course, I think we will head up the Saturday before like usual."

"If you have any special dietary requests, let me know. Otherwise, I'll plan to have the place stocked before your arrival."

"I'm home!" Finn yells from the entryway as we finish up the last of the dishes. "Hey pops, where have you been all night."

Before I can answer, Oliver does, "He's been with Lucy. Celebrating the movie deal."

Finn walks over to me and places his hands on my shoulders, "You've got it bad, don't you?"

"I don't know what you are talking about." I turn back to the more subtle of my two sons. "I'm going to retire for the evening. Going to go over the script some more." Walking out, I wish them goodnight.

"If you have any questions, you should call Lucy!" Finn yells behind me, but I don't bother to acknowledge it.

Twenty-Three

LUCY

IT'S BEEN two weeks since Henry picked me up at the airport and made a romantic dinner for us.

Two weeks since he told me he got the director role for the upcoming *Pride and Prejudice* rendition.

Two weeks since he gifted me the first edition of *Pride and Prejudice*.

Two weeks since we hugged...more than once. A memory that constantly repeats in my mind.

And two weeks since it felt like we were a real couple while we planned the next steps of our fake relationship.

Joining pre-production has kept Henry busy every day since. He's even missed two of our Tuesday nights at the coffee shop. I'm always sure to sit at the end of the table, with an empty seat next to mine, just in case he shows up.

With my classes coming to an end for the semester, I find myself with extra time on my hands. Time I don't want to spend thinking about the way Henry made me feel that night. How my heart swelled when I spotted him at the airport or the butterflies that fluttered when he said he found his Miss Bennett.

No, I must not spend another evening curled up in bed admiring my new books while thinking of how sexy he looked in my small kitchen or the way the muscles in his back moved as he prepared our dinner, and I certainly don't need to think about how good it felt to be in his arms, even for the brief embrace, it was enough to do more damage than I care to admit.

So, in an attempt to silence those thoughts, I volunteer to take over Henry's social media accounts while he is busy with the movie.

Even though his busy schedule has prevented us from seeing each other, Henry calls almost every night when he gets back from work. He lets me know what he did during his day and asks my opinion on decisions he needs to make. I've requested he send me some discreet photos of his day to use for the account now that the production company has officially announced his role. I've posted them mixed in with the throwback photos of him and Max, as well as staged romantic photos.

I message him with a question, one that he doesn't seem to expect by the way he replies.

LUCY

What size shoes do you wear?

Henry is a tall man, I'd guess 6'5", but I don't want to miss the chance to make him laugh at the assumption, so I leave the text without any context.

HENRY

Why?

LUCY

Curious.

HENRY

If you're that curious, you could just ask me out. Rumor has it, I'm usually a sure thing.

LUCY

Don't flatter yourself. I'm only asking because I would like to buy us a matching pair of couples slippers. With us being unable to take photos together, I need props to create the illusion.

English Pervert

HENRY

12.

Have fun fantasizing about my big

Two minutes pass before he finishes his sentence.

HENRY

feet

I don't bother responding, he has work to do. I order our slippers online—sure to adjust my slippers from a US to a UK size. They should arrive in the next day or two.

Until then, I will have to think of something to post today. Looking around my apartment, I fret I've exhausted all possibilities. I'll need to start taking myself out on dates just for more content material. Maybe a call to Ellie would help, to be able to pick her social media director brain.

Although she's never needed to post romantic photos, she's a genius and surely she will have some ideas. I'm also running low on throwback pictures so I'll need to run over to the boys' apartment to check if they have any there.

LUCY

Hey, mind if I stop over this afternoon to grab some old photos of your dad and Max for the accounts?

FINN

If you're coming over now, we can order lunch.

LUCY

Grabbing my shoes now. I'll pick it up. What would you like?

FINN

Sandwiches from the deli would be perfect. I'll call over with my order now. Do you want the usual?

LUCY

Yes, please! See you soon!

As I ring the bell to the townhouse I feel a rush of hope that maybe Henry is home for lunch. The bag from the deli is heavier than I expected.

Oliver greets me at the door and offers to carry the sandwiches in for me. These English gentlemen and their manners, I don't think I'll ever get used to it.

"Thanks for grabbing this, Lucy," he says as Finn goes through the bag, checking each box if it's his.

"Thank you for paying—you didn't have to do that."

Finn hands me the box with my club sandwich, "Anytime," he says before making his way to the table.

Just as we are finishing our lunch, Oliver clears his throat and turns to me. "Dad mentioned you'll be staying with us at his house for the New Year."

"Yes, I can't wait to experience more of England."

Finn chimes in, "His place is beautiful. I think you'll love it."

Oliver smiles and agrees, "I'm glad you'll be there. I have a secret to share with you."

"What is it?" I ask.

Oliver smiles shyly, "I'm going to propose to Hannah while we are all there."

"Oliver! Congratulations, I'm so happy for you!"

Oliver beams, "Thank you. I'm sure I don't have to explain, but this will be a surprise for Hannah. She has no idea. I may need your help distracting her in the coming days while I make preparations."

"Mia knows too. She's already planning all the distractions for you both," Finn says while wrapping up the empty takeaway boxes.

"Perfect! And thank you for including me."

"Of course, you're part of the family now," Oliver says.

"Speaking of family, I'll take you up to the photo albums, Lucy." Finn leads me upstairs to a spare room that resembles an office. I wonder if this is set up for Henry. There is a box on top of a table. "All yours, take whatever you need. I'm working remotely today, so yell if you need anything. Take your time."

I thank him and then get to work. There's an album of the boys as kids, plenty of them playing with two girls who appear to be just a little younger than them with Henry and Max always standing close by. The photos must have been taken by their mothers since I don't see any women in them. I finally come across one of just Max and Henry and take a quick picture of it using my phone.

Then, I move to the next album. Thankfully, Finn and Oliver have held on to this one, but I can also understand why it resides here and not at Henry's home. I can't imagine holding on to a wedding album after a marriage ends in divorce.

I certainly won't post any of these photos, but curiosity gets the best of me as I turn through the pages. With each photo, Henry's joy grows greater. He must have married in his early twenties, and his bride is absolutely stunning. I don't know much about her, but on looks alone, I assume she worked as a model, which I know is his type.

I wonder what ended their marriage—he never speaks about it. Could it be the reason he is so against love? These photos are evidence that, at one time, he was blissfully in love with his new bride. Could he still be in love with her? Maybe he doesn't believe he could find love with anyone but his wife.

She's his ex-wife.

A burning sensation starts to grow in my chest. I allow myself only a moment to imagine what it would be like to have Henry Brooks in love with me. I shake my head in hopes to rattle those thoughts from my mind.

It feels as though much more time has passed since the night we met, and I've become so distracted since returning to London. I've let myself get caught up in the fantasy that I created.

Henry has never wavered in his stance of not wanting a relationship, nor has he done anything to deny the type of women he's interested in. Sure, there's been some flirty banter, but that's it. We are both flirty people—it's nothing more to him…

How much longer can I continue to flirt with him and keep my guard up?

Enough. I am not a part of Henry's romantic life. I'm not a model like this woman. I take another long look at those photos to burn them into my memory.

I am not the woman in these photos.

I close the album and return it to the box. It feels like a cold bucket of water has been dumped on my head, but at least I can approach things with a rational mind going forward.

Monday night has arrived, and I'm out the door to meet Hannah and Mia for drinks.

"I can't believe this is the first girls' night since your trip back to the States with your family! I need details and not the boring stuff you told everyone at the coffee shop," Mia demands. "Did you see your ex? Was there drama?"

"Mia!" Hannah scolds her, "Don't push her." Then turns to me, "We are here to talk if you'd like, but don't feel like you have to share."

"Yes, she does need to share. We are in loving, boring,

no-drama relationships, Hannah. I need drama, something juicy."

"You say that like it's a bad thing, Mia. I happen to love my relationship."

Mia rolls her eyes at Hannah's comment and I just giggle. "Yes, we know you love Oliver, and of course I love Finn, but we need excitement!"

"All right…I did see him," I admit. Mia squeals and Hannah grimaces. I add, "A few times."

Mia shouts, "Are you back together?"

"No, I don't think that's an option for us anymore." I refuse to share the full story with them. I know they would be understanding, but I enjoy not being the girl who was cheated on during her first and only relationship. Or the girl who still allows that ex-boyfriend to hang around in her social circle.

Hannah places her hand over mine at the table. No matter how I try to spin this story, I'll still receive their pity, but I'd rather let them think it's just over a standard break-up than share the less-than-desirable details.

"Did he go crazy when he saw you?" Mia asks. Hannah squeezes my hand tighter.

"It's all right," I tell Hannah and then turn to Mia. "I'm not sure. We spoke a few times, but I kept it brief." I take a sip of wine and speak without thinking, "He did act jealous over the photos of Henry and I… His mom showed them to him." I laugh to myself, but the girls take it differently.

"Who would have thought those photos would benefit you too," Hannah says.

"Quite frankly, I'm getting a little curious about what's

going on between you and Henry myself. I follow his accounts. Did you two really get matching slippers?" Mia asks.

We haven't gone into much detail with everyone, just that Henry started the account to get the director role. I try to shrug it off. "No, the studio keeps pushing for more 'romantic' posts, so I thought of that idea the other day and ordered them myself."

Mia gave me an unsure look, "And you're coming to stay with us at Henry's home over the holidays, correct?"

"Yes, I plan to visit my mom for Christmas, but return soon after and meet everyone there."

Hannah, cheery with the change of subject, replies, "That's so exciting."

"Yes, New Year's Eve has always been my favorite holiday. I'm looking forward to spending it with you all."

"Wonder who you'll kiss at midnight." Mia raises her eyebrows up and down at me.

"Mia…" Hannah scolds her again.

"What?" Mia plays innocent. "It would make for a very romantic post."

Twenty-Four

HENRY

THE EMBERS of the fire flicker while I look at my home in a new light, wondering what it will be like to have Lucy in my personal space. I've been to her apartment twice now, but I have a sense it will feel different when I have her here.

"Henry?" a voice breaks me out of my daydreams. "What are your thoughts on the sketches from the designer?"

Working remotely seemed like the best option for me to get back home as soon as possible, but it's becoming increasingly difficult to concentrate on the meetings as I prepare for my family's arrival.

"Yes, I looked them over briefly, but will review them in more detail this evening." I don't understand why Viewmont is so insistent about holding meetings this week —more than half the people on the call are already at their holiday destinations. Thankfully, we only have two more days of this then break until after the New Year.

"All right, is there anything else we need to address?"

Tom, the rep for Viewmont, asks, and thankfully, everyone shakes their heads. Certainly, I'm not the only one who is eager to get off this call. "All right, enjoy the rest of your day. We will reconvene tomorrow morning."

I shut the laptop and leave it on the end table. I always look forward to this time of year. I enjoy my privacy and peace but it's nice to have guests once in a while. It reminds me of when the boys were little. Now one of them is proposing, and it's such an honor he decided to do it here.

I look over the schedule Oliver sent again. They are planning to arrive Saturday, stay until the twenty-fifth, and then go their separate ways to visit Mia and Hannah's families, then reconvene while they visit with the boys' mother and come back here on the thirtieth to set final preparations for the proposal on the thirty-first. While they are away, I'll pick up Lucy from the airport on the twenty-sixth.

Anticipation and excitement fill my body at the thought of having a few days with her alone. I planned to spend more time thinking about the possibility of a relationship, but work has consumed most waking hours since I last saw her. I need to think this through before she arrives.

Is a relationship something I want again?

I was sure it was something I never wanted to experience again, but now. These feelings are challenging that stance, but can I be a good partner to her?

That's if she's even interested in a relationship herself.

Thursday afternoon finally arrives, and I close the laptop, place it in its carrier bag, and leave it in my study with no intention of opening it again until January third.

While preparing the house for my guests, I've let my mind wander to thoughts of what a relationship with Lucy could be like.

She has never voiced a desire for a real relationship. In fact, she's stayed firm in the idea of only allowing herself to care for fictional men.

As much as I hate to admit defeat, I suppose it's time to consult the only hopeless romantic I know, Max. For someone who lives for the love stories we create on the screen, he's never been able to give himself a second chance at love.

I grab my phone and call him. After a few rings and a quick hello, Max asks, "Henry, how are preparations for the holiday going? Do you need another recipe?"

"Things are going well. How are you? Are the girls in town yet?"

"Yes, they arrived yesterday, and it's so nice to have them home again."

"I know what you mean. I was just thinking about how much the holidays remind me of when they were all little. It's nice to have them under my roof again. Especially being removed from the hassle of the city."

"Well put, Henry. What can I do for you?"

I pause, trying to find the words to express this… confusion that has now taken residence in my head. "I may need another recipe, or a grand gesture idea, or advice."

"Well, it's about time, my friend."

"No need to gloat," I tell him—maybe this is a bad idea.

"Not gloating, simply happy for you. Is Lucy coming to stay with you over the holidays?"

"Yes, but only for New Year's. She is spending Christmas back home with her family."

"Where is Lucy at in all of this? Does she know about your feelings?" he asks.

"I don't even know what my feelings are. I just know for the first time since my marriage, I'm considering getting into another relationship, and it terrifies me. What if I don't remember how to be a good partner? This leads my mind down the road of if I was a better partner, I would probably still be married. If I were to get into a relationship again, would it end the same way?"

"You're overthinking this, friend," Max says. "And because you are giving it so much thought—tells me you care about her."

"Of course, I care. She's become the person I want to speak with as soon as I wake up and before I go to bed. Every time my phone rings, I hope it's her calling."

"Henry…"

"I don't know if she wants this to be more than the friendship it's developed into. When we met she had cited a breakup as one of the reasons for moving to another country and declared she had no intention of getting into another relationship. What if I do something foolish, and things grow distant between us, and it turns out badly?" I ask, and don't let him answer before confessing, "She deserves the best."

"Then give her your best."

His words hit me like a tidal wave. "That simple, huh?"

"Yes, when you love someone, which I think you may be on your way to, if you're not already, it is that simple. You are a different man than you were twenty-five years ago, for many reasons, but most importantly, you are a different man since meeting her."

My life has changed since meeting her in that coffee shop. Not only is my career resuming *thanks to her,* but I'm happier now than I was before. For years, I was content, but now it's as if the sun has come back out, and each day is enjoyable because I can share it with her.

Max continues, "If this is a chance at love, don't you dare let it pass you by." I owe it to myself to try. Max's belief in the idea of love has never weakened, it's such a shame he just doesn't expect it for himself.

"And if she isn't interested in a relationship with me?" I ask now, fearful of those words becoming truth.

"Then you love her in whatever role she needs you in her life. Don't let that love die. It can always grow into something more."

I like this idea of being whatever it is Lucy needs me to be and fill any roles she needs me to fill in her life. It's a soothing way to look at this entire situation, taking the pressure off of me. I just need to be here for her.

And perhaps it will turn into something more.

"Thank you, Max."

"I'm always only a call away, Henry."

We both hang up and after a few minutes of absorbing his words, they have calmed my worries about Lucy's visit.

Friday begins with a call from Oliver. "Morning, Pop."

"Oliver, everything set for tomorrow?" I ask.

"That's why I'm calling. There's been a change to the plan." I didn't check the weather—could he be stuck in London, or did he change his mind about coming out? He continues, "Hannah spoke with Lucy last night."

My heart stops. "Is she all right?" I ask, hearing the panic in my voice. I spoke to her yesterday, but she didn't mention anything.

"Nothing to fear, Pop, she's doing well. There is a bad snow storm hitting New York, and she's decided not to travel. She's staying in London for Christmas."

She's able to come tomorrow.

I smile as I ask, "She's coming with you tomorrow then?"

"Well, I tried to insist, but she is proving a little difficult to convince, worried she would be intruding on our family holiday."

"She'd rather be alone in her apartment?"

"I don't think that's it. I just think she's trying to be polite."

"I'll take care of this," I insist. "She'll travel with you then?"

"Yeah, we were planning to bring two cars anyway with all the luggage and gifts. We have plenty of room," he assures me.

"All right, I'll speak with her and you can let her know what time you'll be picking her up, yes?"

"Yea. Pop?" he asks. "What's going on with you two?

Anything we should know about?" I can't give him the truth. I don't want any external pressures or assumptions surrounding us over the next few days. Once everyone else leaves, I'll try to get an idea of where she stands with the idea of us.

"She's one of your friends and has been particularly helpful to me with this movie deal business. Also, I'm not a complete grinch. I wouldn't wish anyone to spend Christmas alone."

"And that's it?" he asks again.

At least in this, I can answer honestly. "That's it."

For now.

After hanging up with Oliver, I ring Lucy. A photo of us taken by the paparazzi outside that bar pops up on the screen. It's my favorite of the shots, with us both looking into each other's eyes.

"Hello," she answers.

"Hello, Lucy. I just heard from Oliver."

"Oh?" She pauses. "How is he?" She's playing coy.

"Wonderful, he's very pleased that you'll be joining us at my home for the holidays even earlier than planned. As am I."

She lets out an exasperated breath. "Henry, I don't want you to think I invited myself. I decided to cancel my trip but didn't want to crash Christmas with your family. I will be perfectly fine staying in London."

"You're coming," I say, no opening for her to argue. "I'll see you tomorrow."

I hear her begin to argue, "But Henry, that's not necessar—" as I hang up on her.

Oliver and Finn each picked a permanent bedroom when I purchased this property. When Hannah joined, she practically took over Oliver's room. She's made herself so much at home. He's lucky she still lets him sleep there. As for Mia, she was thrilled when she saw the view from Finn's bedroom window. She always says she stays up too late when she's looking out at the small town lit up at night.

Everything is prepared for them. Oliver's favorite toothpaste is waiting in their bathroom, Finn's crackers are in his nightstand drawer, Mia's nightstand drawer is filled with gummy bears, and lastly, I left Hannah a bag of her favorite chocolates by her night lamp.

Lucy will stay in the remaining guest room that is unfortunately located the furthest from my bedroom. I couldn't very well give her a room the others are accustomed to utilizing, but it does bother me a little. *I like to have her near me.* Perhaps this distance will be good for us while she's staying.

I've already straightened up her room like I did for the others, but I look around to see where I can add more personal touches for her without it being too obvious. There's a bookshelf in here, and I've already moved my Jane Austen books onto it from my office. I also added other books I've read recently that I think she may enjoy.

My attention turns to the bed. Images of her in bed start innocent enough but quickly move to images of the two of us tangled in each other's bodies. The memory of her perfume fills my mind. What it must be like to share a bed with her, consumed by her warmth and scent.

That gives me an idea. I quickly run to my room and return with my cologne. Holding her pillow at arm's length, I lightly spritz the cologne on the pillow and then repeat the action with the bed's comforter.

I smile to myself at the thought of her trying to sleep, being tortured like I will be on the other side of the house.

After returning the cologne to my bathroom, I sit on my bed and attempt to settle my nerves. She'll be here tomorrow. I feel like a child waiting for Father Christmas.

Twenty-Five

LUCY

"I'M sorry again about this, Mom." I've apologized repeatedly for the snowstorm. Knowing I have no control over it, I still feel awful about it. She understands, but that doesn't make it any better. This will be the first Christmas we will spend apart, and I hate to think of her alone.

"Oh, stop that. What are you going to do about the weather?" she says. "I promise, knowing you are safe on the ground is a much better way to spend the holiday. I can't imagine spending the next week a nervous wreck, worrying about you flying back and forth during snow storms or being stuck in the airport with delays."

"I'll miss you." My voice cracks as I let my sadness come up after many failed attempts to push it down.

"And, of course, I'll miss you too, darling, but come in after the new year when there are far fewer people traveling, and we will pick a week with clear weather."

"All right, sounds like a plan, Mom."

"Besides, Ellie already stopped by to give me the lists of festivities I'm expected to attend at her family's place over the next week. I'll be plenty busy. And you will be too?"

"Yes, I'm leaving soon to go to Henry's place with Oliver, Finn, Hannah, and Mia."

"That sounds romantic! The holidays with your new man and his family."

"His family, who were my friends before I met him," I clarify. I'm still trying to downplay my fake relationship with Mom. I don't want her to be too upset when I tell her it's over.

"Of course. And do you want me to bring Ellie and her family's gifts to them?"

"Yes, if you don't mind, that'd be great."

"Okay, then. Have a safe trip today. Let me know when you get there safely!"

I still need to grab some breakfast and double-check my bags before I leave. I probably packed too much, but I'll be there for two weeks. Maybe this isn't too much.

MIA

We'll be there in 5 minutes.

It's an hour's drive to Henry's home. There's really no need for these butterflies to be dancing around in my stomach just yet. I grab my coat and check my hair one more time in the bathroom door. Even with being in contact every day, I'm restless to see him again, be in his presence, and beat him in board games, but what I'm looking forward to most is sitting next to him.

I carry each suitcase down separately and then lock up my apartment. Finn and Hannah's cars are parked in front of my building. Everyone is on the sidewalk, and Oliver is talking to someone near the back of Hannah's car. I look at Mia and Finn, and they give me an odd look but don't say anything. Hannah begins to walk over to me as the man speaking to Oliver turns around.

"Lucy!" John yells loudly at me.

John…

John is here, in London. He walks over to me and pulls me into a hug. "Surprise!"

Is this a dream?

More like a nightmare. I shake my head in an attempt to wake myself. This surely can't be happening. Looking around, fear sets in that this is not a dream, and my ex-boyfriend, John, is standing in front of me outside my London apartment.

My head feels like it's going to spin off my shoulders, but I manage to get a couple of words out. "What are you doing here?" I ask quietly as if my friends haven't already seen him.

"I didn't want you to be alone on Christmas. Your mom told mine you wouldn't be coming home. As soon as I heard, I booked a flight. I'm here to spend it with you." He says the second sentence like it was scripted from a holiday romance movie.

I pull out of his embrace and turn to face my friends. They are all looking at me as if I were in a horrible accident. It must show on my face. "Wait here," I tell John as I move him to the stairs leading up to my apartment.

Facing them, "I'm sorry. I wasn't expecting this." I feel

the tears welling up in my eyes. "I'm going to stay back. Have a good holiday." I turn back to John and begin my return to my apartment.

Finn comes up on our side. "Nonsense, you've got to come."

I give him a pleading look, hoping he will let this go and allow me to deal with the disaster that just literally landed on my doorstep. "I can't," I say quietly.

Oliver joins us, "John, it's great to meet you. We are heading to my family's house for the holidays. Would you be interested in joining us?"

No, no. No! I don't want John coming to Henry's home. "No, thank you, Oliver. We couldn't do that," I answer. What is he thinking? Inviting us to his father's?

John ignores my answer and insists, "If that's what you were planning, Lucy, I can accompany you."

Of course, he would.

"No, I think it's better we sort through things here." I turn to John and lower my voice, "In private."

"There's nothing to sort though, I'm here to spend the holidays with you and I'd love to meet some of your new friends," John says to Oliver and Finn.

Oliver agrees for some reason, "That sounds great. John, why don't you ride with us and Lucy, you can go with Mia and Hannah."

Finn continues, "Yeah, give us a chance to get to know you." He has a little edge to his voice that it seems only Mia and I pick up on.

Well, I have a choice, I can break down on this London street and explain to them the embarrassing story that is my history with John, or I can try to save some face and go with them, corner John the moment we get there and insist he leave as soon as possible and hope that Henry can forgive me for this intrusion on his families holiday.

Hannah approaches, "Let me help you get your bags in the car." Mia is frozen like a statue with her arms folded, staring John down as he moves into Finn's car. I nod but can no longer find the words to say to them. Getting into the backseat, I feel my phone buzz, but I already feel sick enough. I don't need to be looking at my phone during the hour-long drive.

How could I have been so naive to think my past wouldn't catch up to me? I thought I could run away, but even an ocean wasn't enough distance to get away from John. What is he doing here? *He's going to say it's because he loves me.* Yes, I'm sure he will say that, but I'm sure he has a text log full of other women he's told the same thing to. Why couldn't he go spend the holidays with one of them? *Because he is going to say I'm the only one he actually wants to be with.* This type of grand gesture may have been successful if it came years ago, but that girl is gone.

A tear falls from my eye, and I wipe it away. So much for the new me, the idea of becoming the person I've always wanted to become. Just like at home, I'll be looked upon with pity by my new friends. The girl who everyone thinks can't get over her ex.

I was finally forgetting my embarrassing romantic relationship past. John barely crossed my mind since I saw him at Thanksgiving. Spending time with Henry gave me hope that there is a possibility for me to have another chance at a normal relationship. Who am I kidding? All of that was fake too. Another tear falls. What will Henry think when I show up with another man? We discussed posting photos of us together for his accounts to show us as a couple spending the holidays together for the first time.

I know deep down, there was never a chance of Henry and I becoming anything more than friends, which even that was questionable some days. But I began to really enjoy that friendship, and look forward to his calls, and just this morning, I was so excited to spend time with him again.

"Are you okay back there, Lucy?" Mia sticks her hands behind her to hold my hand.

"Just surprised," I answer, not able to say much more. "I had no idea," I plead, hoping they know this isn't something I planned.

"Oh, we know. Anyone who saw your face would know," Hannah says. "But surprised good or surprised bad?"

"Just surprised. Still trying to process him being here. With how things were left and even when we saw each other at Thanksgiving, I didn't ever expect him to show up," I say, trying to save face. I need a plan.

Okay, when we get to Henry's, I'll give him my apologies and find a place to speak with John in private, tell him how greatly inappropriate this is, and demand he leave at once, claiming a sick relative or something.

Lost in thoughts, the drive to Henry's home passes quickly, and before I know it we are pulling into the driveway of what is much more than he described to me. He called it a cottage, but it looks like something out of a storybook. Larger than I expected but more beautiful than I could have imagined it would be. Hannah's car pulls up first and Henry is waiting at the side door for us. He looks so handsome…and cheerful.

"Welcome, ladies," he yells to us, but I'm frozen in the car. Hannah and Mia exit and must give him a look of concern, and he moves to open my door. Time to face the music.

"Lucy, welcome. How was the drive?" he asks with caution.

Finn's car pulls up next, and Henry notices the third person in the car pulling his attention away from me. "Who's with them?" he asks.

I lower my head and hold back tears as I say the only thing I can think of, "I'm so sorry." I should have texted him during the drive. I should have warned him, but I was too concerned with myself.

He cocks his head to the side in confusion. Finn breaks the silence as the men exit the car. "Pop, we have an extra guest. Come meet, John." Henry doesn't catch on yet, but Finn clarifies, "You know, Lucy's old boyfriend from the States." Henry looks back at me but I'm too afraid to meet his eyes. I know I'll cry if I look at him, and I can't do that if I'm going to try and blow this all over.

"Hi Henry, nice to meet you, I'm John." Henry takes a couple of steps away from me.

Oliver intervenes to explain, "When we arrived at Lucy's apartment building, John was there to surprise her, so I invited him to come up here and stay with us."

"You did," Henry says with ice in his tone as he takes another step away from me.

John moves to my side, taking my bag and putting his arm around my shoulder before leaning down to ask, "How was the drive? You feeling all right?" I nod and move to put distance between us. He addresses everyone else, "She gets carsick on long drives sometimes." As if he needs to prove our history.

"Right." Henry's voice is more rigid than I think I've ever heard it. "Well, let me show everyone to their rooms. First will be the room for Lucy and her long-lost lover."

Out of reach from John's embrace, I follow behind Henry, neither of us attempting to make eye contact.

Twenty-Six

HENRY

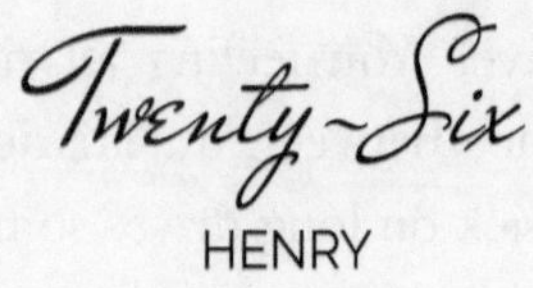

HIDING in my office won't solve anything, but I can't face what is taking place on the other side of this door. How could I have been so wrong about us? Sure, I didn't know if she felt romantically about me, but I thought it was a possibility.

Less than an hour ago, I was bouncing on my feet, unable to contain my excitement for her arrival. All the plans I had made for us, for her. Yes, I may have let my infatuation with her run wild, but it's clear on everyone's faces that no one expected this…*guy* to travel to London.

Now, before I had the chance to declare myself to Lucy, my window closed, opportunity missed, stolen out from under me. I had so much planned—this was supposed to be the beginning of a new relationship for us…if she wanted that. Or, at the very least, a weekend of showing her how much her friendship means to me.

This isn't right. I might not be the guy for her, but there's no way he is…definitely not him.

I refuse to witness the joyous reunion between Lucy

and her American ex…well, no longer ex, I suppose. An urgency to act consumes me, but I'm at a loss for direction. Do I run out and express my feelings to Lucy in front of everyone? Will that look like I'm just doing it because he is here? Until I decide what to do, I have to stay here so I don't cause more damage. My body buzzing with energy, I begin to pace in front of the large window that looks out onto the garden.

How could she do this? Oliver said it was a surprise, more like an ambush, but she should have warned me. She could have called from the car or at least sent a text. No, she doesn't owe me a warning. She doesn't owe me anything.

After a soft knock on my office door, Oliver calls me, "Pop." Coming in and closing the door behind him, "What's going on?"

"What's going on is you invited that man to stay with us." I continue pacing as he watches.

"Did she ask you to? Does anyone even know if she wants him here?" I lean over my desk. "Did you even ask her?" Grasping at the hope that this could all be a misunderstanding.

"What I do know is she was planning to stay in town with him to sort everything out. And if this fake relationship means so much to you, I didn't think you'd want your fake girlfriend spotted around London during Christmas with another man."

How would I have reacted if they arrived without her and then saw photos of her out with another man? "Good thought, Oliver."

He approaches me, back straight. "Look, Pop. I don't

know what's going on with you two, but based on how she looks at you, I'm highly suspicious that it's more than just a friendship to her." He takes a deep breath. "If this is just a matter of convenience for you and you plan to shake her off the moment she's no longer useful, do not get in between whatever is happening between her and John."

I look at him but have no words. Does he think I'd do that to her?

He continues, "I don't know much about their past. Hannah says Lucy barely spoke during the drive here. Do you have any insight? Has she shared anything more with you?"

"No, she's barely mentioned him to me."

"He clearly loves her. He flew here the moment he heard she wasn't going back for holidays."

"Yes, a grand gesture indeed." So much for the grand gestures I had planned for her.

"Just don't lead her on." Exasperation fills Oliver's voice. "We all care about her, and I hope you do too."

"I do." More than he knows.

"Good. Let's get dinner over with and we can all retire for the evening. That should give Lucy time to sort out things with John."

Oliver leaves me to myself in my office. Not ready to face what waits on the other side of the door, I sit in front of the window, pouting, hoping the view of my garden will provide some clarity.

Dinner preparation moves quickly as I've decided on soups and salads for their first day here. We all sit down to eat at my large dining table. One of the boys must have added the extra chair. I certainly didn't do it—he can stand for all I care.

The worst part of this meal is not sitting beside Lucy. She is seated as far away from me as possible, next to him. *That's my seat.* How I long to move near her. The only other time we sat so far apart was the night we met. Since then, I've been unable to tolerate the idea of such distance. When she enters a room, I'm drawn to her like a magnetic force pulling me to her side.

Although I think I am being discreet in my agony, Finn leans over to me, "I don't like him either."

Good, I'm not alone in this, but intrigued about the source of his dislike. "Why's that?"

"Nothing solid—he just rubs me the wrong way." Finn looks to the end of the table where Lucy is speaking with Hannah. "And she doesn't seem like herself. Mia said she barely spoke since his unexpected arrival."

"Let's keep an eye out," I instruct him. Having kept my gaze from her until now, too afraid of what I would see when she looked at *him*. I risk a glance. She looks beautiful as she always does. Maybe this was a mistake. What if she sees my emotions on my face. No, I need to look, to check on her.

While she does appear content, something is off about her. Her posture, while typically exquisite, now looks far too rigid, not as natural as it usually does. When her eyes meet mine for only a moment, I swear I see a flash of something in them. Could it just be that she is sorry for the intrusion, or could it be more?

"Already on it." Finn winks and returns to his meal.

Dinner finishes, and everyone pitches in with the clean-up, but Lucy maintains her distance from me and I do not intrude on her space, still unsure how she feels about her unexpected guest. Oliver suggests a game before everyone retires. Lucy doesn't respond, but John jumps at the idea. I don't hide my eye roll.

In an attempt to be respectful, she may want to play, so I opt out of the game, "Sorry, but I have some work I'd like to catch up on before bed. Have a good night." And I sulk up to my room so I don't have to witness another moment of Lucy with him.

It's helpful to know Finn is keeping an eye on everything. That is, until everyone goes to bed for the night. Fury fills me at that thought. Unable to contain my anger, I slam my bedroom door behind me.

Twenty-Seven

HENRY

UNABLE TO FIND SLEEP, I toss and turn for hours, thinking about Lucy, about her in my home, with *him*. Attempting to distract myself, I turn on my bedside light and grab the closest book. Hopefully, reading can occupy my mind enough to settle it. Of course, the book I grabbed is the cheap copy of *Pride and Prejudice* the studio gave me to make notes on. I flip through the pages and notice Lucy's notes next to scenes she insisted were "required" for the adaptation.

The memory of the airport comes flooding back into my mind.

"I hope you find your Miss Bennett," Lucy says to me.

"I believe I already have," I answer her.

I wonder if she sensed what I felt that day, the spark between us finally morphed into a blaze that I have been unable to contain in the weeks since.

This is no use.

My throat feels dry. Perhaps a drink of water will help me find sleep. Listening closely at my bedroom door, there's nothing but silence on the other side. I'm light on my feet in the open hallway, trying not to wake anyone. My stomach knots as I pass Lucy's room, which she is now sharing with John. I hurry past as if the images of them in there together will disappear the further away I am from the door.

As I reach the bottom step, I notice a figure standing next to the window in the kitchen. Quietly moving closer allows me to recognize the long brown hair that curls under itself at the bottom. Lucy's wearing a white long-sleeved shirt and loose pink pajama bottoms. I look around and feel relieved when I confirm she is alone.

She hasn't turned around yet. If she doesn't hear me coming, I don't want to startle her. I clear my throat and ask, "Couldn't sleep?"

She doesn't say anything, continuing to face the window when she raises a mug above her head.

I walk closer to the kitchen, passing through the living room, when I notice that one couch has blankets and a pillow laid out with a book on it. I recognize the pillow and blanket. They are the ones from her room that I placed out for her…and spritzed my cologne on.

I stop next to her makeshift bed and ask, "What's this?"

She turns around and looks apologetic as she walks toward me. "I'm sorry, I would have asked before doing that, but by the time I got to it, everyone was asleep. I'll have it cleaned up before anyone else gets up."

"No need to apologize. I just assumed you would be upstairs in the embrace of your one true love." *I shouldn't have said that.* It's been decades since I cared enough about anyone to be jealous and I am clearly out of touch on how to handle the emotion.

Lucy meets my eyes quickly, her face void of all emotions, and then walks back to the window. I follow her, watching as she takes a sip from her cup and returns to her spot, gazing at the snow falling outside.

I look around, deciding if I should make a drink for myself, when I notice a packet of hot chocolate powder in the trash. Well, that settles what I'll be making to drink. She keeps her focus out the window. I turn the stove on and pour milk into a small pan. While I'm fetching the chocolate chips from the cabinet, I ask, "Did you have a fallout?"

She takes a deep breath. "I'm trying to figure out how soon I can return to my apartment and arrange for him to return to New York."

A rush of hope overcomes me, but I must not get ahead of myself. "It wasn't a romantic reunion?"

Still facing the window, she explains, "I may have left out the details of our relationship to everyone, but it seems the blanks were filled in with a very romantic story, and when they invited him this weekend, their hearts were in the right place."

My suspicions were correct. I knew something was up with him. "What truly happened between the two of you?"

She sighs and takes another sip of her drink. "He's just someone who has been in and out of my life for years, and I always let him in, but now—things are different—I'm different, and when I saw him today, it felt different."

Her confession is music to my ears. Maybe he's left

already, but no. She wouldn't be sleeping down here if he had. "What did he do when you told him?"

She finally turns to face me as I continue to monitor my pan on the stove. "Well, I haven't yet. I didn't think it was appropriate to get into that in your home. I should have insisted we stay in London." Lucy sighs. "Either way, it won't be easy to convince him to leave so soon after he arrived. He is insistent that we spend the holiday together."

As if I would allow such a display in my own home. "Is he truly so in love with you?" What else could cause a grown man to act that way?

"Shocking thought, I know." She rolls her eyes.

"That's not what I meant."

"I suppose he loves me in his own way, but he also loves the many other women in his life…according to our shared friends." With a pause, she lets me connect the dots.

"Are you the other woman?" I couldn't believe her capable of acting in such a way, but it would explain the secrecy.

She gives a low laugh, "I wouldn't know who was the original woman in his life. He's not known for being a one-woman man."

"How do you know?"

"We share most of the same friends and live in a small town. He's always denied it to me, but since we broke up, I've encouraged him to pursue other relationships. I remained single for a number of reasons —he liked me to believe that he did the same. I noticed his phone was particularly active this evening. Yet, he is here, which only proves he only wants what he can't have."

I'm relieved to hear her regard herself as something he can't have, but still curious how she got into such a situation. I would have never expected her to be the type of woman to get involved in something so…messy. "When did this start between you?"

"About twenty years ago. I was a teenager and foolishly in love."

She was the original woman, the one who was cheated on.

"So what's different?" *Could it be me?* No, I don't want that to be the only reason. I want her to walk away from this guy for more than just me but for herself.

"When I saw him this morning outside my apartment —he didn't seem real any longer. He felt like a memory, no longer a part of my life."

I pour the hot chocolate into a mug for each of us and replace her mug with the one growing cold in her hands. Her eyebrows raise as she holds her stare at me. "My homemade hot chocolate." She smiles and thanks me.

"I can tell him to leave," I suggest.

"Thank you, but I'd rather handle this myself. He's known to get…"

"Violent?" *I'll kill him.*

"Oh no." She laughs a little. "Dramatic…no theatrical is a better way to describe it. Over the years, when I'd attempt to completely cut ties, he would put on a grand show of emotion and declare his love." She rolls her eyes. "I just don't want to put everyone here through that. It's the quickest way to ruin a holiday. I think it would be best for the two of us to go back to London, where I can book him a flight back to New York and get him home as soon as possible…with as little drama as possible."

"And until then, you are going to let him believe everything is fine between you both?"

She sighs and drinks the hot chocolate. "This is delicious, thank you." I nod, pleased by her compliment, and let her continue. "I'd planned to head back to London first thing tomorrow, but now I'm not sure what the driving conditions will be like."

The snow is falling very quickly outside. I hadn't bothered to watch the weather for after they arrived. "Until we can get back to the city, I plan to just keep a safe distance while reminding him that you and I are dating. Still in the early stages, but sticking to our story, nonetheless. He did think he had the victory in hand when you suggested he and I share a room, but I told him you were just dealing with a bit of jealousy." *Little does she know how correct she is.*

"And you will continue to sleep on the couch?"

"Yes, if that's all right with you?" She blinks up at me as her jaw tightens. Does she think I'm going to insist she return to her room and share a bed with him? Absolutely not.

"No, it's not all right that you are spending nights on the couch." *I am elated that she would rather sleep down here than with him, but it's still not right.* "What if we continue to take our ruse a step further?"

"Oh, of course. I promise not to let this affect that. John is still trying to convince me that he and I are '*meant to be together,*' but I have been insistent that we are dating."

How brazen of this guy to come to my home and attempt to steal my girl from me.

"Well, perhaps we should put on a show for him."

"What type of a show?"

"We could fully commit to our fake relationship. Act as if we are the couple we claim to be in the public, even here." I suggest and instantly imagine what it would be like to act as a couple here. Having her in my lap on the chair in my office, cooking together, sharing a bed.

"We have spent weeks telling the four other occupants of this house that this is just a fake relationship, and now we are going to suddenly flip to say we are together. Do you think they would question that? Or feel odd to have to witness us acting as a couple in front of them?"

"We could tell him we've been dating for weeks since I picked you up from the airport." It certainly feels like that, for me, at least. "And that we downplayed it with them because we wanted to see how it went before making it known."

She still doesn't look convinced. "But if that were the case, I probably would have told them in London when they suggested bringing John here or, at the very least, on the drive here with Hannah and Mia."

"We could say you didn't want to say anything about it because we promised we would decide together when to share it with them." She still looks unsure, "It would only be for a day at most while we wait out the weather."

"And what would this entail? I've already reminded him many times we are dating. He just ignores me."

"That's probably my doing, I barely spoke to you since you've arrived and put you in a room together."

"No, it's my fault. I'm so sorry for bringing this mess into your home, especially at the holidays."

"Don't be. You didn't fly him to London. We will take care of this with as little friction for you as possible."

"Thank you. You have every right to be furious with me." I brush off her apology—it's not needed. "I promise I would never let anything jeopardize you or your career. I know how important it is that we keep up this fake relationship."

How I'd love to tell her that I don't care at all about the social media account or the publicity from it. But this is certainly not the time to share my feelings with her, so I simply say. "I appreciate that."

"So, how will this look?" she asks. "My fake relationship expertise only goes as far as posting still photos. As the famous romance movie director, I'm sure you can come up with something."

"Well, we will act as a couple who are at the beginning stages of falling in love with each other. I'll take the lead on most things. With your vast research in the subject, you should be able to follow along with the correct responses."

"It's that easy?" She fidgets and returns her gaze to the snow falling outside under the light in the garden.

First order of business, if we were dating, she wouldn't be sleeping on the couch. I wonder how she will react to my first suggestion.

"Well, something that would certainly authenticate the relationship is someone discovering you slept in my room."

Twenty-Eight

LUCY

I CAN SENSE the brightness of the sun as I begin to wake. I'm so warm, engulfed in the soft sheets of this comfortable bed with an arm around me…

I sit straight up and jump away from the man lying beside me. Terror that it might have been John washes away instantly as Henry greets me with a sexy, just woke-up voice. "Good morning."

I put my face in my hands and allow every memory from yesterday to flood back into my consciousness. John showed up at my apartment, Oliver insisted he come with us, and Henry found me in the kitchen. I told him everything, and he suggested we bring our fake relationship to our inner circle in hopes John would back off. Then Henry suggested I sleep in his room with him so someone could "catch" us to support the lie that we've been dating all along.

"I'm sorry, I don't remember turning over in the night," I apologize.

How embarrassing.

"Not at all—it was quite comfortable having you so close," he says as he sits up, still in his black T-shirt and gray sleep pants. He looks so damn alluring—it's difficult to stop myself from staring. He stands and stretches like he's putting a show on for me. I'm overcome with the reality that I am wasting a highly coveted space in his bed. This spot is meant for a perfect-looking woman who wakes up just as good-looking as he does. Certainly not a mess.

Henry opens his bedroom door and listens for a moment. He shakes his head at me before closing it again. "I don't think anyone is awake, which gives us time to shower."

My jaw nearly dislocates, it drops so quickly. *Gives us time to shower.* That's certainly not what he means, and he definitely wouldn't choose to shower with me. "I can go back to shower in the guest room." I offer to avoid any further daydreams on my end.

Henry stops in his tracks, "Absolutely not." His dark eyes stare into my soul.

"It's no trouble, I'm sure John is still asleep." I make my way to gather my phone and the bedding I used on the couch last night, and he comes to my side.

"No, I can't allow that." He pauses and runs his hand through his hair. "Isn't all of this in an effort to shake him off? I don't think showering in the room next to where he is sleeping would do that. In fact, I'm certain it would be taken just the opposite." I don't say anything as Henry moves to grab towels off a shelf and brings them over to me. "You'll shower in here. I'll wait for you to finish, then I'll jump in."

There he is, stern Henry. I consider arguing with him, insisting he can't tell me what to do. *Even though I secretly like it.* He's right, though. John would see that as an invitation. I concede but realize I don't have any clean clothes in Henry's room to change into when I'm finished in the shower.

"I'll need to run back and grab my things before I can shower," I tell him.

"No, you don't. I have extras of all the products I bought for everyone in the closet. You should be able to find what you need in there." He responds from where he perched himself on the bed, checking his phone.

"I still don't have anything to wear after my shower."

"Sure you do. It's in your hands."

"The towel?" I ask.

"Precisely, what better image of you in a towel running across the house to grab your things?" His jaw ticks, and he swallows. "I mean for getting 'caught,' of course."

Well, it's nice to know one of us is thinking clearly because it's certainly not me. "How convenient for you that I am the one who needs to run around practically naked. What is the difference between me showering in the other room and me showing up in nothing but a towel?"

"The difference is I will be escorting you while you are in nothing but the towel." He smirks. "I suppose if you are so set on showering in the other bathroom, I can always accompany you then as well. That would certainly send a message." He laughs to himself.

Is he offering to shower with me in the room next to John? *No, he's calling your bluff.* "Fine, I'll be quick."

I turn and make my way into a massive shower big enough for five people. *The parties he must have here.* This not-so-subtle testimonial of his playboy life is a grounding reminder of who Henry is and how much I don't fit into his lifestyle.

"Looks like your evil genius plan was unsuccessful," I whisper to Henry as we quickly make our way from my originally assigned guestroom to his bedroom while I struggle to keep my towel in place and carry what I grabbed from the room.

"A bomb could go off, and that man would sleep through it." Henry doesn't bother to hide his frustration as he takes the bag from my shoulder.

I gladly hand it over since he does not feel it is necessary for him to only dress in a towel. Yet, he did select an outfit that is almost as distracting as I imagine the towel would have been. Quietly walking behind him, I savor the view of his sweatpants and the bare muscles of his back.

"Enjoying the show?" he calls back to me.

I ignore his question because it's so obvious I am. "Please hurry, I'm getting cold and would very much like to get dressed."

"Oh, of course," he says as we enter his bedroom. "The bedroom is all yours. There's a hair dryer in the bottom drawer of your nightstand." I head in with another look back at shirtless Henry. A memory that will now live rent-free in my head for the rest of my days.

As I work on drying my hair, Henry showers and dresses. My hair doesn't dry as quickly as it usually does because I'm barely paying attention to what I'm doing.

When he finally finishes, he asks, "Can I borrow the hair dryer for a moment?"

After handing it to him, I turn back to the mirror to finish with my makeup but he catches me staring at him in the reflection.

He smirks, returning the hair dryer, "I'm going to head down and start prepping for breakfast. Join me when you're ready."

"All right," I reply.

I spend the remainder of my time getting ready overthinking my current predicament and how much different things could have gone if John hadn't arrived yesterday. I would still be in Henry's home, but I would be in my own room, using my own shower and sleeping in a separate bed. Dare I say *I don't hate how things have turned out…so far.*

I hurry along with my makeup and give my hair one final fluff before heading downstairs to help Henry with breakfast. I look around for the others, but it is too quiet.

As I approach the handsome man behind the kitchen island, he hands me a tall glass. "I know my skills won't compare to Beth's, but I gave it a try. She was kind enough to give me very detailed directions."

I take a sip of the delicious cold-brew coffee. "It's perfect, thank you."

He nods and resumes his work cutting up peppers.

"You look beautiful this morning," he tells me while I begin to slice the potatoes.

I look around to check if someone is coming, but nothing. "You don't have an audience at the moment. Really no need to act without one."

"In the acting world, there is such a thing called rehearsals," he says as he puts his knife down and moves to wash his hands off in the sink.

"I understand, and you feel that is a line you need to practice?" I say, joining him at the sink, and he hands me a towel to dry my hands.

"I think it is you who needs the practice, Miss Taylor. It's clear you can't even take a compliment."

"A fake compliment," I correct him.

"Fake relationship or not, you look beautiful today." I roll my eyes, and he continues, "Just say thank you."

"Thank you, Mr. Brooks," I say sarcastically.

"I think we have some work to do. How are you going to act around the others?" he scolds me, and I begin to walk away.

He grabs my waist and turns me to face him while he pushes my back against the nearest wall. My breath hitches as I look up at him but before I can think of anything to say, his lips are on mine.

Soft, brief kisses feather my lips. As if it is the most natural thing in the world, I kiss him back, bracing my hands on his chest to steady myself.

As if my action was the permission he needs, he pulls me in closer by wrapping one hand around my waist as the other finds its place between my shoulder blades. While the shock subsides, I ignore all reasonable thought and allow my hands to begin their exploration. The feel of his sturdy body pressed against me isn't enough, it is only a tease, I need more. My fingers find his waist and graze up the side of him as his mouth devours mine.

A moan escapes me as my need for Henry hits new heights. His claiming tongue brushes along mine, and I know my fate is sealed. There has never been, nor will there ever be another who can make me feel this alive.

Our touches become frantic, and the need for more becomes insatiable. He must feel it too, as he breaks our kiss only for his lips to work their way up my neck, biting at my earlobe. My legs grow weak, and my body feels like it is unraveling.

Henry pulls away slightly, just enough for us to catch our breath. Yet, it's too much, my body sways, mourning the loss of his stability. My hands reach for him, but some sense returns, and I quickly pull them back to my side.

I find my footing and he takes another step back, placing his hands behind him on the island for balance. He looks like the lead in a romantic comedy movie, trying to act unfazed, but I can tell he is just as affected as I am. His cheeks are red while his chest is still rising and falling. It does nothing to stifle the lust clouding my mind.

"What…" is the only word I can get out.

"See, look how unprepared you were for that." He stands his breath regaining a normal pattern as he looks down to fix his shirt. "Couples kiss, you know."

"I don't know many couples that kiss like that in front of other people."

"Well, then, I pity those couples," he says with a smirk and continues, "I thought it would be helpful to get the first one out of the way, so when it happens again, you won't look so flustered." And turns back to the island as he wasn't exploring my mouth with his tongue mere moments ago.

He may have a point—I suppose I won't be as shocked if, *when he said when,* it happens again. Although, I can't imagine I'll ever get used to being kissed like that.

As if on cue, Mia and Finn make their way downstairs. Henry informs them he's making omelets and instructs me to work on the potatoes for a side. "Here, just add the ingredients while they cook. It's basically mixing everything together." I nod, still not sure what to say. I keep my head down to allow for the flush of my face to fade before they can notice my overwhelming reaction to Henry.

Shortly, Hannah and Oliver arrive at the table and my potatoes are just about finished. John is the only person missing from the table. Henry looks at me knowingly, and I announce, "I'll fetch him, but while I'm gone, this would be a good photo to post." I point to everyone seated at the table. Henry nods and pulls out his phone as I make my way upstairs.

As I approach the door to John's room, I hear him speaking, but I can't make it out. Knocking loudly on the door, I hear him say, "I've got to go, bye," before opening the door to me.

"Morning, Lucy." John smiles and leans against the door frame with no shirt on and only wearing his boxers. "You know, you really shouldn't have slept on the couch last night. This bed was awfully lonely."

Just wait until he finds out that I didn't sleep on the couch or alone.

"Breakfast is just about ready. Make yourself decent. Then we can discuss plans about getting back to the city." I turn on my heels without another word.

The others are already seated at the table, their plates stacked high with the impressive spread Henry has laid out for us. John finds a seat at the table and I offer to make him a plate. I have a feeling it's best to keep as much distance between him and Henry as possible.

I place John's breakfast in front of him. Capitalizing on our close proximity, he wraps his arm around my waist, but I turn out of it as soon as I can.

I barely have a moment's notice before Henry walks over to me. He turns to face the table, "I think it's about time, don't you, Lucy?"

Panic over what my friends' reactions will be overcomes me but disintegrates just as quickly when Henry's arm moves behind my back and slips his hand into my jeans' back pocket.

Without waiting for my reply—*I'm already blowing it*—Henry looks at them all and announces, "We are together, it's serious, and we decided to make it exclusive a few weeks ago." He leans down to me for a kiss, and I meet his lips like it is something we've done a million times. "And now you all know." He looks directly at John and says, "Especially you."

The rest of the table just look amongst themselves with smirks on their faces, maybe Henry texted them earlier to give them the heads up. Not a single one of them looked puzzled by this announcement.

John, however, acts shocked by this news, even though I told him again last night that I was sleeping on the couch to be respectful of my new relationship. He stands and begins to pace, looking only at me as if Henry isn't even in the room.

"What about us, Lucy?" he pleads, and so begins the much-anticipated revival of his interpretation of *I Love Lucy…Taylor*. "I know you needed to do this London thing, but haven't you gotten it out of your system yet? You can't just throw away twenty years of what we have. I love you."

I can sense Henry's anger building in him. The muscles in his arm tighten as he moves his hand from my back pocket to around my waist, pulling me closer to him. Embarrassment floods through me, and I just want to go hide in bed… *Henry's bed, preferably.*

Henry looks at me and gives me the "Who does this asshole think he is" look.

John continues by listing "big" moments we've shared over the years, starting with senior high prom then moving to the holidays and our family vacations, all evidence for his argument that we are meant to be together.

How convenient that he neglects to mention that the majority of those twenty years have been spent with us as acquaintances…old friends at best, considering he cheated on me when we were together.

But I can't bring myself to say those things. I should have cut him out of my life the moment we broke up, but instead of dealing with him, I just let him continue to invade my friend group once again. Yet, I'm starting to be relieved that it did end that way. Because if he had never cheated on me, I'd have married him and never found my way to London or to Henry, *even if it's not real.*

John then proceeds to make his biggest mistake yet. He turns to address Henry, puts on an apologetic look, and says, "I understand, man. Lucy is great, I can see why you're interested, but there is no comparison for something that just started when we have a connection that is built on a twenty-year foundation."

My cheeks reddened from embarrassment—I can't look at Henry. I'm too afraid. How I wish John would stop talking, but of course, he doesn't. "Lucy and I are meant for each other. No fancy mansion in England is going to change that."

A bit of reality hits and fear takes hold of me as some of John's words begin to make me question things. I don't want to be with John, I know that more than anything, but haven't I said that before, many times?

Sure, I have a new great life here in London, but what can I expect when Henry wraps his movie? We will go back to being friends, if that and I will return to my apartment.

What if I lose my friends when I lose Henry? No one can be sure of their future, but mine does have the possibility of becoming sad and lonely and deciding to move back to New York. Then what? John would be there, and I would fall directly into the same trap I've always found myself in.

Henry must notice my internal crisis, and he squeezes me close, "Are you all right?" he whispers, and I nod while trying to regain my mental footing. Leaning into Henry, I feel a little stronger.

This is John's doing. He has a way of getting in my head and making me question myself. There is no denying it. He's been a staple in my life, which is why I've never been able to completely distance myself from him. He knows exactly what to say to me that will make me cave. I always fall back into the headspace that I'll never be able to do better than him.

Not this time—I've found myself a *fake* British boyfriend who is perfectly content to be romantically connected to me in the public eye. And when this arrangement comes to an end, I may meet someone new. Sure, I may not find anyone else who kisses as well as Henry, but I certainly could find someone else, maybe someone to fall in love with.

That's enough for me. Even if clinging to this fake relationship is what will help me finally break ties with John, so be it. I'll deal with the fall out when it comes.

Until then, I will savor every moment.

Twenty-Nine

HENRY

LUCY WASN'T EXAGGERATING, this guy really does put on quite the performance. To an outsider, this passionate display could be fitting for the final scene in a romantic movie. A high school sweetheart flying across an ocean to declare himself on Christmas to the only girl he's ever loved. Except, from the sounds of it, she's not the only girl, not by a long shot. Unfortunately for him, this isn't a movie and it will not end as he hopes. I am the director here, and I will be sure to be the one who gets the girl in the end.

If he truly loved her and wanted to make a real go at it with her, he should have started with an apology, but instead, he stands here and attempts to manipulate her with lies and false promises of true love. Even if I weren't hoping to win her heart, I wouldn't want her to end up with a person like this.

John's reasons for them to be together are only based on the past and his feelings. Not once has he asked if she loves him. He speaks as if it is assumed.

He doesn't deserve the kindness she's shown him since his arrival, let alone her affections.

It's time to make something clear to this man—she comes first. This is her life, her heart, and her decision. With a firm tone, I say, "This is Lucy's choice."

Before we spoke last night, I would have followed Oliver's warning to not get in the way of her being in a loving relationship just for my career and newfound popularity. Now, I know she has moved on with her life and decidedly wants to leave him in the past. It is only because of his irrational decision to board a flight without her permission that she is even acknowledging him at this moment.

She has made a new life here. With any luck, my role in her life will continue to grow. *Hopefully, growing to the point I will have many more opportunities to taste those luscious lips of hers.*

To show I value her choice, I move to unlock our hands, but Lucy holds on tight. My heart swells, and I feel the smile break free on my face as she meets my gaze. She doesn't say anything, but I can see her mind racing behind her eyes. She can't find the words but still manages to demonstrate her choice. I let myself hope that our kiss earlier meant just as much to her as it did to me.

Elated to know where I stand, she picked our relationship over her ex. *Fake relationship…fake for now.* I shake my head to get rid of those thoughts. Now is not the time. Blurting out my feelings and intentions while she is combating his unwelcome advances is not how I want to do this. She deserves so much more, which I will be happy to deliver.

Turning to John, I offer, "You are welcome to stay until the storm lets up and the roads clear." I pause and look down at Lucy, then back to John. "There is no reason we can't enjoy each other's company until then. But if you do anything to upset her or make her feel uncomfortable, you will be removed at once. I don't care if I have to lease a helicopter to come get you—I won't stand for you upsetting her."

John's reaction is not what I expect, he's obviously not taking my threat seriously. He turns back to Lucy, taking a step closer before addressing her directly. "I would never want you upset or uncomfortable, you know that." He turns back to me. "Thank you, Henry, I look forward to spending more time with Lucy."

It's as if he still believes he has a chance with her. My words barely affected him. *Maybe he would absorb them a little more if they were delivered by my fists.* Thankfully, he knows enough to return to his room for now.

The others begin to clear the table. Finn says to Lucy and I, "You both should take a couple of minutes."

Hannah follows his lead, trying to extinguish the awkwardness lingering in the air. "Let us take care of the cleanup. The two of you cooked an extraordinary breakfast."

Grateful for the opportunity, I walk with Lucy's hand in mine to the living room and pull her down onto the sofa next to me. She curls up against my side as my arm finds its place around her. "Thank you," she whispers.

Before I can worry if I handled that in the way she wanted, she rewards me by snuggling against me. I'll never be able to enjoy sitting in this spot again unless I have her in my arms, just as she is now. "He's exhausting," I say to her with a low laugh.

"I told you." Her body relaxes against mine. I wonder if she is aware of the physical cues her body is giving me. Each one increases my hope that she wants this thing building between us.

We sit like this for what must be an hour, quietly coming down from the theatrical performance we were just pulled into.

In a quick text to Oliver and Finn, I ask them to meet with me in my office. I learned years ago not to go around knocking on doors. We are all adults, and privacy is important when multiple couples are under one roof. We have a few items to go over for New Year's Eve, and I'm sure they will want an explanation about Lucy.

"Close the door, will you, Finn?" I ask, sitting on the edge of my desk. The boys sit beside each other on the large windowsill.

With a deep breath, I go into the fabricated story Lucy and I agreed on last night about our courtship. "I'm sorry I didn't say more about Lucy and me earlier. It's just we weren't sure where it was going and wanted to wait before telling everyone which would bring added pressures."

"Yes, I suppose that makes sense." Finn squints his eyes and tilts his head.

"Well, whatever it took, Pop. I'm just happy you got here." Oliver smiles. I give him a questioning look, and he continues. "It was a little obvious."

"What was obvious?" I ask.

Finn chimes in, "That you've been obsessed with her since you met her."

Oliver continues, "You can't keep your eyes off of her. Everyone's noticed."

"Then what was the point of the speech you gave me yesterday, Oliver? About how I better not be leading her on and how you think it's one-sided?"

Oliver laughs, "I was trying to make you jealous, hoping to push you to finally make a move."

Finn continues, "But it appears you already made your moves…" and then he winks.

"Yes, well, I think that's about the extent I'd like to discuss Lucy," I tell him. "What should we do with her ex while we wait for the snow to settle?" I ask.

Oliver speaks up, "Aside from his history with Lucy, he seems like an all-right guy."

"We were planning to take a walk in the snow today, maybe make some snowmen. I can invite him out with us." Finn suggests, "Mia, like every year, put off wrapping the gifts for her family until today, and Hannah offered to help. That would leave time for you and Lucy to have by yourselves."

"What is the plan for John's departure? Do you need us to take him back to London?" Oliver asks.

"No, Lucy plans to take him as soon as the weather breaks. I offered to get them a car service. It might be Christmas Eve by the time the roads are cleared. She insists I stay here with you. She plans to return the same night." Even as I say it with confidence, my stomach still tightens. I'm not comfortable with this plan, but Lucy has asked me to trust her. He's taken up space in her life for too long—she needs to close this door. She's been right about him so far.

Thirty

HENRY

WHEN THE BOYS and I finish up in my office, they ask about lunch. Thankfully, I had the house stocked before the snow started. We head to the kitchen, and I pull a deli tray out of the refrigerator. Over the years, I've perfected the meal schedule during their holiday visit. Putting the most effort into fun breakfasts and delicious dinners, I keep lunches as simple as possible.

Later in the afternoon, I find Lucy in my office, sitting on the windowsill with a book open on her lap. Grabbing a book for myself, I sit across from her. While she is lost in the created world, I take this moment to admire the view before me. Lucy looks so at home here. It's as if she picked this house herself. She only looks up at me when it's clear she finished her page.

"How are you doing, my dear?" I ask.

"Better now. I thought it would feel different after telling everyone that we are in a relationship. I assumed they'd have questions and want to be more involved. Yet, so far, Hannah and Mia are acting like it's not a big deal.

Which is very unlike Mia." She worries her brow and looks down at her closed book. "Do you think they don't believe us?"

"No, I think it's quite the opposite, actually." I try to reassure her as I move closer to her, leaving only an arm's length between us. "When I spoke with Finn and Oliver, they said they were expecting it. I believe they used the words 'It was obvious' in regards to our feelings for each other."

She keeps her face looking down, but her eyebrows pop just the slightest. Then, she changes the subject. "Too bad they didn't realize we shared a bedroom last night. Maybe that would have gotten the shock we were hoping for."

She finally looks back up at me. "Maybe now that they 'know,' I should sleep on the couch. You are their father, and I am their friend. Maybe the insinuation of us sharing a bed would be off-putting for them."

"No," I laugh. "We will continue to share a room. As long as you are comfortable with that. They are all adults. I'm sure they can handle the concept of us sharing a bed."

She nods, "If you say so. Oh, I'll need to get the rest of my things from John's room."

"Let's get those now. I think I saw him in the garage on the phone on my way in here," I say, standing and holding a hand out for her to join me. She takes it, and my heart flutters a little. Is she noticing the gestures I am making when others aren't around? Can she tell what I'm trying to tell her without speaking the words?

As we make our way to the staircase, the anticipation of sharing a room with her again overtakes me. Visions fill my mind of sleeping next to her and waking up with her in my arms, our bodies becoming intertwined throughout the night.

My need for her is growing stronger every moment. We've already broken the seal with the kiss in the kitchen this morning…why not another…why not now?

She only makes it to the first step before I stalk up behind her. Hooking my forearm, holding her tightly around her shapely hips, I pull her forward, flush against my chest. My right hand slowly travels upward, varying pressure from my palm to my fingertips, grazing over her body.

Her mouth-watering cleavage tempts me, peeking out from her low-cut top as I brush over it. I want so much to linger, but this part of her body deserves far more attention than I can offer here on the main staircase.

My thumb hits its destination under her chin, pushing it upward, causing her head to tip back onto my shoulder as my hand closes gently around her neck. Her ass presses against my growing firmness. My hips instinctively push back, creating a tortuous friction that makes me pull her closer against me.

My nose dips to the base of her neck, inhaling her scent. *I need more.* Pressing my lips to her skin, my tongue darts out to taste her. She shivers as a moan escapes her lips.

I look around to check for an audience, and this time, I am relieved to find we are alone. Something protective comes over me. I do not wish for another living soul to witness her in this way. This lust is my undoing and should be for me alone to enjoy. Even as we are alone now, someone could find us any moment at the bottom of the grand staircase. That's not enough to stop me, but I decided to shield her just to be safe.

Keeping her close, I whip her body around to, once again, use the wall behind her to cage her in. In these brief moments, while our eyes are locked, I watch her expression, those hungry brown eyes staring directly into mine as her cheeks and neck are flush. Lucy's breath quickens its pace with anticipation, causing her breasts to rise further from her top.

Prolonging our kiss is infuriating to my own body, but seeing her in this state is worth the wait. Her enticing lips part the closer I stalk toward her. Her gaze confirms what I had been hoping for. Her lustful look mirrors my own feelings, consumed with desire.

Our lips reunite, and it takes less time for her shock to succeed and return the kiss than previously, which makes me ravenous.

Lucy's hands explore my body more forcefully this time as my tongue dips between the seam of her mouth. Her decadent taste consumes me. I devour her while my hand runs down her back to the curve of her ass, grasping onto it, using my hold to bring our bodies as close as they can possibly be.

I can't remember the last time I was so turned on, so voracious for a woman. Surely, she can sense how desperately I need her as I press my hips into hers. She responds in the most seductive way, lifting her leg and wrapping it around the back of my thigh.

My mind is now starting to agree with my body that it

is time to move this to the bedroom. I take that as my signal to break the kiss as much as it pains me.

This is not the right time.

Her eyes don't meet mine at first. Does she feel the loss of our connection like I do?

Lucy looks just as disheveled as I do. My restraint is barely hanging on, I want to tell her how I feel, but I can not let our story begin while her ex is staying in my home, declaring his love every hour.

It has been my life's work creating the most memorable declarations of love for millions. She deserves the most romantic setting I can imagine, not this mess. It will all be over soon. She will put him on a plane and return from London just in time for us to have the house to ourselves for days. And in those days, I will set the most romantic scene, one that is deserving of the beginning of our love story.

"You're improving," I say in hopes of diffusing some of the tension.

"This isn't a matter of skill. It's adjusting to the ambush!" Lucy says as she smooths down her shirt and attempts to straighten her hair. I take a deep breath to calm myself as I watch her hands move over her shirt and pull it into place.

How I long to rip that shirt from her body.

I turn away before addressing her to make sure the proper words leave my mouth. "Well, as your partner that everyone knows well about, it shouldn't be startling that I kiss you at random moments," I remind her, and I know it will only continue now that I've had a taste. Each moment

I don't have her lips on mine, I'll be waiting for my next chance.

"Easy for you, you know, when you're going to strike," Lucy playfully scolds me, and my body heats all over again, imagining an unplanned assault from her.

"I welcome you to pounce on me whenever the need comes over you, with a kiss or any type of physical display of affection." I can only hope that she takes me up on this invitation. *And soon.* I lean in, "My body is yours to do whatever you please with it." I wink as I grab her hand and continue up the stairs.

We make our way to the bedroom I had originally designated for Lucy, but fortunately, she didn't get to use this room. I much prefer her to stay with me, and I don't know if that would have occurred if not for this odd situation we find ourselves in.

She repacks the few items she's got out since arriving and then turns to the door as we hear John's voice coming up the stairs. "I told you, I'm away at a work conference."

Lucy's face darts to mine, but then she just shrugs and shakes her head.

I stand in the doorway as John approaches. I can hear a woman's voice loudly coming from the earpiece of his phone. He nods at me and I move to allow him entry and then return to my post, watching how he will navigate this phone call in Lucy's presence.

Lucy gives him a brief smile as she lifts one of her bags over her shoulder. She then turns to the bookshelf and grabs a few of the books I left out for her. I don't bother to contain the smile on my face. It's the little things, intentional or not that Lucy keeps doing that reassure me.

As she wheels the larger suitcase to me in the doorway, she holds up the books and asks, "Is it okay if I bring these?"

Play it cool, Henry. "Oh sure, I forgot they were even in this room," I take hold of her larger suitcases, and we make our way back to my bedroom without acknowledging John.

The first thing she does is pull multiple chargers out of her bag and plug them in next to the nightstand on her side of the bed. *Her side of the bed.* Then, she immediately charges her e-reader. I smile at her dedication to the machine. If I can not win her heart, I suppose losing to the greatest fictional men of all time is a proud defeat.

Thirty-One

LUCY

BEFORE OPENING MY EYES, I bask in the warmth and comfort of this bed. The mattress is just the right combination of soft and firm. The comforter and sheets lay delicately across my skin and certainly kept me warm throughout the night. I'm sure it cost a small fortune, but could one really put a price on the perfect night's sleep?

The weight of the comforter shifts on top of me. My eyes shoot open, and I look down. It's not the weight of the blanket I am wrapped up in—it's Henry. His arm lays loosely around my chest while his leg is tucked between mine. Then his breath warms my skin as his head rests on the crook of my neck.

As the shock of our sleeping positions subsides, the desire I've been suppressing roars back to life. Every inch of my body is urging me to turn into his embrace, to face him and wake him with a kiss.

How did I get here? Could I still be sleeping? Is this a dream?

Could this be a reality for me?

If the fake relationship, production company, social media, and ex-boyfriend were removed, could I have a future with Henry? One where *we* wake up in this bed every morning?

I give myself one brief moment to hope but then come back to reality. If that's something I want, then first, I need to fix all those issues that need to be removed, starting with John.

I don't want to wake Henry, on the chance he may too feel awkward about how we ended up in the night. *I just don't want to risk seeing the disappointment on his face when he wakes up snuggling me.*

Delicately as I can, I slip out from under his embrace and head to the bathroom, closing the door quietly behind me.

During my shower, I remind myself not to cling too much to the hope of us being together. It's desperately becoming something I want, but I don't want it to be tangled up in all of this. I've had my fill of complicated relationships, and that's the last thing I want with Henry.

I hear a loud knock over the running water. "Almost done in there?" Henry asks.

"Just another five minutes," I yell back and hurry to make up for the time I spent standing under the showerhead daydreaming.

When I exit the bathroom with my towel tied tightly around my waist and my hair up in another, I am greeted with quite the show. Henry's smile lights up before disappearing under the T-shirt he pulls up and over his head on the way into the bathroom. "Oh, good morning," he says to me over his shoulder. I clutch my hairdryer and move over to my nightstand to plug it in.

I rush through my hair and makeup routine so that I can be downstairs in the kitchen by the time he exits the bathroom. I have a feeling he might walk out in nothing but his towel, and I don't know if my heart can take that after waking up in his embrace.

Blissfully distracted by the large view of the snow-covered property, I wait for Henry to join me.

"The usual?" Henry asks.

"Yes, thank you." My gaze remains outside. Even with all the trouble this snow has caused, I can't bring myself to be too mad about it. "Beautiful view."

"It certainly is," Henry agrees. "Snow looks lovely too," he adds.

I turn to him and roll my eyes.

"We could take a walk this morning if you'd like," Henry suggests.

"That sounds great—I love being out in the snow." Back in New York, when the snow fell, it meant an unexpected reprieve from the classroom. Mornings were spent shoveling. Leaving the rest of the day to spend relaxing with a movie or a book.

He leans against the island. "Could be a good place to take a picture for the social media accounts."

Oh no. I've completely forgotten about the accounts since I arrived. Panic fills my system. "Henry, I'm so sorry. I haven't posted since I arrived." I scramble to put my coffee down and pull my phone from my back pocket.

Henry takes my hands into his. "Lucy, it's okay. I

posted." I look up at him. "Just an old photo of Max and I, then yesterday I posted a picture of my bookshelf."

"Oh, well, then I guess it's caught up." Glad he remembered all of this, but I feel a little pinch of hurt that he didn't forget it when everything else was happening. I need to take this as a reminder of where his priorities lie.

"What do you say to posting a photo of us in the snow then?"

"Great idea. I'll get my gloves and new hat." I run upstairs to grab them from my suitcase before he can notice the emotions that must be playing on my face as they race through my mind.

While warming up in the big chair by the fire, I scroll through the selfies we took in the snow. They look perfect, just as romantic as the experience was for me. In most of them, it would be nearly impossible to recognize us underneath the hats, scarves, and sunglasses. Once we realized that, we took our sunglasses off, making our matching pink noses more noticeable and adorable. I think this might be the best one to post. As I move to hit the share button, I see the option to make this photo my home screen. It takes only a second before I give in to the temptation. No one but me will see it because a lilac photo still acts as my lock screen, but I like knowing it's there.

The day continues on, and still no sign of plow trucks to clear the roads. Tomorrow is Christmas Eve, so they must plan to have them clear by then. At least, I really hope they will.

It's time to prepare John for our anticipated departure tomorrow.

I make my way to his room but stop at the first stair as if the magnetic pull from yesterday's kiss with Henry still resides in that spot. *If this is what you want, you have to clear out all the mess first.* Right, I continue up the staircase and knock on John's door.

"Hey, it's me. Can we speak for a moment?" I ask.

John opens the door quickly and motions for me to enter with a smirk on his face. He must assume I am here to rekindle our relationship, but it's just the opposite. I enter but stop only a step inside.

"The snow has stopped, and the plows should be coming around shortly to clear the roads. With the possibility of ice, I'd rather not travel after dark." He looks at me, confused. My patience with him is running out.

"Plan to leave first thing tomorrow. I've arranged for the driver to be here at 8:00 a.m. sharp. It will take us at least an hour to get back to London, and then the driver will be able to return to his family's celebrations fairly early. Once we get to my apartment, we will book you the next flight out of London."

"You're coming with me tomorrow morning?" he asks.

"Yes, you don't very well know your way around the city, and honestly, John, I don't trust you after showing up here, so I plan to watch you get on that plane myself."

"I think after we get away from this mansion and finally have time alone to talk things through, you'll see things a little differently," he says confidently.

"John, don't start this."

"Lucy, I'm looking forward to leaving tomorrow

morning. I think spending time, just the two of us, on Christmas Eve in London will be just what we need."

"There is no more we, John." This conversation is more exhausting than the hours I just spent in the snow. *That's because those were with Henry, and time with Henry never feels like this.* "I am with Henry now. I am just accompanying you to the airport tomorrow afternoon. Understood?"

"Absolutely, and I look forward to our time together," he answers with a smirk.

Exasperated, I turn and leave, closing the door behind me. Henry is leaning against the railing opposite John's door, looking as handsome as ever. He doesn't say anything as I walk across the landing and into his arms.

"The girls are looking for you. They are in the lounge downstairs." His tone is soft as he speaks. I nod but remain in his embrace. He kisses the top of my head. "After you're done with them, I'll meet you in the kitchen, and we can start on dinner."

Reluctantly, I pull out of his arms, "Okay, see you then." I head down the staircase, turning back to look at him when I reach the bottom stairs. He smiles down at me.

"Lucy!" Mia shouts, "Where have you been? We couldn't find you."

I slump my shoulders as I land in the chair next to Mia and Hannah on the loveseat. "Unfortunately, dealing with the ex-situation."

"How's that going?" Hannah asks.

"As frustrating as ever, but hoping to have it resolved in the morning."

"You're planning to take him back to London on Christmas Eve?" Hannah asks.

"Yes, that's the plan. I need to rid myself of the parasite as soon as possible and by any means necessary."

"The what?" Mia asks as she's laughing.

"The parasite." I smile. "That is the nickname my best friend Ellie gave John years ago. It is fitting, as you now know, he is very difficult to get rid of."

Laughter erupts among us. "We've all got crazy ex stories, Lucy, but I think this one wins the award for the worst," Mia says, wiping the tears from her eyes.

"I, unfortunately, will accept that award." I stand to take an obnoxious bow.

Hannah, always the kindest in our group, changes the subject to something unknown to her that Mia and I have been trying to find a natural way to bring up. "Don't forget we will still need fancy dresses for New Year's Eve. The snow has deprived us of our shopping days before we leave to visit our families. Since we don't plan to get back until the thirtieth, I'm not sure if that will give us enough time to shop."

"We could each plan to shop while we are at our next destinations, then come back to show off what we find," Mia suggests.

Perfect, Mia. "Yes, that way, we don't have to panic about finding the perfect dresses at the last minute, and we could plan to go to the salon on the thirtieth and get manicures and pedicures. New nails for the New Year," I suggest.

"Oh, that sounds fun," Hannah agrees. This is almost too easy. "But I'm still worried about finding the right dress. I was thinking maybe we should order a couple online, in addition to your idea, Mia, just to be safe."

Mia and I both agree.

"Have them delivered here so they will arrive while you're gone and ready for you when you get back," I suggest.

"Yes, let's do that now. We still have time before dinner," Mia suggests, and we each pull out our phones and begin our online shopping for the perfect New Year's Eve dresses. Mia and I fabricate how dressy we are planning to look to make sure Hannah looks radiant on her big night.

Thirty-Two

HENRY

LUCY LEAVES to find the girls, smirking up at me from the bottom step. I never had a favorite step before, but I sure do now. We may not have said it or anything close to it, but I am certain what's happening between us is real. She is mine.

And certainly not his.

I remain in the hallway for a moment to cool my anger. In any other scenario, I wouldn't allow this man to share the same air as Lucy, let alone continue to undermine her like this. Every instinct I have tells me to throw this guy out of my home this instant and let him fend for himself, free to die in the cold for all I care.

I should just walk away. I trust her to handle this, but it's killing me to stand by and not defend her. The need to protect her from an asshole like him, *assholes like I am, or was until she came into my life,* grows stronger every time he opens his mouth.

I move closer to the door but still try to convince

myself I don't need to intervene. Then I hear him on the other side. "Hey baby, I miss you so much."

The last strand of restraint I have snaps—I grab the door handle and barge into the room. "Call her back," I say as he takes me in with shock across his face.

"I'll call you right back. Something just came up." He hangs up with looks up at me. "What the fuck, man? You could knock."

I laugh under my breath, how dense could this guy be? "We need to talk," I tell him, standing tall in front of him with my fists clenched at my sides. "No, Actually, I'm going to talk, and you are going to listen, very closely."

John laughs and stands up to face me but leaves an adequate distance between us. "If you're worried about Lucy and I going back to London together... I can't really blame you. It's nothing you did wrong, but when two people are meant to be together. Nothing can change that."

I want to grab him by the shirt and throw him up against the wall, *but Lucy would be upset if you did.* And this guy would surely put on a show after it. Instead, I take a step closer to him and deepen my voice. "From this point on, if you find yourself in Lucy's company, I expect you to be respectful to my partner. That includes hearing her when she tells you she is no longer interested. I overheard your phone call. Does that woman know you are in another country trying to win back your ex-girlfriend?"

"You don't know what you're talking about, old man. At the end of the day, no one has ever compared to Lucy, I'm here for her and she will understand that once I can get her alone and talk some sense into her." He tries to get out of my reach but fails as I move closer, backing him into a corner. Before he can make a scene, I deliver my final warning.

"If I hear that you have made one step out of line with her tomorrow, I will come to London and remove you from this country myself." He rolls his eyes at me but doesn't argue. "Do you understand?'

"Sure," he says as I take a step back, allowing him a path to sit on his bed. He picks up his phone and begins ignoring me. There's no use staying any longer with this immature man. Leaving I slam the door behind me. Needing to work out this angry energy, I head to my personal gym in the basement. Thirty minutes or so with the punching bag ought to work.

The alarm sounds on my phone, and I remove the gloves from my hands. I take a few drinks from my water bottle as I head to my bedroom. The workout did help to get out some of my aggression, but I know I won't feel completely at ease until all of this is settled. I head directly for the shower, and choose to leave the bathroom door ajar on the off chance Lucy may find her way up here.

With each passing hour, it's becoming more and more difficult to suppress my feelings for her. It's a particular form of torture to sleep next to a woman and not be able to express my feelings both verbally and physically.

That is, if she has changed her mind about only being interested in fictional men. *I think she has…*

Thinking back to our kiss on the steps, when I had

encouraged her to jump me next time. Maybe I shouldn't have done that. What if that put too much pressure on her? It was also poor planning on my part, knowing that if she does make a move, my restraint will completely disintegrate.

She deserves better.

I've spent far too long in the shower. Turning off the scalding hot water, I dress quickly and head down to the kitchen to meet her.

Standing in the same spot I found her the other night, Lucy looks out the window as the sun sets over the snow.

Finn and Mia are at the table whispering about what I can only assume are more proposal preparations. Honestly, I don't care what they are speaking about. I'm just ecstatic to have an audience for me to put on a show.

I walk up behind Lucy and wrap my arms around her hips, recalling the last time I did this. She stiffens at first, then relaxes against me. Leaning down, I place my chin on her shoulder and follow her gaze.

"I love the snow." Lucy releases a deep exhale.

Just then, two lights appear to be making their way down the road. As the truck gets closer, it's clear there is a plow on the front.

"Thank goodness," she says, "I was beginning to think they weren't coming."

"Should be clear for your travels tomorrow," I reassure her. "Are you sure you don't want me to come with you?" I ask again, hoping she changed her mind.

"No, I think the entire ordeal will go more smoothly if I go alone."

While I'd love to insist on accompanying her, I understand this is something she needs to do for herself.

Oliver and Hannah enter the kitchen, with John following behind them.

"What's on the menu tonight?" Finn comes around the table to lean on the kitchen island.

Begrudgingly, I let Lucy go and begin the dinner preparations. "I planned one more night of Italian before we switch to the Christmas meals tomorrow. Build your own pizza night. I have the dough fresh from a local bakery and I'll leave out the ingredients for you to choose from."

Lucy helps me chop up the peppers and mushrooms. Then, I separate the dough and preheat the oven as she shreds the cheese. My mind wonders again what it could be like to have her here for every holiday to come.

Once the ingredients are set out, we step back to allow everyone else to make their own pizzas. I take the opportunity to pull Lucy's back to my chest. It's not enough, overcome with my need to be closer to her, I lean forward and kiss her cheek while I wrap my arms around her.

Dinner moves quickly, and as soon as the dishes have been cleared, Oliver suggests a game before bed. Thanks to John's company we have too many players for most games and can't switch to teams, as it would still leave John by himself *as he should be.*

With Lucy sitting next to me *where she belongs,* she must notice the distaste showing on my face as I look in John's direction. She places her hand on my leg and pulls me out of my internal disdain.

"Why don't we sit this one out?" she asks, but I'm too lost in her eyes. We spent the evening sharing endless displays of affection for our audience, but I didn't even notice if they were looking most of the time. The last few hours have felt so natural. "Henry?" she asks again, "Do you agree?"

"Of course," I answer. I don't even remember what the question is, but I agree.

"Yeah, maybe it is time for you two to call it a night. We've all witnessed enough of your dallying for one night," Finn interjects from the opposite side of the table, sitting next to John, who is glaring at me. Finn continues, "Take it upstairs. We'll see you in the morning."

Lucy turns to smile at me, and slight sorrow fills me, knowing our intimate touches and excessive flirting will end the moment we are out of the presence of others. She stands and I follow behind her, grabbing her hand while we wish everyone a good night. She walks closer to John but doesn't release my hand.

"Enjoy your evening, but be sure you are ready to leave first thing," she instructs him.

He turns and looks up at her as if she is the only person in the room. I'll be glad to be rid of him. "I can't believe you're bowing out so early. It's not because you know you'll lose, is it?"

Her brows fall as she responds, "It's not going to work."

"Oh really, the Lucy I know wouldn't turn down a chance to show off her superior game-playing skills… seems to me you've lost your touch," he says as he smiles and moves his gaze up and down her body.

My instincts whisper in my mind to punch this guy square in the jaw. I move closer to her, but she has an answer ready for him. "I'm just done playing your games, John." *That's my girl.* Finn and Mia squeal at the table as John laughs it off but returns his attention to the board game. With her hand in mine, Lucy follows me up the staircase to our room.

Closing the door behind us, I watch Lucy as she moves to the dresser and begins to take her earrings off. I can't take my eyes off her. Each declaration she makes against him fills me with hope, not to mention how fiercely attractive I find it.

Wanting a front-row view of the show she is unknowingly putting on for me, I sit in the chair next to my fireplace. Silence fills the room as she pulls her sweater over her head to reveal a black fitted tank that blends with her matching leggings to accentuate her perfect hourglass figure.

Fighting my body's desire to go to her, I reposition myself in the chair, forcing myself not to stand. If I got up, I would be on her in an instant. I want to kiss her again, I need to kiss her again, I need her…

She looks over her shoulder at me. She must have felt my eyes on her. No need to deny it—I meet her gaze and smirk. I may not have confessed my feelings in full to her yet, but I will never hide or deny my interest. She smiles back and asks, "Do you mind if I get ready for bed first?"

"Not at all." My mind floods with ideas of all the things I can do with her in this room and the connecting bathroom. Visions of her in my shower…watching the water cover her body.

She nods and faces away from me just for a moment before turning and walking toward me. Time slows as she stops in front of me. Lust and desire fill her eyes as her breathing increases, causing the neck of her tank to move even lower than it already is. I notice white lace peeking out the top, and I'd give my life for a look at the rest of it.

That's when she crawls into my lap, stretching a leg out on either side of me. In all of my fantasies about this moment, I could never have imagined how powerful it would be when she finally made her move.

Now that she has, I am lost to her.

Instinct guides my hands to her thighs, rubbing up and down, tightening my grasp at the top, near her center.

Her hands weave over my chest before moving to my shoulders and ending around my neck. A low growl escapes me as she brings her mouth to graze mine.

Her name escapes my lips in an exhale. There's so much I want to tell her, how she's changed me in the short time we've known each other, how she deserves this new life she designed for herself, and how much I am falling in love with her. Yet, "Lucy" is the only thing I can get out before her mouth collides over mine.

Her fingers weave through my hair, and my hands move from her thighs. One to her waist, pulling her into me, and the other capturing her firm ass. As if that isn't bliss enough, she begins to roll her hips forward. I mirror her movements, lifting up beneath her. She rewards me with some of the most sensual sounds I've ever heard.

She begins to gasp as she breaks our kiss but keeps our bodies connected everywhere else. She shakes her head as if trying to pull herself out of a haze. "I was just…" She stops, trying to catch her breath. "You said to catch you off guard. See, it's disorientating," she says with a wicked smile, still breathing heavily, her forehead resting on mine while she tries to recover, but I don't want this to end.

Pulling her chin up to look at me, I plead with her, "Don't stop, please."

Genuine astonishment flashes across her face and it hurts too much to acknowledge that I still haven't let her know how wanted she truly is.

This isn't how I planned to declare my feelings and I certainly don't want her to think as though I am only declaring them to move forward physically, but I can't keep my feelings in any longer, I must tell her. With a hard swallow and a deep breath, I decide to tell her now, "Lucy."

Thirty-Three

LUCY

HENRY'S JAW ticks and his throat flexes, igniting a stream of naughty thoughts running through my mind. He looks into my eyes and begins to speak. My name escapes his lips with a heavy breath. I know more will follow, but this isn't the time. I'm not ready for him to tell me this doesn't change anything, or that we can just have a fun night without any strings attached, or worse, that this does mean something to him too. I'm not ready for any of it.

Before he can say anymore, I crash my lips onto his, silencing him in the most alluring way I can. I linger, memorizing the feel of his mouth on mine. It's as if our minds finally quiet and allow our lust for each other to take over.

I don't realize Henry is standing beneath me until my legs straighten to the floor. He reaches back, and the lights in the room go out, leaving only the fire to illuminate our night. Never breaking our kiss, his hands graze over my body. Henry backs me up until my knees touch the mattress. He hooks a hand under my knee and dips me back as if we are in the middle of a dance floor—secure in his embrace, he lowers me to the bed.

Lifting his body away from mine, only to seductively look me over head to toe and back again. I can't help but squirm under his intense stare.

I worry that he may take this moment to speak again—discuss what we are about to do. He watches me closely as if he can hear my thoughts. Respectfully, he does not utter another word.

Henry nods. I return the gesture to let him know I want this. We don't need words—the seductive look in his eyes and the sexy smirk he is wearing is all I need to know he wants this.

He wants me.

Moving like he's stalking his prey, he crawls over the top of my body. Desperately, I find the bottom of his shirt and move to pull it over his head, revealing his strong chest.

Granting me only a second to admire him before his attentions are on my neck, his kisses alternating between soft and rough. Letting his tongue slide from my ear to my collarbone, where he bites down just hard enough for me to feel the pleasure shoot down throughout my entire body.

Suddenly, I am hyper aware of the fabric stopping us from being skin to skin. I quickly try to remove it, but before I have a chance, Henry beats me to it. A feral noise emits from his throat at the sight of my bra, and it sends more shivers throughout my body.

He looks up at me with an exaggerated questioning

look on his face before directing his gaze to my lower half. Sitting up to kneel above my legs, he brushes his fingers gently over my sides across my hips and down my legs only to move them back up, stopping at my waistband.

With a wink, he drags my leggings down to reveal the matching half of the lingerie set. A wicked smile grows across his face as he stands to toss my leggings on the floor. His chest is panting with such force. Willingly, I am falling under his trance. I'll never be able to look away.

Henry clears his throat and snaps my attention back to his alluring face, his eyes filled with a mix of desire and desperation. *I need him.* He grabs my wrist until I'm seated as he stands above me. My bra is gone in moments as his mouth devours mine before he pushes my body back down.

His hands clasp around my ankles and slide my entire body to the edge of the bed before he drops to his knees in front of me. I pull my elbows under me to watch as he slips his fingers between the remaining strands of lace at my hips. Removing them at an agonizingly slow pace, until I finally feel them glide over my feet and drop onto the floor.

Parting my legs, he takes his time with each to kiss, bite, and tease up my legs while slowly inching closer to my center. My body is ablaze with need for him.

As his warm tongue finds its target, a soft moan escapes my lips. Never will I consider removing him from this position again. *It is where he is meant to be.*

Feelings of bliss overcome me, building from a pleasure that only he can deliver. "Henry…" I call to him, plead with him, for what, I do not know. I only wish to worship this man who compares to no other. His hands tighten around my hips, pulling me closer to him as he moans against me.

The urgency of his efforts vibrates through my core, sending me over the brink as the frenzy of pleasure overcomes me. A tingly warmth continues to spread to every inch of my body as he slows the movements of his endeavors.

A smile stretches over my face as Henry comes to lay beside me on the bed, placing soft kisses on my heated skin.

When he reaches my neck, I feel like a feather, no longer weighed down but floating from the ecstasy of Henry's attention. I no longer remember where we are, how we got here, or what I was worried about. At this moment, it is only Henry and I in the world.

I attempt to sit up but feel slightly lightheaded. Henry notices and sits up next to me, pulling me into his arms. A glorious place as he is still shirtless, but sadly, his pants are still in place. Underneath my skin, lust and exhaustion are battling it out over what our next move will be. I want, no *need* Henry more than ever, but fatigue is slowly winning the battle. I do not recall ever feeling such pleasure before.

"Time for bed," Henry says as he turns my body to place my head on my pillow. *Yes, sleep. This already feels like a dream.* My body is so relaxed it would take moments after closing my eyes.

No, I can't be this girl, the one who only takes and leaves him…ignored. "But we haven't—"

"We are going to bed because we have had an amazing and eventful evening," he responds as he moves around the room, bringing a set of my pajamas over to me. "Do you need help getting these on?" His sly smile is gorgeous, proud his efforts left me in such a state, *as he should be.*

Finally regaining some feeling in my legs, I move them over the edge of the bed and stand to pull on my pajama shorts. As soon as the matching top is over my body, Henry directs me back into bed. "I'll run down and get you water. I'll be right back."

I watch as he pulls a shirt on as he walks out of the room, admiring the view of his ass as I drift to sleep.

Waking in Henry's arms is becoming a routine that I am getting far too comfortable with. *It could all end once John is gone, and I am free to go back into the guestroom.* My chest begins to hurt at the thought of losing the closeness I'd found with Henry. He's sleeping soundly behind me with his arm tucked around my waist. I look around and notice the glass of water he must have fetched for me last night.

Last night. I feel myself smile simply at the memory. Henry wanted to say something last night, but I stopped him. Hope begins to grow that something real might truly be developing between us, but I don't want to start it this way.

I need to get John out of this country before I even consider anything with Henry. Checking the clock, it's just after 6:30 a.m. A shower will clear my head to get focused on the day ahead.

Slowly moving out of Henry's arms, I place my pillow under his arm in hopes that my absence won't wake him.

With the door closed, I shower as quickly as possible and dress quietly. Once I am finished, I make my way back into the bedroom and find Henry still asleep.

I stumble around the low-lit room, grabbing clothes from my drawers, hoping they match since I was too preoccupied to pack last night.

An odd outfit or two is more than worth the distracting activities.

With my overnight bag in hand, I take one final look at Henry peacefully sleeping. No need to wake him. I need to do this on my own—for both past and future Lucy, it's time to cut John out of my life once and for all. I kiss Henry on the forehead and leave the room, closing the door behind me.

Placing my bag on the floor in the hall, I knock on John's door.

No answer. *Of course.*

Turning the handle, I'm relieved the door isn't locked. John is still asleep and clearly hasn't packed at all. This will be easier if I do it myself. I move around the room and throw his clothes into his luggage and duffle bag. Stopping in the bathroom, I grab his toiletries and put them on top of his luggage so he doesn't forget them.

Now, to deal with him. I leave a single outfit from his luggage and put it on the end of his bed before I give him a *not-very-gentle* push to wake him up. It takes three attempts, but he finally opens his eyes.

He tries to pull on one of my hands in a poor attempt to get me to sit on the bed with him. He mumbles with a groggy voice, "I knew you'd come to your senses. Are we making a run for it before the old man finds out you'd rather be with me?"

I would love nothing more than to give him a detailed play-by-play of last night explaining that he is no competition for Henry, but instead, I throw a pillow on his face and say, "Get up."

He slowly sits up on his elbows, looking disorientated.

"The car is coming for us in thirty minutes. We are heading directly to London. If there aren't any flights out today, I will set you up in a hotel." He looks at me with a smirk, and I remind him again.

"This is my life, and you are no longer a part of it. Get ready, now."

I exit the room before he can say anything else that will piss me off. It is his fault I am leaving this beautiful home and Henry. *It's also his fault that you shared a room with Henry in the first place.* As well as that has worked out, it's time for him to go.

In the kitchen, I find a note on the refrigerator door.

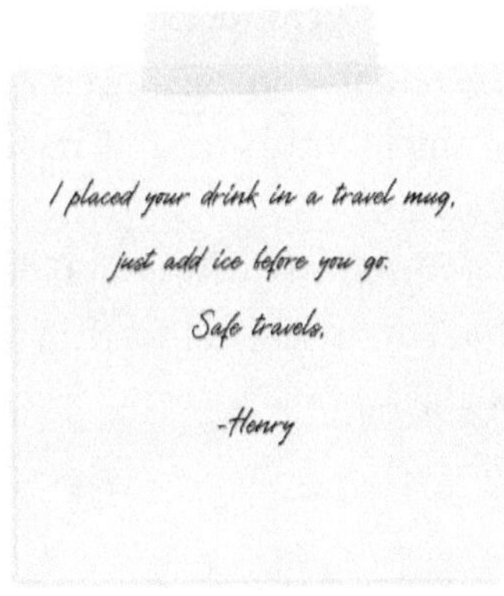

Smiling, I open the door to find my cold brew coffee on the top shelf with a bottle of water next to it. Henry must have prepared these when he came down last night after our…physical pursuits.

Before I can begin to reminisce about the sight of Henry kneeling before me, John makes his way downstairs. As we walk together to the garage, John's phone rings and he ignores the call, only for it to begin ringing again.

"Feel free to take that," I say.

"No, it's not important." He sets the ringer to silent and returns it to his pocket. "You and I have far more important matters to discuss."

"John, get it over with now because I do not plan to spend the entirety of our drive discussing this."

"You don't even know these people, let alone that man." I ignore his statement and check my phone to see if the driver is close. "Tell me what I need to do, Lucy." He pulls the phone from my hand and stands in front of me. "You know how much I love you."

"John, it's over, it's been over for years, and now I'm with Henry." He remains unconvinced. "But you should know, I could be single for the rest of my life, and I would feel the same. It's over."

He turns away from me with a huff just as our driver pulls up. I couldn't be more relieved to see him. Finally, the beginning of the end.

Thirty-Four

HENRY

SOMEWHERE BETWEEN SLEEP AND CONSCIOUSNESS, memories of the night before fill my mind. Lucy stalked toward me before climbing on top of me, kissing me to the point of madness. When I could no longer restrain myself, I gave into my lust, devouring her on my bed.

Everything in my body told me to keep going, to finally make her mine, but thankfully, I stopped it when I had. She needs to know how I feel before I claim her completely.

The way she moved beneath my touch confirms that she feels the pull between us just as strongly as I do, but I need to know if it's more than the physical attraction.

Sharing her pleasure was enough for last night, but today is a different story. Not another moment will be wasted on uncertainty between us.

There will be time for flowers and romantic dinners later, now I need to express my admiration. I'll wake her with soft whispers, declaring my affection for her.

Rolling over, I slightly open my eyes to find her as my arm falls across an empty bed.

"Lucy?" I call toward the bathroom.

No answer.

Her e-reader sits in its place on her nightstand. She never goes anywhere without it. Even when we were in London, she always had it on her. London. She's taking John back today. She must be downstairs, waiting for the driver. I grab my phone to check the time and find a text from her.

LUCY

Didn't want to wake you, leaving for London now. Thanks for the coffee! I'll text you with updates as I have them. Talk soon!

Loneliness overcomes me as I dress for the day. She left her e-reader here, a clear sign she plans to return soon, hopefully tonight.

Moving through the house, it feels empty.

I stop to peek in the spare bedroom that John occupied, it's as if he were never here. It looks just as I set it for Lucy before they arrived, except for the books she brought with her into my room. I smile at the memory of her pulling them off the shelf and clutching them in her arms as she walked across the hall.

Even with everything that we shared between us last night, I can't overcome this feeling of jealousy as she spends the day with another man, one she has a complicated history with. My instinct was to insist I go with her, but after all he's put her through, I know how important it is for her to end this on her own. It's not her that concerns me. It's him and his persistent pursuit to win her back.

Standing at the counter, the sound of the coffee brewer starting up is the only noise in the house as my gaze sweeps over the snow-covered garden.

Thankful for the brief privacy, I begin what I expect will be a long day of repeating "everything will be fine" to myself.

Oliver and Finn, accompanied by their partners, gradually make their way to the kitchen. It was decided days ago that today will be a simple breakfast, everyone skims through the pastries and fruit before taking a seat at the table.

I draft a quick text to Lucy, trying my best not to sound too desperate.

HENRY

Be safe.

I hit send, even though I have so much more I'd like to say. Those words are not meant to be shared in a text message.

Finn breaks my concentration, "Lucy and John leave already?"

"Yes, a little more than an hour ago," I answer.

"That guy was something else," Hannah adds, shaking her head.

"Last night, he was really putting on the charm. I think he was even trying to win us over to his side," Mia adds, then meets my gaze. "Of course, he didn't, Henry.

You have nothing to worry about. We all know you're much better for her than he ever was."

"Even after *twenty* years…" Finn mockingly repeats John's favorite piece of evidence in his case, causing laughter to erupt around the table.

Oliver turns to me with a serious expression. "How are you holding up with all of this? Her leaving with him can't be easy."

"It's not."

He nods, "Why don't I come with you to town? You said you had to pick up a few things, and I'd like to get some flowers to bring to Hannah's mother."

Oh yes, I almost forgot this was our cover story for leaving the house today to make final preparations for his proposal. "Yes, thank you. I'd appreciate the company."

The first stop in town is at the bakery. I have a smaller order of pastries to be delivered on the twenty-seventh for Lucy and me, then a larger one to be delivered on the thirtieth for when everyone rejoins us.

Oliver finalizes the order of a dozen double chocolate cupcakes, Hannah's favorite, for New Year's Eve. I coordinate with the bakery to be the contact person for deliveries, giving my cell for them to text upon arrival so we can be sure to sneak them in without Hannah noticing.

Next, we move to the florist. Oliver orders a customized garland to decorate the banister of the staircase and large vases to sit on the bottom steps filled with red roses.

To Oliver's surprise, I also place an order for a few bouquets of fresh flowers to have around the house for Lucy.

Before we leave, I remind Oliver that he needs to get the flowers he announced at the breakfast table he was picking up to bring to Hannah's mother.

"Thanks, Pop. It completely slipped my mind."

***

The rest of the day is spent cooking with everyone pitching in. As we set the table, I take a photo of the arrangement and post it to my account with a caption Lucy came up with, "Happy holidays from my family to yours." Dinner is a success.

After dessert, we move to the lounge and settle in for our Christmas Eve gifting. Once my gifts are open, I excuse myself like I do every year and give the two couples privacy to exchange between themselves.

Checking my phone again, it's nearing midnight, and I've only received two additional texts from Lucy today. The first briefly said everything was fine. The second confirmed she wouldn't make it back here this evening but would call tonight.

My phone battery is almost dead, so I grab my charger and plug my mobile in, turning the volume up as high as it can so I don't miss her call while I am in the shower.

Stepping under the powerful streams, I let the warm water consume me while trying to remain positive.

Everything is all right.

She can handle this.

There's nothing to worry about.

If something was wrong, she would have called.

Everything is all right.

I keep repeating these rational thoughts over and over in hopes of drowning out the many more irrational ones that refuse to go away. I stay in the shower longer than normal to delay the inevitable, having to sleep in my bed alone.

I turn off the water as my skin begins to raisin. Using a towel, I dry off my hair and then wrap it around my waist. The phone screen is dark as I walk back to my nightstand. The screen lights up when I tap it.

MISSED CALL: LUCY

1 NEW VOICEMAIL

Not waiting to listen to the message, I call her back immediately, but it doesn't ring. It goes straight to her voicemail.

Hanging up, I listen to the message she left.

"Hi Henry, it's been a hectic day. I'm sorry to be calling you so late. Everything is fine, but I can't give you the full story now. My phone battery is about to die, and I forgot the charger at your place. Hopefully, I'll be able to find a shop that's open tomorrow to buy another. I'll call again as soon as I can. Merry Christmas, Henry."

Hearing her voice settles my nerves. She isn't avoiding me. She said everything is fine, but didn't mention John at all. Is he already on his way to the States, or is he squatting in her apartment?

She didn't sound stressed, only tired.

If something were to happen, she would have no way to reach me. I could get in my car now and drive to her apartment. Not in the middle of the night. She's probably sleeping already. Now is not the time for me to make these decisions. I'll try to sleep tonight and hopefully hear back from her first thing.

If not, I'll go to her.

<h1 style="text-align:center">Thirty-Five</h1>

LUCY

BEEP...BEEP...BEEP.

With one eye open, I feel around until I find the button to silence my alarm clock. I'm still not recovered from yesterday, and I'm certainly not ready to take on today.

I suppose yesterday could have gone worse, but it certainly doesn't compare to the prior days I've spent with Henry.

When we arrive back in the city, we stop at my apartment to get lunch and check the flight schedule. After tons of double and triple checking the air carriers, we realize we missed the only flight directly to the Syracuse airport today. There is an option for a flight with three layovers and it would take almost as long for him to arrive if he just took the flight that leaves this afternoon. As much frustration as he's causing me, I don't want to subject anyone to spending that much time in airports and on planes on Christmas Day.

However, there was a line. Just because I have been kind about the flight doesn't mean I want to spend Christmas Eve with John. I'd rather spend it alone in my apartment, and that's exactly what I do.

The only hotel that still has rooms also has their restaurant open, and we are able to have dinner before I return to my place. Not that I want to eat with him, but all the other restaurants are closed, and I don't have much to eat in my apartment.

After dinner, we say our goodbyes, I hand John one of the room keys.

"Keeping the other in case you get lonely?" John asks.

I roll my eyes, "Not in a million years. I doubt my phone battery will survive the night. I won't be able to call and make sure you're up in the morning."

"I can get to the airport myself, no need for you to come." His tone is deflated.

Could he finally be conceding?

"I would prefer to watch you step onto the plane myself, but since I can't get through security, I'm at least going to get you to the airport."

He shakes his head and hits the button for the elevator.

"Good night."

I turn to leave and hear him yell behind me, "Merry Christmas!"

After a quick shower, I dress and check my phone once more. It's dead, not turning back on.

I was only able to get a couple of texts to Henry and then a call to him before bed. Not only did I leave my charger at Henry's house, but I forgot to charge the phone the night before. I suppose that's Henry's fault for… distracting me…in the best possible way.

I totally forgive him.

With my coat wrapped tightly around me, I start my walk to John's hotel, looking for an open shop that could sell a charger.

Christmas morning in London is absolutely beautiful. How I wish my phone had some power left to take photos. With the streets almost empty, there wouldn't be anyone to feel annoyed with my tourist behavior. No luck with the shops, and the chilly weather is getting the best of me. I finally grab a cab to drop me off in front of John's hotel.

Walking in, the lobby is busier than I would have expected. The rich smell of fresh baked goods and sweets hits my nose as I turn with relief to see the restaurant open once again. We'll stop there to eat before we leave for the airport, that's if John could get ready quickly.

The elevator takes me up to the third floor, and I don't need to look much before a room door opens, and a beautiful red-headed woman exits with John close behind her. I turn back to face the elevator to give them privacy during their goodbye.

And there is the proof, what my friends have been warning me about since John and I broke up years ago. I always believed them over him. I've witnessed him flirt on many occasions, but he would always deny it. *How's he going to deny this one?* As he likes to cite on a regular basis, we have a twenty-year history. That history should be enough for him to be honest with me.

As the elevator doors close with the woman inside, I make my way to John, who is still standing in his doorway. *Well, this may get awkward...* "Lucy, let me explain—"

We don't need a production here in the hallway. "I don't need an explanation, but I want to say something.

For someone who claims to care about me and our twenty-year history so much, you could at least be honest with me. It's been over a decade since we broke up, I am in full support of you moving on. Honestly, that might be the catalyst that would allow us to be friends. But the deceit is a deal breaker for me, and you, of all people, should know that." *That felt good to say.* "The restaurant is open downstairs. I'll grab us a table. How long do you need?"

"I'll be down in twenty," he says, and we each go our separate ways.

After a quiet breakfast, we take a cab to the airport. I notice a small strip of shops next to the airport entrance, but as we get closer, it's obvious they are all closed.

When we enter the airport, the large screen states that John's flight is delayed by two hours, but that's not the biggest problem. The lobby is filled with people in line trying to get their tickets changed.

We take seats against the window and wait. "You don't have to stay," John says as a beautiful set of twins in front of us decide that this moment is a good time to test the limits of their vocal cords.

I raise my voice so he can hear me over them. "It's okay, I'll wait with you a little longer."

Above everyone, the monitors hang a Happy Christmas sign, reminding me that the chances of me finding a shop to buy a new charger today will be impossible. I can't call Henry because I didn't think to write his number down, but I can at least call my mom. "Could I use your phone to call my mom and wish her a Merry Christmas?"

"Of course." John hands his phone over.

My mom answers after a couple of rings. "Hey, Mom! Merry Christmas," I say.

"Honey! Merry Christmas. Did you get a new phone?" she asks.

"No, it's actually John's phone…" I don't give her enough time to connect the dots. "He came to London to visit me, and he's heading home today, but my phone battery died, so he let me borrow his. I promise everything is all right."

"Ohhh…well, when you get a new charger, I look forward to the rest of that story."

"Sure thing. I hope you have a nice night with Ellie and her family. Send them my love!" Sadness fills me. It still doesn't feel any easier not being with my mom on Christmas.

"Okay, sweetie, call me when you can. Love you!"

"Love you too, Mom." I hang up and hand his phone back.

John lowers his eyes, focusing on the zipper of his travel bag, and asks, "Don't you have someone else you need to call?"

I shrug, "I don't have his number memorized."

"Technology." He shakes his head and tsks.

After another hour, the lines begin to move as John turns to me, "I don't want to leave this on a bad note."

I look at him. "John, there's no hard feelings on my end, but if you want to end things on a better note, you can apologize and stop trying to interfere in my personal life, especially because I really don't care about your romantic relationships." I laugh a little. "Your unexpected arrival was quite the surprise and certainly frustrating at times, but it wasn't the worst thing that could have happened."

"I'm sorry. I guess I was just always certain that we would end up together, and when you finally moved on, the future I was so certain of was now in jeopardy. I didn't even think to ask if you saw the same future."

"John, we are different people now than when we were together. I doubt we would even enjoy being in a relationship anymore." I try to reassure him.

"So this is it? Is it actually over?" he asks.

"Yes, it certainly is. But that's not a bad thing. We will always be a part of each other's life story, but now it's time for the next chapters."

"Your chapter will be starring your fancy British director boyfriend…"

"And your chapter will have plenty of leading ladies, I assume."

He smirks and shakes his head. He opens his arms for a hug, and I give in one last time. I watch as John crosses through security and walks to the gates.

I turn toward the exit but only make it a couple steps when I hear someone calling my name. "LUCY! LUCY!"

It's John yelling and waving at me from his side of the security gate. As I walk toward him, John hands something to a guard and points to me. The guard catches up to me and hands me a white box. I look down, and it's a charger for my phone.

I look up to find John and yell, "Thank you!"

He replies, "Merry Christmas!" And turns back to his gate.

Bursting through my apartment door, before I even take my coat off, I run to the nearest outlet in my kitchen and plug the phone in to charge. When it doesn't immediately come back to life, I decide to take a quick shower. It's the perfect opportunity to wash off all the nonsense from John and get refreshed for what's to come when I return to Henry's home.

Still contemplating my next move, I decide to let my phone charge a little longer while I put on something comfortable. On my way to heat up some soup, my phone rings, and I rush over, hoping it's Henry but disappointed it's not. It's Ellie.

"Hello! Merry Christmas," I answer.

"What is going on? Your mother just told me you called her from John's phone because he came to London to be with you. How long has the parasite been in the UK? And why didn't you tell me sooner?"

This is going to be a long conversation, so before I get into it all, I ask, "Can you hold on a minute." I pull my phone from my face to send Henry a quick text.

LUCY

Merry Christmas! All is well, John is on his flight, and I was able to find a charger. I'm back at my apartment. Will call you later.

Before I get into it with Ellie, she hands the phone to my mom again, and I wish her and Ellie's parents a Merry Christmas.

Then for the next two hours, while making and

enjoying my soup, I share almost every minute since John's arrival with Ellie. Yet, I keep the details of my spicy night with Henry from retelling. I like having that memory all to myself.

After we finally hang up, I notice a text from Henry.

HENRY

Well, that is some very good news. Get some rest and we will catch up tomorrow. Happy Christmas, Lucy.

As much as I'd like to talk with Henry, I'm drained from the past two days. I make my way into bed and finally feel like the weight of having my ex here has been lifted.

Tomorrow is a new day with endless potential.

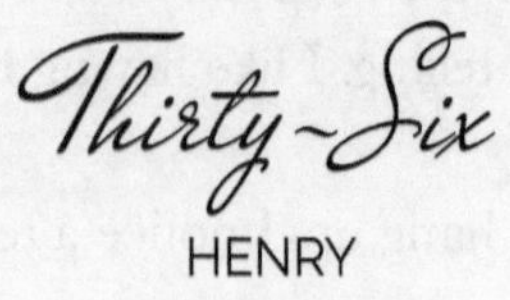

CHRISTMAS MORNING COMES JUST as it always does with a delightful breakfast of freshly made pancakes, a tradition I started when the boys were young. Now we continue it while everyone stays in their pj's. Except this year, something is missing…no, *someone* is missing.

It's been roughly three months since meeting Lucy, but this group of five doesn't feel right anymore without our sixth.

By mid-afternoon, everyone is in their rooms, getting ready for their travels, and I sit in my office to complete the next of my Christmas Day traditions, calling Max.

He answers with a joyous tone, "Merry Christmas, Henry!" Nothing makes Max happier than spending time with his daughters. Now that they are older and have busy lives of their own, he spends the entire year waiting to have them home to enjoy the holidays together.

"Merry Christmas, Max! How are the girls doing?"

"Wonderful as always. And the boys? Are they enjoying their holiday? Oh, and Hannah and Mia too?"

I fill him in on all the major events but am careful to leave out the proposal preparations just in case Hannah is walking by my office. I told him about it not long after Oliver told me, but I don't think his girls know either.

Next, Max asks about Lucy. I go over what has taken place since her arrival on Saturday, only leaving out the more torrid details.

"I haven't spoken to her since she left and yesterday it was just a few brief texts and a voice message." I can hear the stress building in my own voice. "I'm thinking of driving back to London after everyone leaves."

"Hmm," Max replies.

"All right, out with it." I need his opinion—I'm too in my head over this. "You don't think I should go?"

"I think this sounds like something she had made it very clear she wants to settle on her own. She'll let you know if she needs you."

"Well, that's the issue, without a charger, she has no way to reach me." I'm beginning to hear the desperation in my voice. "I can bring her the charger she left here. I'm certain she won't be able to find one with all the shops closed on Christmas Day."

Max pauses for just a moment, then gives me one of his hypothetical questions. "You seem to know her pretty well at this point. If she at all sensed things were taking a turn for the worst, would she have told you yesterday?"

"Yes."

"And did she sound confident in her message last night that everything is fine?" he asks.

"Yes." He's right. "But what do I do until then?"

"Henry, you've been on your own for a long time…entertain yourself. I'm sure you'll hear from her soon."

"Thanks, Max." We then continue our conversation. Max tells me about the new recipes he's trying out for the holidays. I thank him for the ones he's shared with me. We speak briefly about the movie and when production will start.

"I've already begun practicing my lines, '*For what do we live, but to make sport for our neighbors, and laugh at them in our turn?*'" Max says in his British accent. He continues, back in his natural American accent, "I'm looking forward to working with you again, Henry. I think it will be your greatest work yet."

"Thank you, Max. The feeling is certainly mutual. "

We say our goodbyes and a notification for an email appears on my phone screen.

```
From: Mark Hill
<mark.hill@hilltalentagency.com>
Subject: P&P - Meeting /Social Media
Promotion
Henry,
I heard from Viewmont Productions and I
want to go over a few things with you.
When can you meet?
-Mark

To: Mark Hill
<mark.hill@hilltalentagency.com>
```

Subject: Re: P&P - Meeting /Social Media
Promotion
If it's urgent, we could have a phone call
tomorrow.
-Henry

From: Mark Hill
<mark.hill@hilltalentagency.com>
Subject: Re: P&P - Meeting /Social Media
Promotion
That works, I plan to go into the office
tomorrow afternoon to catch up on some
things and take advantage of a day when no
one else will be working. I'm not
complaining, but it can be tough to get
things done when the phone calls and
emails don't stop coming in.
-Mark

To: Mark Hill
<mark.hill@hilltalentagency.com>
Subject: Re: P&P - Meeting /Social Media
Promotion
If you're in the office, I can meet you
there. You can expect me to be there at
2:00 p.m. tomorrow.
Also, It's Christmas Day. Put your phone
down and enjoy the day with your family.
-Henry

If this week had gone as I originally planned and Lucy

had been with me, I'd have told Mark not to expect me until January. But he just gave me the perfect excuse to head back to London. With Max's advice in mind, I won't call Lucy until tomorrow morning and ask her to attend the meeting with me.

With a new sense of hope, I make my way out of my office just as everyone else is bringing their bags to the back door.

"All set?" I ask.

"I think we are," Oliver answers.

"One more thing before you leave, I've got a meeting with my agent in London tomorrow. Is it all right if I head to the townhouse tonight?" I ask.

Smiles grow on each of their faces—all but Finn tries to be discreet about it. "Oh, a meeting with your agent? No need to make up meetings, Pop. Just say you're off to see Lucy. That you can't bear to be apart from her for another moment."

"All right, that's enough." No use arguing with him. "Off you go. Safe travels to you all. And don't forget to let me know when you arrive."

I help them get their bags into the cars, but before they get in, I have another request.

"Don't mention my being in London in the group chat…" They start cheering and clapping before pulling out of the driveway and heading on their way.

Just as I'm walking back into the house, my phone buzzes. It's a text from Lucy saying she found a charger and will call later.

Wanting to get a head start on my trip as soon as possible, I can't risk her calling while I'm in the car. I text back, telling her to get some rest and that we will catch up tomorrow.

I move quickly to my room to pack a couple of days' worth of clothes to be sure. I remember to bring my charger and put her e-reader and its charger in my bag too. She must be missing it terribly. Locking up the house behind me, I jump in the car and head to London.

I wake thirty minutes before my alarm is scheduled to go off. I try to lay in bed a little longer but my body thrums with energy, forcing me to move and start my day. Quickly showering and dressing for the day, I check my phone for any messages from Lucy, but nothing yet. I don't want to arrive while she's sleeping, so I text to make sure she's awake.

HENRY

Good morning.

LUCY

Good morning! Do you have time for a call?

HENRY

I'm a little tied up at the moment. How about in about 45 minutes/hour?

LUCY

Sure, that works for me.

After stopping at the florist, I arrive at her apartment in exactly forty-five minutes. I move to stand next to her building and call her. She answers on the first ring.

"Hello." Her voice is music to my ears. I don't think I ever want to go that long without hearing it again.

"Hello, there," I reply, trying to play it cool.

"How was your holiday?" she asks.

As I reply, I ring her doorbell. "Better than yours, I assume."

"Oh, can you hold on one moment? Someone's ringing the doorbell." She sounds frustrated at the interruption.

"We really can't catch a break, huh? Tell them to go away. I've been waiting days to speak with you," I tell her, smiling like an idiot outside her front door.

"Oh, it will only take a moment." She speaks into her phone, and then the intercom buzzes and as her voice comes through, "Hello?" I let it echo through the phone.

"Special delivery for Miss Taylor" I say into both the intercom and phone.

"Very cute," she says into the phone while she unlocks the front door and I make my way up the first flight of stairs.

Her apartment door is open with her mobile still in her hand. I rush to her and pull her into my arms as I kick the door shut with my foot. Resting my head in the crook of her neck, I hold on tight.

Reluctantly, pulling away, "These are for you," I say, as I bring the flowers from behind her back. "I missed you… quite a lot."

She closes her eyes and smiles while breathing in the scent of the roses in her hands. "I missed you too." She looks up at me and asks, "Have you eaten?"

"Actually, I was going to ask if you'd be interested in

going out to grab something to eat, but first, we have a meeting to get to."

"A meeting? We have a meeting?" she asks with wide eyes.

"Yes, Mark—"

"Your agent," she interjects with a coy smile.

"Yes, that Mark reached out to meet with me today about the social media accounts and some requests the production company has for them. As you are the mastermind behind my new public persona, I thought you should be included. That's if you'd like to be." I'm not letting her out of my sight today. Even if this meeting was regarding another matter, she'd be coming with me.

"All right, let's head to the meeting."

Just as I had planned, the car I ordered with my usual driver is waiting outside her apartment. Lucy gets in and speaks with the driver. "Hi Tom, how was your Christmas?"

"Great, thank you, Lucy. And yours?"

"Better now that Mr. Brooks is in town." She squeezes my hand and smiles.

Tom addresses me, "Good to see you again, Mr. Brooks."

"Yes, and you too, Tom." I look between the two before remembering that it was Tom who picked up Lucy and John on Christmas Eve morning to bring them back to the city.

The car makes it through the busy streets of London to Mark's office. Lucy continues to hold my hand as we walk into the building. I can't recall if I've ever held hands with someone for this long before, but I never want it to end. As we enter the lobby, I notice the front desk is empty.

Mark shouts and waves to us from his glass-wall office. "Come on back, Mary is off for the holidays."

"As you should be, Mark. Is a quiet office really enough to come in on Boxing Day?" I ask.

"If you must know, I plan to take some time off, and my flight leaves tomorrow," he shares, looking at his monitor. "So, I wanted to tie up some loose ends before I go."

"That's great, where to?" I ask.

Still not making any attempt to look up from his computer, "Somewhere warm."

Fine, I suppose it's his personal business. I clear my throat for his attention, "Mark, this is Lucy Taylor."

Mark begins to look a little uncomfortable. "Nice to meet you, Lucy." He finally looks up at her and asks, "Do you plan on staying for the meeting?"

I interject, "Mark, you mentioned this meeting is about my social media accounts. Lucy is the one behind all of them—she has been since the first post. Anything you have to say can be said in front of her."

Mark stands and takes a deep breath, "Viewmont Productions marketing department called. They love what you've done with the accounts and how much you've engaged the audience before filming has even begun."

"That's great," I say, but it's clear there's more as he's looking everywhere but at Lucy.

"They are suggesting we use your accounts and popularity to make the fans part of the production experience. The idea isn't just for you but also for the actor playing Mr. Darcy." He pauses, his stalling is wearing on my nerves.

"What's this idea?"

"With your new reputation as a romantic man, the production company wants to give fans a chance to win first-hand experiences in the world of *Pride and Prejudice*, even bringing them onto the sets..." He takes a deep breath.

Then, he rushes to get the next words out of his mouth as quickly as possible. "Contests to win a date with the leading man and the director of the movie, but for that to feel believable, they suggested it would be better if you were single or appear to be unattached and looking for a new leading lady. It would give the viewers the idea that they could become that leading lady themselves." He finally peeks at Lucy from under his bowed head.

I turn to her and see that the color has already left her face.

Thirty Seven

LUCY

AS THE WORDS leave Mark's mouth, he keeps his eyes on his desk. This production company needs to make up their minds. First they didn't want him to be known as a single man, that he wasn't viewed as romantic enough. Now that he has established himself as a smitten and fully committed man, they want him to be single and ready to mingle again.

My body begins to shrink into itself and my ears begin to ring. I always knew in the back of my mind this was temporary, so foolish of me to think it could end any differently. How silly I was to spend the last hour basking in the closeness with Henry. I was worried that it would stop once John had left, but it didn't. Until now.

Henry begins to address Mark, but I stop him. "I think I should leave you two to discuss this in private."

Mark agrees, "Yes, I think that's for the best."

Henry shoots him a look and then takes my hand. "Lucy, stay."

Looking into his eyes, "Just as I needed to…handle

things myself the last two days, I want to show you the same respect. This is your career and your job. I don't want you to have that discussion with me in the room." I look back to Mark. "Hear what he has to say. I'm going to head back to my place and give you some space to make the best decision for yourself."

I don't want him to think he owes me anything because that one night we shared in his bedroom. *If anything, I owe him for that night.*

"Lucy…" Henry says as I smile and make my way out of the office. I spot Tom's car and walk in the opposite direction. I don't care to explain to him why I'm coming out of the meeting so soon and by myself.

Thankfully this part of London is even busier than it normally is during the week. Shops are packed as I move through the crowd of people carrying bags all around me. Finding a cab only takes a moment. I ask the driver to take me back to my neighborhood with plans to stop at a grocer on the way to my apartment.

There is a very real chance I will be staying in London instead of returning to Henry's home with him. Either way, I am sure he will invite me to return with him, but is that something I can put myself through?

It's my own fault for developing this…crush on Henry. He's always been upfront about things with me. We got into this mess with the mutual understanding that neither of us wanted a relationship. We started this for the movie production company, so it's only fitting that they dictate when it's over as well.

Just because our fake relationship may be over, that doesn't mean we can't still be friends. *But I want to be more than friends.* Can I sustain the type of torture, having feelings for a friend who doesn't feel the same? Is my great love story to be an unrequited one?

He will most likely go back to his casual dating, and I can go back to devoting my affections to fictional men.

My mind drifts to Henry in Mark's office. I don't regret my decision to leave. I couldn't live with myself knowing he made a particular decision only because I was in the room.

When I arrived at his home with my ex-boyfriend without giving him notice, he immediately gave me space with minimal sarcasm. But that night, he let me talk and explain it all to him without pressure. Not to mention the endless patience he showed as the days continued until I could finally get John back to London. He deserves the same respect from me in this situation.

My phone buzzes and I hurry to check if it's Henry, but I groan when I find it's just an email confirmation of John's check out from the hotel room with the invoice of the charges attached. Well, at least he didn't order any room service.

An hour passes without any word from Henry. So I decide to distract, *more like torture,* myself by putting on the movie adaptation of *Northanger Abbey* that Henry directed.

I plug my phone into my charger, and before I leave it on my coffee table, I make sure my ringer is as loud as it can be. Then, I lie down on the couch with my favorite blanket and attempt to let Jane Austen's story consume me. Max is a wonderful Mr. Tilney, and when my mind wanders to his love of cooking and then to Henry making those recipes for me, I stop myself and focus only on the characters.

Just as Catherine is getting kicked out of the Abbey in the middle of the night, I hear my text alert. It's from Henry. No text, just a photo of two coffees, one cold and one hot, sitting on a familiar-looking table.

I drop the phone back onto the table and move quickly to get ready. My heart is pounding. I don't even waste a moment to text him back. Running around my apartment as quickly as I can, I throw my phone in my pocket and head out the door.

I round the corner to the coffee shop and find Henry carrying two coffee cups in the direction of the trash bin, a hot drink cup and one clear cold cup that looks to have an iced coffee in it, just the way I like.

"I hope you aren't wasting a perfectly good cold brew coffee." I'm out of breath from running.

He freezes when he looks up at me. I immediately start to explain, "I'm sorry. I just saw your text. I probably should have replied to you, but I came straight here."

Henry smiles and walks back to the table we sat at when he first asked for my help to win over the production company and Jane Austen fans. Once seated, he asks, "So tell me, how did things go after you left on Tuesday morning?"

So anxious to hear about what he decided with Mark, I'm having trouble recalling Tuesday. Oh yes, with John. I answer with a quick recap of events.

He seems satisfied, Henry then asks, "So, do you have any plans for dinner?

"No, not yet," I answer. Still waiting for him to discuss the meeting.

"Perfect!" He stands, fixes his coat and clears his throat. He holds his hand out, I take it, and he tugs me up to stand in front of him. "Lucy, will you have dinner with me tonight?"

It's that moment, the one where you never think you'll experience yourself, one you believe to be just out of your reach. Happiness fills me as I look into Henry's eyes.

"Lucy?" he asks again, "will you have dinner with me tonight?"

"Yes! I'd love to, but Henry, what happened at the meeting with Mark? With Viewmont Productions' request?" I can't let this go any further. I need to hear it from him.

As much as I want this dinner to be the first of many dates for us, it could also just be a parting gift to let me know he's decided to follow through with the production company's plans. If that is the case, I'd rather hear it in the coffee shop than at a dinner with him that feels like a date.

"Oh, that, I told him to let them know they could fuck off," he answers with a shrug.

"What? What about Viewmont Productions?" I ask.

"Oh, well, I appreciate the role they played in all this to begin with, but I'm not letting them interfere any further." He slips his arms around my waist and pulls me toward him, *but not close enough.*

"Interfere in what…" I ask slyly.

"Well for starters, I am finally able to ask you on a

proper date. And you've accepted, so I believe that makes us…a thing?"

I know I'm smiling like an idiot. "A thing you say. And what does this thing involve…exactly?" I tease him.

"Well, dinner tonight and then all the other perks that come with us being together," Henry says, looking every bit the cool and collected man he is.

"I look forward to these perks."

After the perks I received Monday night, I can't wait to experience the full package.

Henry pulls my face to his and kisses me more passionately than I would assume is acceptable in public. "There's a perk."

We walk hand in hand to the restaurant. Of course Henry requests a booth so we can sit next to each other. The meal is good, but the company is delicious.

I ask if there will be repercussions with the production company if they are upset about him refusing their marketing proposal.

"Mark and I looked into it. They can't infringe on my personal life that much. They are welcome to suggest anything they'd like, but they have no power to enforce it. There won't be any repercussions. Let that young actor do it if he's single and interested."

The way he shrugs it off makes me giddy as a tingling rush moves throughout my body. I almost jump with happiness. Then it hits me, "So is all of this, the coffee shop text, taking me out to dinner. Is this just your way of directing the romance in your own life?"

He laughs at me. "Lucy, I don't think anything that

has occurred in the last week is things I would have planned for us." That's a fair point. "Yet, it was enough to make an interesting movie. Plenty of plot twists." He winks. "While I am utilizing my expertise in the subject, real life provides too many variables, but I will try to maintain great levels of romance while we tackle anything else that comes at us."

The honesty in his tone melts my heart. "Well, John is one less thing you'll have to deal with," I reassure him.

"At least not until we visit your family and friends back in the States." He has a serious look on his face. I hadn't considered him coming to the States. "I need to meet your mom and your feisty friend, Ellie."

"Of course. We can plan for a trip over the summer. Ellie works for a baseball team. We can watch her in her element."

"I look forward to it," he says with his arm around me.

The check comes, and we make our way out of the restaurant. We've been sharing a bed for days *and doing more than sleeping*. I shouldn't be nervous to ask, but I keep my eyes down. "Would you like to stay at my place tonight?"

"Thank you for the offer, but I had other plans." I look up at him, my fingers fidgeting at my side while I wait for him to continue. "If you're up for a late-night road trip, I thought we could avoid the traffic and head back to the house this evening…together."

"Yes, I'd love that. I just need to grab a couple things from my place." My heart begins to hum as I try to keep my face somewhat collected.

"The boys' townhouse is on our way. We can stop there, grab my bags, and take my car back to your place before we leave."

"Sounds like a plan," I say following his lead, so thrilled to be heading back to his place tonight together.

Thirty-Eight

HENRY

IT'S NEARLY 2:00 a.m. when we pull into the driveway of my home. I look over at my beautiful passenger as I pull our joined hands up to my lips. I gently let my lips brush against her knuckles and imagine placing such kisses over every inch of her body. The moonlight shines through the windows and lights up her sleepy face.

We will have days with the house to ourselves before everyone returns. No need to rush things tonight.

I want her well-rested for what I have planned for us.

"Why don't you get the door and head in." I hand her the house key. "I'll grab the bags and be right behind you."

We don't linger for long, heading directly up the stairs where Lucy stops at the first door. "Now that this room is vacant, will I be staying here?"

"Absolutely not. Keep moving." I direct her toward my room.

She does as she's told but continues to tease me. "Are

you sure you want to move that fast? We've just been on our first date tonight."

"You and I both know we are far beyond that." I smile as she puts her bags down and stands in front of the dresser. The memories of the last time she stood in front of that dresser come flooding back into my mind. *I'm trying to be a gentleman and allow her rest before I ravage her tomorrow.* "Unless you forgot, which I can assure you, I'm more than ready to refresh your memory."

Her eyes grow wide at my offer but then close tightly as she fights off a yawn. It's adorable. Gone is the need to devour her, *well not gone, but pushed aside for now,* and all I want is to get her into those cute pajamas she wears and hold her in my arms all night while we sleep.

"All right, sleepy. Time to get ready for bed." She frowns but moves toward the bathroom. I catch her arm and pull her back to me, with her back to my chest. Lowering my mouth to her ear as my hands softly graze over her arms. "You're going to need to be well-rested for what I have planned for the next three days." She squirms against me, a strained laugh escapes my lips, and I release her before I change my mind.

As we crawl into bed, I pull Lucy up against me. Her scent fills my lungs as I bury my head in her shoulder. My lust begins to stir once again, but I ignore it as I feel her body relax against mine. I whisper softly, "I'm so glad to have you back."

"I'm glad to be back," she says with a sleepy voice before taking my hand and pulling it tighter around her body.

Lucy stirs beside me, in the same position we fell asleep in, but doesn't wake up. My anticipation for the day won't allow my mind to settle back into sleep.

I make slow movements toward my side of the bed and quickly make my way off of it in an effort to not wake her. I have texts from both the local florist and bakery shops asking to confirm the deliveries I scheduled for this morning in a half-hour's time. The deliveries completely slipped my mind, but thankfully, I woke up early enough to receive them. I confirm with both via text and head into the bathroom to take a quick shower.

At the back door, the deliveries arrive together. The small box of fruit-filled pastries and half a dozen iced cupcakes are more than Lucy and I will be able to finish before the next delivery arrives in a couple of days. At least she will have a variety.

The flowers are beautiful. Three vases are filled with fresh bouquets. Pastel-colored petals sit delicately surrounded by deep green leaves exploding out the top of the vase. I hope she likes them.

Leaving one vase on the kitchen island, I place another at the center of the large dining table and bring the last one upstairs to place on her nightstand. Something beautiful for her to wake up to each morning. Just as I place them down she stirs beside me.

"Good morning," I say as I sit on the bed next to her as she stretches.

"Good morning. What are the flowers for?" she asks.

"You, of course."

"They're beautiful." She moves to sit next to me and leans over to smell them. "Thank you."

When we shared a bed before, she woke before me each time. Watching her in this somewhat disheveled state stirs something in me. *I'll have plenty of chances to take her first thing in the morning. Today, we have plans.*

"Enjoy a shower, I'm going to head downstairs." I kiss her cheek and rise to leave. Knowing my restraint only goes so far, and I am certainly not strong enough to watch her enter the shower without joining her, I force myself to head downstairs.

After sharing the fresh pastries, I suggest a short walk. "I know how much you enjoy the snow and I'm not sure how much longer we have until it melts," I explain, but it's clear on her face she doesn't need any convincing to spend time in the winter weather.

"Of course, I'll just run upstairs to dress a little warmer." She smiles and runs along.

Was it presumptuous to start putting her things in my closet?

Yes. Did I do it anyway…also yes.

I take her for a shortened version of the walk I usually take—we can do the regular route when the weather warms up.

"It's beautiful here, Henry," Lucy says with the excitement of a child visiting their favorite theme park for the first time.

"Everything you pictured in your books?" I ask.

She looks back at me. "Much better." And leans in for a quick kiss.

She looks lovely bundled up in her winter attire, a puffy black coat with a faux-fur hood. A large olive colored scarf wrapped around the bottom of the hood, her thick sunglasses and her long brown hair flowing out the sides of her hood.

"I had some thoughts for dinner," I tell her.

"Oh, what do you have in mind?" she asks innocently.

You.

"I'll do the cooking." I pause. "Even though we are planning to stay in, I thought we could still make a date of it." I watch as she follows me. "I can wear my suit, you can wear a dress. You do have a dress here, don't you?"

"A couple." She gives me a wicked smile. "And I have the perfect one for tonight." A quiet giggle escapes her mouth, and it sends an electric jolt through my body. The last time she wore a dress comes to mind.

Off the shoulder, exposing her long neck.

The slit that highlights her gorgeous long legs.

I can only hope this one looks similar.

"Well, it's a date then," I confirm, and she pulls close to my side, wrapping both of her arms around me.

Thirty-Nine

HENRY

LUCY'S BEEN UPSTAIRS for hours. She insisted on her privacy as she got ready, and I reluctantly obliged. With my suit in hand, I head to my temporary dressing room for this evening, Finn and Mia's room.

With some more time to kill before I need to begin preparing dinner, I decide to text Max.

I shower quickly but don't dress in my suit just yet. I hang it in the bathroom downstairs to change into at the last minute. I don't want to get anything on it while I'm cooking. I made Lucy promise not to come down until I texted her that everything was ready.

The chicken sizzles in the pan as the pasta cooks in boiling water and I mix the ingredients for the sauce together. I choose to add less garlic than the recipe calls for. Max must smell like it for days after if he uses this much. Tonight, it is necessary that I have fresh-smelling breath.

The meal comes together rather quickly and I'm plating it in no time. The table is set, wine glasses full, with glasses of water next to them, as I know she likes.

I dash into the bathroom, leaving my cooking outfit on the floor in a pile. I put my suit on quickly and take one final look in the mirror before I pull out my phone.

HENRY

Dinner is served.

I take my place by the table and watch for her to reach the top of the stairs. The first thing I notice is the long leg that breaks free of her skirt with a black strappy high heel at the end. My gaze travels up to the top of her hip.

She'll never wear this anywhere but in our home.

She descends the steps slowly, exactly as I'd film it for a movie, and her hand slides effortlessly down the banister. The top of her dress is a solid form that is exceptionally low in the bust, which leads me to believe if she moved any faster, she may risk falling out of it. Her shoulders are bare apart from her hair that falls in loose curls around her.

I move to meet her at the final step, holding my hand out, but she hesitates and then looks back at me, eyes filled with desire.

"It's now my favorite step too," I confirm.

She smiles and allows me to walk her toward the table. With these heels, she is almost as tall as I am. *Sexy.* Her brash gaze moves up and down my body.

"Enjoying the view?" I ask.

"Very much," she answers.

I pull out the chair at the head of the table for her. Candles fill the table, and I move to dim the lights in the room before claiming my seat next to her. It's immediately apparent I'm no longer very hungry for the meal I've spent an hour preparing. It tastes just as it should, but I'm craving the more appealing woman sitting on my left.

Discussion during dinner is minimal—she compliments the food and I bask in her praise. Conversation flows as it always does between us. Yet, when we both go quiet, I can almost hear the buzz of lust filling the air between us.

It's not long before we are both ready to abandon our meal and proceed to the rest of the activities. Before we head upstairs, I suggest we retire to the lounge. I refill our wine glasses and walk her to the loveseat in front of the fire.

With the lights still low, I imagine us being in this setting every night, enjoying the privacy of our home together. Dinners with us dressed up for each other, wine in hand, and no need to restrict my attraction to her.

I take one final sip and then abandon my wine glass on the end table. It's taking up prime real estate in my hand, and right now, I'd much rather use it to caress Lucy's delicate skin.

Leaning closer to her, running my hands down her legs until I hit the cuffs of black fabric that rests around her ankles. Without notice, I pull them up onto my lap, and her body follows, forcing her to lie sideways facing me.

That's better.

My hands began massaging her legs. Fortunately for me, when I turned her, the skirt bunched to the side, and the slit opened up further to give me adequate access to both legs. She smiles at me over her wine glass but doesn't make any indication for me to stop.

"Have you worn this dress before?" I ask.

God, I hope no one else has ever seen her in this dress. I'm certain no one else will in the future.

"No, this is the first time," she says as she flexes under my touch. "I just got it."

"Oh, really? For what occasion?"

I hope she purchased it for an evening with me.

"I purchased a couple of dresses for New Year's Eve. Yet, when this one came, I realized it might not be right for that occasion."

"I believe you have successfully found the right occasion for this dress." I inch my hands higher on her thighs. Her shoulders shiver.

As I move my firm touches back down her legs, I hook my hand under her left knee and bend it to bring her calf up and over her other leg. Those strappy black shoes with the dangerously high heels sit in my lap. A great debate wages in my mind.

Should I remove them and gain access to additional areas of her body to massage?

Or do I leave them on and have her wear them while I strip the dress off her body?

Yes, the shoes stay.

Lucy tips back her glass and extends her neck as if taunting me with a piece of her I cannot reach. Well, that just won't do. With great ease, I return her feet to the floor and rise from the loveseat. There will be plenty of nights to sit among the fire, but for now, it is time we move to the bedroom.

I take her empty glass and place it on the end table before holding out both hands to help her stand. I can't imagine walking in those shoes is very easy, but after two glasses of wine, I'm slightly concerned for her safety. "Those shoes look like a hazard."

"Oh, you don't like them? Should I take them off?" she asks.

I pull her flush against me so she can feel just how much I enjoy the shoes. "I love them. And they are staying on." My voice comes out deep with my directive. "I'll be close by as we make our way upstairs."

"What a gentleman." She leans in to kiss me but moves to my neck without warning. I allow myself a small preview of what's to come. Tightening my arms around her, one hand to pull her closer to me, the other to stroke her bare back.

Goodness, this dress is tight. How I long to release her from it.

Her hands explore my chest. With my jacket still in place, she slips her hands beneath it and begins to slowly unfasten each button of my dress shirt. Pleased with my decision to skip the tie tonight. Her lips move agonizingly slow in a downward movement toward the opening she has created above my chest. "Lucy…" My arms continue to caress every inch of her body within their reach. Her tongue slips past her lips and draws a slow line back up my neck until she meets just under my ear. Moving upward, her breath on my ear. "Yes, Henry?" she whispers.

Exhaling the breath I didn't realize I'd been holding, I take a step back. I need to regain my senses and be alert enough to assist her up the stairs. My hands are on my hips as I shake my head, I look up at the mischievous smile on her face.

"Upstairs." This is the only directive I give before taking us hand-in-hand to the staircase.

"We are taking these slow. No need to rush and break an ankle," I say to her with a smile. I could whisk her into my arms and run up the stairs, but this somewhat awkward moment may be the perfect time for another awkward conversation. "When we reach the top of the stairs, I'm not going to want to stop and talk. I plan to worship every inch of your body without any interruption. I've acquired protection, so that's taken care of."

She smiles beside me with one hand on the banister and the other holding mine. "I almost forgot about that. I honestly haven't been…active…in quite some time."

"Well, prepare for that to change." I wink at her and she laughs.

"I am still on the pill, though. I didn't want to give up the other perks of it," she says with a shrug as we reach the top step.

"I'm also all clear...since my last…interaction." Lucy drops her gaze at my statement. I hate how this is upsetting her. Could she be wondering how long it's been for me? I need to put her mind at ease. "In fact, that was the same interaction that you caught me walking home from."

"Let's not talk about that morning, I don't really want to think about that right now." Her voice is pleading, I understand why, but I continue the discussion.

"I don't necessarily want to either, but I think you need to know something about that morning and the evening prior."

I continue as I stalk toward her. "I was falling for you even then. Like a child refusing to acknowledge my emotions, my feelings were hurt when you left that night. I only went home with her because you pointed them out earlier."

I keep moving, forcing her back until her shoulders touch the wall behind her. "When I saw you that morning, my regret consumed me in such a way I never felt before. Since that moment, I haven't cared to look at anyone but you."

I feel her body rise and fall as she breathes again my chest. Placing my hands on the wall around her, I bring my face as close to her as possible without letting our lips touch. "Lose the dress."

"Here?" she asks and looks around like she will find people standing in the hallway.

"I plan to have you in every room of this house, and since it's just us tonight, there's no harm in starting here."

Lucy regains her footing and stands with a straight posture. She tucks her hands under her right arm and pulls aside a strip of fabric that is covering a small black zipper.

She tortures me by pulling the zipper down in a slow-moving motion, staring directly into my eyes, but I break the connection to watch the trajectory of the zipper. It ends where the slit at her hip begins. She lets it go and the dress falls to the floor around her.

I freeze in place as I take in the sight of Lucy standing in front of me. All that remains of her attire is a black lace panty that hangs around her hips and dips down to disappear between her legs. She doesn't move to cover herself under my stare but proudly stands in those black heels. She is perfection.

Shaking my head, I pull myself out of the trance and offer her my hand to assist her while she steps out from the dress that has pooled at her feet. I walk her into my bedroom. No need to close the door tonight—her screams will echo through the entire house.

As soon as we come to a stop, she removes my jacket and makes quick work of the remaining buttons of my shirt. I'll allow her to continue removing my clothes, but after that, I'll be taking my time with her. Anxious for my turn to come, I remove my belt and throw it to the floor. She finishes with my shirt and begins to pull it from the waist of my pants as I push them to the floor. Lucy stands back to admire my naked body. As her eyes fill with desire, I commit this image to memory.

I move past her to the bed. "I'd like to revisit the other night when you were in my lap. I think we are better dressed for the occasion now."

She exaggerates her movements as she places a leg on either side of me before she seats herself in my lap. With one final look into each other's eyes, it's as if a starting pistol fires in the background, and then the race is on.

My hand tangles it in her soft locks as I claim her lips with the hope that this is the only mouth I will kiss for the rest of my days. Our passion continues to build as her fingers cup around my neck and her pointer fingers graze over the scruff of my beard. The simple movements across my face are grounding in this moment of chaos.

Endless emotions flowing through my mind begin to settle at her gentle touch, evidence of one simple truth. I am hers.

I could kiss this woman for the rest of my life, but I want more.

I slowly lay my back on the bed taking her with me. She takes the lead as she rocks her hips against mine, with only the delicate lace between us. Her focus switches between my mouth and my neck, and I can't help but submit to this moment of bliss.

Frustrated at the lacy barrier between us, she lifts her hips, and I let out a sigh at the loss of contact. Her hands move to remove the item, but I pull them back to me. "That's my job," I scold her and use my strength to flip us over, with Lucy's back to the mattress and it allows me to hover over her.

I crash my lips into hers, as a lustful need engulfs my entire body. Possessively, I claim her mouth with my tongue, so sweet and addicting.

Kissing down her body, I linger at the spots that elicit a sweet moan from those beautiful lips.

Sure, that dress accentuated her cleavage, but I far prefer the view and access I have without it. My hands cup her as I move between them, licking and sucking until she is writhing beneath my touch.

Moving to shower her belly and hips with attention, I

use my knee to separate her legs. When my exploration finally hits its destination, I fall to my knees in front of her once again.

I hear a soft sigh as my tongue makes contact with her most sensitive area. I would give everything to spend my days here, drowning in her sinful moans and exquisite taste. I do not tease as much as I did the first time, we have other items on the agenda tonight.

Slowly, I allow my fingers to slide inside her, matching the rhythm I set with my tongue. Soft at first, growing more rapid with each gasp from Lucy. It's not long before her sighs turn into panting, and panting turns into begging, and then it all concludes with her screams of ecstasy.

Her legs continue to tremble as I climb back on top of her, eager to feel her around me. "How are you, my love?" I ask.

Her head moves back and forth, still trying to catch her breath. With a gentle touch of her hand on my chest, she finally looks at me. "I need you."

I do not hesitate to follow her command. Positioning between her legs, I slowly ease into her. I hold for a moment, watching her face, waiting for her cue to continue. "Henry…" How I love to hear her beg—I can't deny her. Quickly finding my pace as I am completely surrounded by her warmth.

In that moment, all restraint, worry, distrust, and caution leaves my body. I was meant for this woman and I will do everything in my power to meet her every need for the rest of my days.

She wraps her legs around mine, meeting my rhythm, digging her nails into my back desperate for each thrust.

I want to tell her how much I love her. No, that has to wait. With one hand holding my weight from crushing her, the other grips her hips. *I am in love with her smile, with her eyes, with her hopeless-romantic personality, with her kindness.*

"Henry…" she moans.

I'm in love with the way she says my name, especially while we are connected like this. I'm in love with the way her body moves to meet mine, desperate to close any space between us.

I lose track of time, lost in this woman who has turned my entire life around. Her pleasure and mine mix together in pure euphoria as we rise and fall in sync with one another.

"Lucy…"

"Yes," she answers as if she understands completely.

With her approval, my movements become frantic as I submit to the bliss of our connection. The next moment, I'm falling over the edge, plunging into an existence that is consumed by Lucy.

My Lucy.

Mine.

Forty

LUCY

"**WHAT HAVE** you and Henry been up to since you got back from London?" Mia asks with a devilish look in her eye.

"Aside from the things you saw in the posts on his social media accounts?" I ask, but don't leave time for her to answer. "Enjoying the peace and quiet." As if I'd share the details of how we spent the last three days enjoying each other on every surface of this house, including the kitchen island she is currently leaning on. Of course, we made sure to do a deep clean before they all returned from visiting their relatives.

"Well, that's incredibly disappointing and boring," Mia huffs and rolls her eyes.

As always, Hannah is the voice of reason with a kind smile, "I think it sounds romantic."

Not wanting to linger on this topic any longer, I suggest, "If we head out now, we can get drinks on the way to the salon."

"Yes, please," Hannah agrees as she puts her coat on.

Then, hooks her arm with mine. "Thanks again for surprising us with this. A stress-free girls' day is just what I needed after all that traveling."

Little does she know, this day was planned weeks ago. Like most women, Mia and I were sure she'd want her nails done when showing off her new ring. Also, with the numerous photos we'll be taking, she'll be glad to have that fresh-from-the-salon look.

I give her hand a squeeze in return before we all enter the car. I choose to sit in the backseat. Unexpectedly, I start to recall the last time I sat here. I can laugh about it now because it's over, but John showing up without notice had me spiraling on the drive out of the city. I wonder if things between Henry and I would have progressed as quickly if I had come alone. *It might just have been the best thing that could have happened.*

Turning back to me, Mia suggests, "I'm thinking of tea to take to the salon and then grab coffees on the way home. It's going to be a late night, ladies."

Mia is the queen of partying, which is why she was the one to coordinate the order of events for tonight including after the proposal photos and phone calls. I'm certain she could run the world if she tried.

Hours later, I text Henry from the back seat of the car.

The remainder of our drive passes quickly. I don't say much to avoid mistakenly spoiling any surprises. I sit quietly until we find ourselves parked next to Henry's home. Mia is the first to jump from the car, with Hannah and I following.

Mia and I are fantastic actresses. "What are you all doing standing out in the cold?" Mia asks.

"We did some decorating for the New Year's Eve celebrations," Oliver shares.

"It should be a surprise, and we are quite frankly still in the middle, and it looks a mess. We only want you to see the finished product," Finn explains.

Henry stands there as he would, not saying much but going along with it all just the same.

I argue when they pull out the blindfolds. "We just got our hair done for tonight. You can't put those on us."

"What if we promise not to look at your decorations?" Hannah asks.

Henry speaks up, "All right, how about if we cover your eyes with our hands?"

Oliver continues, "And when we get to the stairs, you can face the wall and walk up sideways."

"I'm recording this." Finn laughs to himself.

I face the girls, and we form a huddle like a team preparing for the game-winning goal. After a moment of fake deliberations, we agree and get our boys to stand behind us to cover our eyes.

As we enter, Henry silently lowers his hands down so I can get a look at it all. Vases of red roses sit on every flat surface with gold confetti placed around them. A garland made of white hydrangeas wraps around the banister of the staircase. Mia is peaking too, and we exchange silent looks, making our eyes wild while keeping our lips firmly sealed.

Once we are all at the top of the stairs, our eyes are once again covered, and we receive our instructions. Oliver begins, "None of you are allowed to leave your rooms unless escorted by one of us."

Next to speak is Finn with a tone similar to that of a drill sergeant. "You ladies have mobile phones, use them. If you need to speak with each other, call her, text her, I don't care if you video call each other but do it from your rooms."

Henry sighs behind me. I lower my hand behind me and rub his leg. His breath catches as he lowers his head to rest on my neck.

Finn continues, "If you wish to contact your hunky fella, the same means of communication are required. We will have our phones with us at all times, should you need us."

"Please know I will be available to meet any and all needs you may have," Henry whispers softly, the heat of his breath brushing against my skin before he clears his throat to address the others. "We will be starting dinner preparations and plan to serve at 8:00 p.m. I do believe the next two hours should provide plenty of time for each of you to relax and get dressed before the festivities begin."

Finn speaks up one final time. "You will be escorted into your rooms now."

I laugh, "I think you're enjoying this too much, Finn."

"I think it's sexy," Mia says in a seductive tone.

Henry and I walk a little faster into our room. The door closes with a loud noise as Henry signals to the others that we are inside. Two similar sounds follow.

"Your hair is lovely." His fingers comb through my hair as his gaze locks on mine.

Placing a finger under my chin, tipping my face up to his, he leaves soft kisses around my lips. With each touch, my need for him grows stronger. We have plenty of time, perhaps we could grab a quick shower…together. Before I can suggest my steamy idea, a thunderous noise coming from the other side of the door startles me.

"No funny business, Pop!" Finn yells.

Oliver joins in, laughing as he says, "We have things to do!"

Finn pounds on the door again. "Give the lady a rest!"

Henry kisses me one more time before opening the door to his sons, laughing in the doorway.

I wave silently, not wanting to give anything away.

With more than enough time to get ready, I decide to pick up my e-reader. Our days have been filled with waves of uncontrollable pleasures, which hasn't left much time for reading. *Not that I'm complaining.* The only book I've read is *Pride and Prejudice*, to discuss the adaptation with Henry. I think it's time to revisit Captain Wentworth—surely, he misses me.

Tonight is New Year's Eve. My favorite holiday is one most people overlook, but that's one of the things I love about it. I like that I'm the only one who makes a big deal about it because that makes it feel more like it's just for me.

Yet, after tonight, it will always be special for Oliver and Hannah as well. I can't wait to see the look on her face when he gets down on one knee.

Next to my new bouquet of flowers is the alarm clock with the time showing ten minutes before 8:00 p.m. Butterflies start to dance in my stomach as my excitement builds. I'm all about being ready early, but now all I have to do is sit and wait until Henry comes to fetch me.

Getting dressed this evening is nothing like the other night when Henry cooked for me. My hair looks different thanks to the amazing hair stylist at the salon we visited this afternoon. My makeup is done and I've selected a black sequin dress that covers much more of my body, well at least my top. The dress has flowing long sleeves and covers most of my neckline. Yet, it does show a lot more leg, cutting off a couple of inches above my knees, so I paired it with black tights and my knee-high boots.

The guys all got ready in the spare bedroom so as to not risk us seeing the decorations before it was time.

Three loud knocks strike the door before Henry enters

the room. My breath catches as he stalks toward me. I notice he is wearing the same suit he wore the other night.

He notices my recognition. "I had it dry cleaned. For you," he says with a mischievous smile.

"Well if I had known," I tease. "Let me go change into the dress I wore then."

Turning toward the closet, he quickly pulls me back. "That dress is for my eyes only," he says with a growl behind his words.

"Yes, sir." While curling into his embrace, we are once again interrupted.

"Pop, let's go. Time to get out here with your girl," Oliver yells, his words rushing out quickly.

"The rest of us are waiting on you," Finn yells.

We move quickly hand and hand out the door, but to keep up the act for Hannah, Henry adds, "Just had to get her blindfold on. All set. Here we go."

Next, Finn goes in to relieve Mia with similar announcements about her eyes being covered when they really aren't.

The four of us huddle at the bottom of the stairs, waiting for Hannah and Oliver to arrive.

Silent smiles are exchanged as we watch Hannah with her blindfold on at the top of the staircase. Rather than taking their time, Oliver sweeps her up in his arms and carries her down. We all nod and signal that the cameras are hidden in position, and we all have our phones ready behind our backs.

Placing Hannah on her feet, he kneels beside her.

"What do I do now?" she asks.

He opens the ring box in her direction, clears his

throat, and answers, "I'll take the blindfold off now." But it's really Mia behind Hannah, gently pulling at the loose knot behind Hannah's hair.

When she notices Oliver kneeling at her feet, Hannah's face changes to stunned before she brings her hands to cover her nose and mouth. The quintessential proposal pose, according to Mia, who is currently shining a smug smile my way.

Oliver's nerves are getting the best of him. "Hannah…I…I had a huge speech that I've spent days trying to memorize, but now I don't remember any of it."

Her sweet laugh physically eases him enough to continue. "You are my life and my better half. I never want to spend another day without you. I love you and will continue loving you for the rest of my life, if you'll have me." An anxious squeal escapes Hannah's lips and he smiles up at her. "Hannah, Will you marry me?"

"Yes!" she screams as she throws her arms around him, almost knocking Oliver onto the floor.

He catches her and stands without letting her down. "I believe this belongs to you then." He holds up the ring.

She slips down his arms and holds her hand out. After we all capture a photo of him placing the ring on her finger, Mia begins to shoo us away from the couple. "Privacy, the newly engaged couple needs their privacy." We follow her lead to the lounge to sit and wait for their return.

When they come over to us, we all hug and congratulate them. Hannah is giddy as she shows off her new ring.

Mia has a tight schedule and insists they make all the

necessary calls now. "Get your calls in now before everyone's phones start blowing up with New Year's wishes.

Turning on Henry and I, she directs us to start getting the dinner out while she preps the area where she wants to pose Hannah and Oliver for photos.

Hours fly by with all the celebration throughout the evening and before we know it, we are all crowded around the large clock that hangs above the fireplace.

Together we count down the final seconds of the year. "Ten… Nine… Eight… Seven… Six… Five… Four… Three… Two… One… Happy New Year!"

Henry pulls me into his embrace but doesn't kiss me immediately. He touches my forehead with his and whispers, "Happy New Year, darling," before closing the distance between us. I stifle a groan as he deepens our kiss, remembering that we are not alone.

I'm so ready for us to be alone.

I quickly devise a plan and put it into action immediately. As we exchange Happy New Year's with everyone, I yawn twice.

Then we all go to our phones to check the incoming messages from friends and family. I call my mom, even though she still has hours before the new year arrives for her. "Happy New Year, Mom," I yell into the phone.

She laughs, "Happy almost New Year to you too, sweetie! Are you having a nice night?"

"I am, I'll send you some photos from the proposal," I offer.

"Yes, please send them over."

My phone beeps in my ear, and I pull it away and notice Ellie is calling.

"Mom, I gotta go. Ellie is calling, but call me tomorrow."

"I will. Goodnight, Lucy."

"Night, Mom."

Swiping my finger across the phone, I can hear Ellie yelling before I bring it to my ear. "Happy New Year, Lucy! How's the future?"

I laugh, "It's exceptional, Ellie. The only thing missing is you."

"That sounds about right," she agrees. "All right, well, I'm in the middle of making our snacks for the family, so I gotta go, but *Happy New Year*!"

"Thanks, Ellie. Happy New Year to you too!"

And then, with an "Okay, *bye*," she hangs up.

As I return to the group, I feign a large yawn, covering my mouth for everyone to see. Henry picks up on it quickly and plays directly into my master plan. "Well, I'm sure you all plan to party for a few more hours, but I think it's time for us to call it a night." He squeezes my hand, but little does he know what's waiting for him once we are alone.

We say our goodnights and head back to our room.

I close the door behind me and stalk up behind him as he strips out of his suit jacket. "Hello, there."

He turns with a sharp inhale, "I thought you were tired…"

"Well, that's what I wanted them to think. I just wanted to ring in the new year with you…alone…in the shower."

His eyes grow wide. "Who knew you were such a skilled actress?" He kneels in front of me and begins to pull down the zippers on my boots, guiding my legs free while his strong hands wrap around my calves. As he rises, he tucks his hands under my dress and pulls it up over my head. It's my turn to even us out—he is still wearing far too much clothing…for a shower.

Once we have stripped each other bare, he takes my hand and walks me to the shower door. He walks in to start the water but instructs me to wait. The room begins to fill with steam as he tucks me against his body, with his arms behind my back. Following his lead, I nuzzle into him.

His touch creates an electric buzz throughout my body when he looks into my eyes and says, "I want you to know something, Lucy. You have changed me, so very completely, much more than I could have imagined the night we met in that coffee shop. Each moment in your presence, whether I knew it or not, altered who I am. No longer the content man who sought out companionship at arm's length." His brows furrow, and he looks away briefly, then smiles at me.

"Now, I want nothing but to be by your side each and every day. To live as those fictional men do from Jane Austen's stories, breathing only for my one true love." He grins. "Even before I got the director role, I stopped caring about this movie weeks ago. Suddenly, after years of wanting that film, I knew it meant nothing if I didn't have you in my life."

My breath catches as I have to fight back the tears that pool in my eyes at his confession. He holds my chin gently in his hand, rubbing his thumb across my cheek, "Lucy, I love you." The words sound more like a promise than a statement.

If only I could come up with something half as romantic as his declaration, but all that comes out is, "I love you too, Henry," I answer as my voice cracks.

His kiss is urgent and demanding. We move quickly into the shower, consumed by our love for each other... and the endless amounts of steam.

Epilogue

LUCY

ONE YEAR LATER...

IT'S as if I escaped reality and found myself as the main character starring in one of Henry's romantic movies. *Romantic comedy with all the twists and turns we've endured in the last year.*

Here I stand, admiring my home in this small English town while snow falls in light flurries around me. Henry swears I brought the snow with me last year because that was the first time he had so much snow since buying this place. I'll gladly be its source and I hope it returns every winter.

We practically moved in together right after the New Year celebration. While he was working on the movie, he stayed at my place in London for an easier commute, and whenever he had extended time off, we stayed here.

For Valentine's Day, Henry had the spare room that was once originally planned for my stay, but I never slept in, converted into a home office for me. More thankful than ever for my remote teaching position—it never prevents me from traveling with him. Although, after a year on the movie set, I am considering another career change.

I've suggested getting rid of the London apartment, but Henry insists on keeping it for the memories and a permanent place to stay while we are visiting everyone in the city.

Even the townhouse will be switching tenants soon. Oliver and Hannah are shopping for their own place, still deciding if they want to live in the city or not. Mia has decided to move in with Finn, neither wanting to leave the city anytime soon.

Now that filming has ended for Henry's adaptation of *Pride & Prejudice* and is in the middle of post-production, we are spending more and more time away from the city. We did get to fly back to New York a couple of times during the year for Henry to meet my mom. They got along so well. I think he may be more competitive now that he's trying to fit into our family.

Ellie switched teams at the beginning of the year and we got to see her in action at a couple of their games. She certainly has her hands full with a player that's benched with an injury or something. Although, I teased her the entire time that he's secretly in love with her. *Payback.*

The backdoor of the kitchen creaks as Henry emerges in his sexy winter outfit. Only he can make a tracksuit, puffer vest, and ski cap look just as sexy as a three-piece suit. His salt-and-pepper facial hair accents perfectly with the all-black outfit.

I shiver, thinking about how much I love it when that

beard glides over my bare skin. I'd stay out here all day just to gawk at this man.

My leading man.

"With your love for the snow, I'm surprised you moved to England, darling. I'm sure there are other locations that get more snow." He stands behind me, leaning forward to place his chin on my shoulder. "But I'm not complaining."

"Yes, but the rare snow here makes it all the more special when it arrives," I share.

"Very special, indeed." His nose snuggles against my ear. "Dinner is just about finished. Do you care to join me?"

"Of course." Holding his hand, we trudge through the snow back to our home. Henry kept tonight's dinner a secret.

As soon as we walk into the kitchen, the smell of garlic fills my nose. I look around and notice he is preparing Max's chicken Alfredo recipe, one of my favorites.

I remember when Max offered to make it for me himself when I was visiting the set and Henry became adorably jealous. I politely declined.

"Well, It's just about the anniversary since the last time I made it for you, so I thought it could become a tradition of ours after Christmas when we have the house to ourselves." I'm still adjusting to the quiet since everyone left this morning to visit their relatives.

With that being said, I welcome the privacy and having him all to myself. Henry will never cease to amaze me with his unlimited supply of romantic ideas.

That reminds me. "Should I run and put that dress on

again? I do believe many firsts happened that magical night a year ago," I tease.

"No need for the dress, I think tomorrow will be our formal date night in the evening. I have a new recipe I want to try." He looks up from his pan. "Less garlic than this one."

With a laugh, I reply. "Well, I'm very much looking forward to the abundance of garlic in this meal." I peek over his shoulder to see the sauce before gathering the place settings for us.

The first bite of fettuccine melts in my mouth as I devour the endless flavor. "You are an exceptional cook," I praise him.

"If it weren't for Max's recipes, I wouldn't know where to start, but he's a good teacher." Henry smiles at the mention of his friend.

"Good dancer too…and perhaps he's finally found the perfect dance partner." I play coy.

"Did you plan that all along?"

"Two people meet…at work, you could say. And that job requires them to…spend a lot of time together. I really don't have control over that. I think the universe is to thank for it." I shrug but silently bask in the match I helped create.

"I don't think either of them would describe it so smoothly. If Max had his hair, he certainly would have pulled it out after those first couple weeks working with Luna." Henry shakes his head.

"I'm sure the same can be said about our rocky start, sweetheart," I point out.

"Yes, I suppose you are right about that." He puts his

fork down to ponder. "Maybe the best relationships are those with a difficult start."

"Difficult start…very conservative way to describe it."

"Either way, they seem very happy now." He returns to his meal.

"They do," I agree.

After dinner, we move to the loveseat with glasses of wine in front of the fireplace. I'm bundled up with a blanket.

Last January, I found a large bag of throw blankets in one of the linen closets.

"Henry, why do you have so many throw blankets hiding in this closet?"

He comes behind me, "Oh, I forgot about those. I ordered them when you agreed to stay with me for the holidays. I noticed you have them covering your entire apartment."

My heart melts at this thoughtfulness. "Why are they all in the closet?"

"I think in the rush of everything, I forgot about them."

They aren't as prevalent here as they are at the London apartment, but I do have them strategically placed throughout the house.

"I know it's months away, but you'll need to start thinking about what you want to wear to the movie premieres," Henry reminds me. "I'm going to insist we go custom." I hate to think of the cost of a custom dress, but he's pretty set on this.

"Are you getting a custom tux?" I ask.

"Of course."

"How silly of me to ask." I roll my eyes.

"Yes, I'll also need to know if you plan to invite

anyone. Perhaps your mom or Ellie might want to attend the American premiere?"

"I can definitely ask Mom, but I don't know if she'll be up to all of the chaos. We'll have to check if Ellie can get the time off—summer is prime baseball season time."

"Oh, yes. I was also thinking we can host a mini-premiere here."

"Really?" I'd love to have my family join us here with Henry's.

"Yes, we can make popcorn, I'm sure Mia can think of some themed drinks, and you can require a book quote to be admitted inside."

I can't imagine what Henry would say when I met him last fall if I suggested such a thing. But that is not the man that sits beside me now.

This man has let his walls crumble and helped me to tear down mine. He's so much more than a romantic partner, he's truly become my partner in life. Anything that comes our way, we face together.

Henry has turned into the very fictional leading man he mocked so much when we met.

No, even better than those fictional men.

Henry is very real and all *mine*.

Acknowledgments

I am so thankful and fortunate to be writing the acknowledgments for my second book. So much has changed in the last six months, but I still find myself with endless gratitude to those who have been listening to me go on and on for *years* about this book or as those close to me know it "The Colin Firth Book."

To the guy playing guitar in the room across from me, thank you for always keeping your endless support close by and providing the soundtrack to my author journey. I am never at a loss to think of an affectionate gesture or a caring word because of the extraordinary love you show me each and every day.

To my friends, who have read snippets of this story via photos of my computer screen that I text to them in the middle of their work day asking "How does this sound?" or even worse, when that photo is of a spicy scene and I simply asked "Cringe?", thank you for always answering. Thank you for not blocking me when I've flooded your inboxes with Colin Firth pictures in the middle of the night. Most importantly, thank you for always being there for me.

To my alpha reader, editor, formatter, proofreader, cover artist, my person, Cassie. Thank you for your patience, understanding, and guidance through the publishing process. When I was starting to consider delaying the release date for this book because I couldn't get the right cover you swooped in and saved the day yet again. You are my partner in this publishing journey and to simplify a very complex thing, I could not do this without you.

To my author friends, Cait, Maggie, and Taryn. Thank you for offering to beta, providing exceptional feedback, answering my endless questions and most of all believing in me. I am so very grateful to have the support and friendship of such amazing individuals.

To my beta readers Alyssa and Amber. I can not thank you enough for the time you have taken out of your lives to support me and provide invaluable feedback. In addition to you both, thank you to Whitney and Fern, I greatly appreciate the social media love you have shown for me and my books. Most of all, thank you for your friendship. I am so very lucky to have you in my life.

To my family, thank you for your excitement when I mention my books and displaying your copies proudly. Thank you to those who, on my request skipped those spicy chapters, Mom, Michael and LT. For those who read them anyway (Nana, Aunt Barb, and Danna), I'm sorry, it's just going to keep getting more spicy so read at your own risk! Thank you for your love and support.

E.G. Verot spends her days in the world of education but her evenings reading, writing, and loving books of all flavors and spices. She has a TBR list longer than she cares to admit. She has been longing to share the characters from her daydreams with you for many years. She lives in the Northeast area of the United States and looks forward to the winter weather all year. When she is not reading, she can be found spending time with her pets, crocheting, and enjoying her life with loved ones.

Our story begins in England during the early 1800s, or as it is more commonly known, the Regency era.

Marriage is common amongst the residents of England, love is a rarity.

Margo began her journey in society as a teenager, inconsiderate and so consumed by her own fears that she was unaware of the hurtful effect her words had on someone very important to her. She now finds herself nearly a decade older and is just now realizing the error of her ways. When she meets a young friend who finds herself in a similar situation upon entering society, Margo tries to share her mistakes in the hope that another will not repeat them. Will she be able to save a valued friendship once lost?

Edward however had a very different outlook on love when he was younger. So much so that he made himself vulnerable to utter heartbreak…a devastation he has never recovered from. Now, he is forced to come face to face with the woman who broke his heart when his sister decides to spend her summer holiday at Margo's country estate.